NISEMONOGATARI

FAKE TALE

PART 02

NISIOISIN

VERTICAL.

NISEMONOGATARI
Fake Tale

Part 02

NISIOISIN

Art by VOFAN

Translated by James Balzer

VERTICAL.

NISEMONOGATARI, PART 02

© 2009 NISIOISIN

All rights reserved.

First published in Japan in 2009 by Kodansha Ltd.,
Tokyo. Publication rights for this English edition
arranged through Kodansha Ltd., Tokyo.

Published by Vertical, Inc., New York, 2017

ISBN 978-1-942993-99-5

Manufactured in the United States of America

First Edition

Second Printing

Vertical, Inc.
451 Park Avenue South, 7th Floor
New York, NY 10016

www.vertical-inc.com

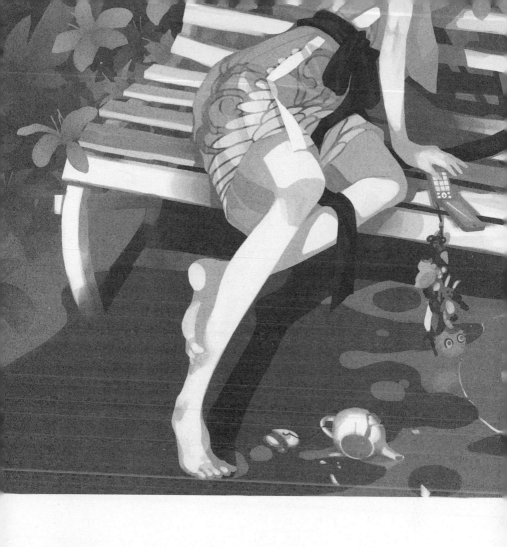

FINAL CHAPTER　TSUKIHI PHOENIX

FINAL CHAPTER
TSUKIHI PHOENIX

001

By revealing the true nature of Tsukihi Araragi, I will at last reach a full stop in our tale. As aggravating as she is clever, the story of my littler little sister will mark an end to this episode about me and the friends I've grown so close to. Not that our lives end with this story, or that the world ends with us. When all is said and done, our lives will be spared—besides, whether life, or the world, having an end promises any salvation is something we'd all do well to think upon more often. To long for an end that never comes, to wish to stop and to be unable. Don't people experience and endure such a hell on an ordinary or extraordinary basis all the time?

Take me, for instance. Koyomi Araragi.

During spring break, I was attacked by a vampire—a legendary vampire, an ironblooded, hotblooded, yet coldblooded vampire, the king and slayer of aberrations. My blood drained, my life and being drained, my physical body drained, my mind and psyche drained, afterwards nothing was left.

Correction. A monster was left behind. What was me was subtracted from me, and a monster remained. Hide as I might I could not hide, run as I might I could not run, and die as I like I could not die—it was the beginning of two weeks in hell.

The truth is, even now, I can't truly say that those two weeks of hell are entirely over. Of course—even without bringing up my own unusual circumstances, there is something unreal about a word like "end" in the first place.

There is no shortage of people who choose to take their own life— but in a broad sense not even that act can truly be called an end. When the dust settles a suicide becomes its own departure point, the origin of yet new developments.

Even if justice eradicates evil…

A new evil will simply be born.

Evil may be eradicated, but it cannot be exterminated—in fact, it is quite possible for the new evil that arises to have started out on the side of justice.

Now, if my other sister, Karen, heard me say that, she'd be none too happy. In fact, her own brother or not, she'd probably make my face unhappy with her boot. She'd do so spouting that she wasn't kicking me, the righteous blood flowing through her was.

But eventually she'd learn. Even if I never told her. It's nothing difficult.

Even raised in a peaceful, happy-go-lucky nation and with only a normal education, she'd learn—that at the end of the day, justice is no more than a setup to be overhauled by some new justice.

Everything is an opening act, to everything.

The revolutionary can't become a settler.

Backs are turned without fanfare, promises are broken without scruple, debts are left totally unpaid, and the weak are hardly protected.

Those are the rules.

The rules of this world.

However loudly my two sisters, my pride and joy, proclaim justice, the concept of justice is rooted in fighting evil, in being hostile to evil, so it's inevitable.

Evil, too, has its reasons. Evil, too, has family.

Faced with this reality, few could persist in their righteousness without a shadow of doubt—and you'd be hard pressed to call those few just.

Ultimately, justice and evil aren't binary opposites.

It isn't a dualism, nor is this humanism.

When we start down that path, we never get started and never get finished.

We languish—and that's how it goes.

Even supposing that a person can be just, it's only in still images and commemorative snapshots rather than vids—eventually, the passage of time degrades meaning and significance. Negates the original sense.

Of course, this isn't all bad—everything I've said hints, too, at the possibility that what exists as evil can likewise turn into justice. There is still room for penance, and for change.

Instead of stubborn pessimism, it's probably best to accept that hope—just as after descending into hell, I found Tsubasa Hanekawa and Hitagi Senjogahara, there is no telling from where salvation might come.

It can come from anywhere. We could put it this way: It is because nothing ends that salvation exists.

This placeholder might seem little more than hypocrisy, but I don't see the harm in it. In fact, we might say that it is a clear and present representation of this final tale, replete with fakeness.

Well—in any case, I don't want to be bombastic here on top of all that.

Let's not speak, then, of justice and evil or of good and hypocrisy.

Of endings and beginnings.

Of living and dying.

Why put on airs?

We have no thesis. We won't discuss noble themes.

The story I am about to tell is simply that of my sister.

Tsukihi Araragi. One half of the Fire Sisters.

My younger younger sister, my littler little sister.

In the second grade of middle school, born in April, fourteen years old, blood type B, prone to hysteria, cunning, subject to mood swings—

And also, immortal.

The tale of a mere fake.

002

"Hey, Koyomi, do you know the sure way to win at rock-paper-scissors? I bet you don't. Of course not, I mean look at you! If I weren't around to teach you stuff, you wouldn't know anything at all. Ahaha. Well, what can I do. I guess I can be nice and teach you. I'll lend you a hand, and the shirt off my back, streaking butt-naked until you get the whole picture."

Karen Araragi.

My little sister, who's in her last year of middle school, said this suddenly, with absolutely no preface, while doing a handstand.

A handstand. Which was actually typical of her.

By the way, just so there are no misunderstandings, allow me to clarify that it was not as if we were in our living room at home, or in Karen's own room, or even in a gym or some other sports facility— we were in the middle of a residential neighborhood, atop a section of paved surface commonly referred to as a sidewalk.

Beneath the brilliant, glittering sun, perched above the asphalt, my sister, believe it or not, was upside down. In a way, it was even more embarrassing than if she had gone streaking.

The Nike Shox she was wearing, supposedly designed not only to absorb impact but to spring off the ground as you stepped, served no purpose at the moment.

"Huh? What are you blabbering on about? A sure way to win at rock-paper-scissors? You expect me to believe that? I mean, there isn't any. That's about as ridiculous as you."

An acrobatic posture is an accomplishment in its own right, but since I'm hardly the type of person who enjoys being gawked at by the whole neighborhood, I'd have preferred to put at least three miles in both physical and emotional distance between myself and a mysterious schoolgirl standing on her head (if it were up to me, she'd either stop that or stop being my little sister), but I didn't have much of a choice and answered her instead.

Maybe this stupid way of walking was part of her fitness regimen, but for my own part I was doing everything I could to get her to knock it off. I aimed sharp kicks to her head from behind whenever I saw an opening, but she seemed to have eyes on her back like the hundred-eyed goblin and managed to dodge each and every strike.

I guess a martial arts junkie like Karen was just cut from different cloth. Without real gaps in her defense, I wouldn't be able to kick her head—well, not that that was my goal.

I sure wouldn't have minded landing one, though. It sounded like a great way of repaying her for her daily antics.

By the way, Karen's hair was styled in her usual, old-school ponytail, but when she did a handstand, her long hair wound up touching the ground and dragging along, so she wrapped it around her neck like a scarf while she was upside down.

If I could grab the end and give it a tug, I could choke her nice and good. I'd given that a few tries as well, but of course my attempts had all ended in failure.

Given that it was the height of summer, August fourteenth, with about a week left of summer vacation, a scarf of hair seemed like it would be too warm, or even hot (plus her face was just inches away from the baking asphalt), but perhaps it was precisely what Miss Karen Araragi's Spartan nature craved.

A woman on fire—she even liked to call herself "a human fireball." The first character in her name meant fire, but I almost wanted to scrunch it together with the second to yield the one for phosphorus.

"Heheh. But there is a way. As surely as I exist."

With that declaration, for a moment Karen appeared to sink, but then ricocheted up like a powerful spring, performed an agile, elegant somersault, and returned her body to the right way round.

Karen Araragi, the woman in the jersey. I forgot to mention that she's also quite tall.

Even though she's a girl, still in middle school, and what's more my little sister, Karen is taller than me (incidentally, I stopped growing in the second year of middle school, can you believe it), so when she stood upright, her eyes hovered higher than mine—um, in which case, maybe she ought to spend the whole rest of her life standing on her head? Was I self-centered to think so?

"Listen," she said, "knowing it will completely change your rock-paper-scissors life. I'd kind of like to keep it to myself, but it's thanks to you that I'm enjoying this fine day. Not that I'm trying to pay back that debt, just think of it as a special, cool gesture."

Heck, I haven't even shared this with Tsukihi, she added with a cheeky grin.

Her legs never stopped moving. She was marching backward at a brisk pace.

She was indeed agile, but it hardly surprised me at this point—when it came to physical prowess, including her sense of balance, she was a regular monster. Despite being human, maybe she was more monstrous than a vampire.

She wasn't the Fire Sisters' "enforcer" for nothing—without even recalling the whole bee commotion from the other day.

Compared to her ongoing training, walking backwards was almost normal.

It's just that being seen with her tends to get very embarrassing. Generally speaking, though, that means everything.

"I don't have a rock-paper-scissors life, let alone completely changing it."

"Oh, but you might. Even morning, day, and night. Don't reject possibilities, okay? Imagine the advantages of being great at rock-paper-scissors. For instance, Russian roulette. What if an argument over who goes first comes down to a game of rock-paper-scissors?"

"The probability would still be the same."

Pretty remedial stuff she ought to have learned by her third year of middle school.

More to the point, when was I ever going to be forced to play Russian roulette? Once things came to that, I was most likely well on my way to kicking the bucket, no?

"Huh? The probability is the same? Are you sure? Isn't the person pulling the trigger first at a disadvantage?"

"What if he doesn't get a bullet? Then the chance of shooting yourself heightens."

"Huh? What? Help me out here."

"You see—"

"What does 'heightens' mean?"

"That's what you don't understand?!"

Was a simple word like "heightens" not part of her vocabulary? How did she ever manage to survive for fifteen years?!

And your backstory is that you have good grades!

"Heightens… Heightens…" she muttered. "Hmph. That sounds like the name of some demon."

"You're thinking of Hiten!" I hollered like a straight man, although to be honest I wasn't sure if it was a demon. I considered myself a utility player when it came to fielding a joke, but I was rusty about some shows.

"Wait, the Dutch scientist who studied Saturn's rings and wrote a pioneering treatise on probability, Christian…"

"I think you mean Huygens… It's not even pronounced the same way. Besides, why would you not know what 'heightens' means and come up with Huygens?!"

"Hrrm, then who could it be... I feel like I've come across it somewhere." Her arms folded, Karen got sidetracked into recalling some random name—search as she might, she was lost now.

"Hey, you want me to believe that someone with such a poor vocabulary actually knows a foolproof way to win at rock-paper-scissors?"

"It's not about knowing, it's about feeling. When it comes down to it, what you know or don't know doesn't matter, it's what you can *do*, and *do* do..."

"Well, true..."

Just look at Hanekawa. She's certainly a treasure trove of knowledge—but what's so amazing about her, so exhilarating, is how she applies it.

The *veni vidi vici* of knowledge. No half-measures for her.

No wonder there are all kinds of crazy rumors about Hanekawa, like that she took the ancient Chinese imperial exams while in middle school, or that she passed the German A-levels over summer vacation as a high school freshman (I spread those rumors, by the way).

"So Koyomi, I might not know my probability theory, but I've survived Russian roulette and that's what really matters."

"You've played Russian roulette?!"

It wasn't a hypothetical!

Seriously, it wasn't a hypothetical?!

If it was true, and she survived, that meant her opponent blew his brains out!

Officer, we have a criminal case! A case involving my little sister!

"Hm? Oh, don't worry," Karen assured me. "Once we were down to the last chamber, my opponent chickened out and gave up. Bzzz, end of game."

"I guess it's fine, then... Wait, no, that's so not fine."

You Fire Sisters... I knew they got up to some insane stuff, but not that they'd been in a conflict where firearms made a showing...

Did I need to go to the cops for real?

"That Italian Mafioso was a pretty tough cookie, though."

"What was an Italian Mafioso doing in our little country town?!"

"Mostly sightseeing, apparently."

"Sightseeing!"

"You know how delinquents go on a school trip and get into a big fight with the local high school thugs in some manga? It was that sort of thing."

"What sort of thing?!"

If all this was true, it went well beyond playing at defenders of justice.

What had I done to deserve such a sister? Forget about justice, this slant-eyed Ponytail Head was defender of jack squat.

"It got pretty exciting toward the end! A real party—that's how it got to Russian roulette. Ahaha, a Japanese girl playing Russian roulette with the Italian Mafia. That's so globalist, you forget who's from where."

"In that case, how about we exile you and strip you of your citizenship." It was time for Karen to leave Japan, if she cared about peace. "Hm? But wait a sec. If your opponent had the last chamber, that means you went to bat first, no?"

It was odd to be speaking of Russian roulette like it was baseball, but anyway, for the last one to fall to her opponent, she had to have been the first to place the gun to her head... But didn't that mean she'd lost at rock-paper-scissors when they were deciding the order?

What happened to her sure way? Unless maybe it wasn't one on one? If there were three of them—

"Koyomi, you idiot!"

Karen hit me. Across the face, for no good reason.

When it came to violence, my sister never hesitated. She studied at a dojo geared toward actual combat, and her skills were beyond first-rate, but when it came to mental composure she was a rank amateur.

Sadly.

"In a serious battle where lives are on the line," she proclaimed,

"I'd never use anything as underhanded as a sure way to win at it! I embody justice!"

"If that's how you feel, when does your method ever come into play?!"

What a pinhead. She'd forgotten what she'd told me only a minute ago.

Well, once we started talking about Russian roulette, the rest was probably all nonsense. The whole premise was bankrupt.

"What's my name?!" yelled my sister.

"Uh, wasn't that the line of an incredible villain?"

An incredibly funny one, too. What Jagi lacked in strength, he made up for in impact relative to his fictional brothers.

Such a contrast with Raditz.

"I think I get it," I said. "This sure way of yours must take incredible kinetic vision, like seeing how your opponent's fingers move and reacting in the blink of an eye."

As unbelievable as it sounds, apparently some people out there are capable of such extraordinary feats. I heard it from Hanekawa, so it's probably true.

Huh, so maybe if it was right after feeding Shinobu my blood, I could pull it off too?

"Tsk tsk tsk. What sort of sure way is that? If you got your eyes poked, it'd be useless."

"Why would you be playing rock-paper-scissors after getting your eyes poked? Who'd ever want to under such harsh conditions?"

"A real martial artist is prepared for all contingencies. I aim to be as omnidirectional as possible."

"Well, I'm not a martial artist, let alone aiming to be whatever an omnidirectional one is. What sort of unprincipled mastery is that, anyway? And if they poked your eyes, how would you know if you've won or lost?"

Your opponent could just lie. Anyone willing to go after your eyes would hardly flinch at the idea of telling a lie.

"What's essential is invisible to the eye, Koyomi."

"Don't be sounding like the Little Prince to fudge things." Speaking of which, I always thought they should add a footnote to that famous line: Not everything invisible to the eye, however, is essential. "If your eyes got poked, I guess they went with scissors."

"Haw! Seriously though, the sure way I've come up with works even if your opponent tries to lie. Heheh, I should win the Nobel Prize for this!"

"Really? Because I can't think of anything stupider than believing that every clever idea qualifies for a Nobel Prize."

"Heh, squawk all you like, little birdie, but after you hear my method, you'll never ever say 'Rock and paper and scissors, I win!' like a grade schooler again."

Combining the three into a single hand gesture—with the middle and index fingers opened to make scissors, the thumb lifted to make paper, and the last two fingers clenched in rock...

"Ah, when I was a kid, we used to call that a 'pistol'..." But forget about never saying it again, I'm pretty sure no high schooler ever did it. In fact, did anyone who was already in middle school?

"A pistol? Oh, right. It looks like a gun. Huh. But my method even works against people who claim victory that way... Let's see, if not the Nobel Prize, then I deserve, uh, uh, the Pulitzer for this..."

"......"

Didn't she even know what the Pulitzer was? Without my noticing, had she fallen behind? My sister who was supposed to be smart having turned into a total blockhead at some point was kind of depressing...

Did my sisters feel the same way when I turned into a slacker after starting high school?

Talk about sad. It made me want to go easier on them.

"All right, all right, lay it on me," I said. "Your sweet big brother Koyomi is ready to listen, Karen-chan."

I raised my hands in the air. Not in celebration, but in surrender.

Until I let her tell me her method, our conversation, though maybe not our legs, would stand still. It was like some flag you had to trigger to proceed in a game. Like a YES/NO question that keeps popping back up until you finally choose YES.

I doubted it was a quest line that I needed to clear to beat the game, though…

"Okay! Since you insist, Koyomi, I'll teach you. In practice, too. Ah, but you probably need some motivation. We should make a bet."

"No thanks, that sounds like too much trouble."

"Come on, otherwise you might try to be a sore loser and say you lost on purpose or something."

"Losing on purpose at rock-paper-scissors would be as impressive as a sure way to win…"

What a pain in the ass my sister could be. Couldn't she just jump out into the street for no reason and get herself run over?

"All right, Koyomi, how about something physical? A dare. Whoever loses has to piggyback the winner."

"Piggyback…"

"Yeah, all the way to where we're going."

"……"

Hell, why not? I was pretty sure there was no sure way to win at rock-paper-scissors, and if I did win, she could carry me piggyback. It would be a fitting punishment for all her nonsense.

What's that you say? Even if there's no sure way to win, I might still lose normally?

That would be that.

All I had to do was not honor my end of the bargain (grin).

Alas, unlike in the little baby world of middle schoolers, any contract not executed on paper wasn't much of a contract at all in the adult world of high schoolers.

What guy in his right mind would parade around his own neighborhood with his taller (and maybe also heavier) sister on his back?

"Fine, then," I said. "I agree to your terms."

"Hm? You accepted awfully quick."

"Nah, I'm not plotting anything. Trust your big brother. He's the type of man who never goes back on his word, yeah?"

"That's right. I sure am proud of you." Karen nodded and flashed a pleasant smile.

Promises with my smarter little sister, Tsukihi, were another matter, but having broken thousands of them with Karen by now, your guess is as good as mine as to where her trust came from.

I was starting to worry if she was seriously stupid.

"All right," I said. "Rock—"

"Ah, wait, wait, wait," Karen interrupted me mid-stance. "The match has already begun at that point. I need to be the one to say it. That's stage one of my method."

"Stage one... Sounds pretty overblown for just a game of rock-paper-scissors. How many are there?"

"Two."

"La-a-me!"

Just two.

Maybe you needed to mind your step, but they weren't actual stages.

"Is it," I asked, "in order to control the field? Some kind of spiritual thing—like Feng Shui? Not that I get Feng Shui...which means 'wind' and 'water'? Anyway, whatever. Knock yourself out."

"Okay, let's do this." Karen drew back one arm. "Rock..."

Then she yelled—

"Paper!"

And stuck her hand out in rock shape.

"......"

Obviously, I hadn't made my move—or rather, never had the chance.

Karen stood there with her hand in a fist against thin air.

"Heheheheh. Do you get it, Koyomi? Do you? I go 'rock,' then stick my hand out at 'paper.' That way, since your opponent is still waiting for 'scissors,' you get them to throw late! An ultimate technique that uses the name of the game to force your opponent into dropping the ball! In other words! Regardless of whether he plays rock, paper, or scissors, he's thrown late so I win automatically! Now! I'll be accepting my piggyback ride!"

Whereupon I punched my sister in the face. How's that for rock?

It was no love tap either, but a demonic iron fist.

My punch wasn't half bad. My sister had her own iron defenses, but since she was so busy grandstanding, it connected squarely. They say people are at their most vulnerable when they're certain of victory, and I guess that wasn't a cliché for nothing.

"Bullshit," I scolded. "Who in the world is going to recognize such a win? If you pull that with the Italian Mafia, they'll shoot you dead on the spot."

"Nrgh, but it seemed like a pretty good idea when I thought of it just now."

"You just thought of it!"

Well, I'd figured as much. But the confidence with which she talked up an idea she'd just thought of... Even if she was my sister, I had to hand it to anyone who could bluff that hard.

Still, she'd given it hardly enough thought. It was too simplistic. Couldn't she see that I'd get mad?

"Karen, you lose for breaking the rules. A piggyback ride isn't going to cut it. As punishment, you have to carry me on your shoulders."

"Ack. I guess," Karen readily accepted my harsher punishment.

I called her Spartan, but actually she was a flat-out masochist. I often wondered if she bugged me whenever she had the chance because she wanted to be punished.

"All right, Koyomi. Get on my shoulders."

She crouched down for real—and I started to think that maybe I was the one being punished here. Was I about to travel around my own neighborhood, my own territory, on my sister's shoulders?

I didn't need to go to the police, they'd come to me. What was I gonna tell them?

"Hrrm, you know…maybe we should just forget about this, Karen. With all the studying I've been doing I've put on some weight lately."

"How much do you weigh?"

"About…125 pounds."

"That's nothing. Anything less than four hundred pounds is light as a feather to me."

"You live on the Moon or what?"

Four hundred pounds. Even on the Moon that'd come in at around sixty-five pounds, still pretty heavy for some people.

"W-Well, Karen, even so. On your back is one thing, but your ponytail would get in the way of carrying me on your shoulders. It'd stick right into my belly, so I'd have to lean back, and I might end up tipping over. And if you undid it, your hair might get wrapped around my legs, and that might get pretty painful."

"Hm? Ah, my ponytail. Maybe you're right."

"Don't you think?"

"Yeah, you have a point. Like always, my big brother knows best."

She stood up immediately as if she'd given up—perhaps trying to persuade her hadn't been a waste of time, but I also knew better than anyone that Karen wasn't the type of girl to listen once she got an idea into her head.

As soon as she got out of her crouch, she reached into her jersey pocket and pulled out her key to our house.

The key? Why would she pull it out now?

"Hm? Koyomi, haven't you ever used the teeth on a key to cut through packing tape and clothes tags?"

"Uh, yeah, I guess I've done that before."

When there weren't any scissors around—but it's not like there was any packing tape to cut… Wait a second, scissors?

Scissors, like—

"Hup."

It was already too late.

With the key in her hand, Karen stretched her arm behind her, placed the teeth against the base of her ponytail, and snagged them back and forth like a saw to hack through her hair.

As casually as you or I might peel a banana.

In contrast to her casual air, the noise was hideous and grating.

".........nkk!"

"Hum hum... Ah, and there's a garbage can right there." *Whoa, I feel lighter,* she remarked in between her humming as she half-walked, half-skipped over to the bin, into which she lobbed her severed and curled-up ponytail.

Like it had been nothing, she returned the key to her pocket.

"All right," she told me, "now you can get on my shoulders!"

"That was badass!"

She was a stone-cold badass...and a total moron! My sister really was a blockhead! Depressing didn't begin to cover it!

She ditched her trademark hairstyle since grade school just to carry me around on her shoulders—in other words, just because she'd cheated at rock-paper-scissors. Or to put it even more starkly, just because she'd lost at rock-paper-scissors!

"Y-You! You you you! Your hair looks so...jagged!"

"Hrm? Ah, who cares. I'll just swing by my usual hairdresser tomorrow. Well, come to think of it, they might be closed for the *Obon* holidays."

"If they saw what their customer did to her hair, they might close down for good!"

Karen's head looked like a retired sumo wrestler's...

I don't think I'd ever been so surprised in my life. Not even when I got turned into a vampire.

"You've had that ponytail since grade school! I thought that was your thing?!"

"I don't know, it was long and a pain to take care of. It got in the way whenever I was trying to sleep and I always had bedhead when I woke up. Honestly I've been sick of it."

"But you kept it anyways?!"

She really was a masochist! Since grade school! The real McCoy, a masochist through and through!

"Still, don't just throw your hair in the bin! The collector might think that something terrible happened! 'A woman's hair is her life,' haven't you heard?!"

"Hrm? Nope."

"You dunderhead!"

Such unfathomable stupidity! Was she the kind of moron who'd write "Merry XXX" on her Christmas cards and actually send them out?!

Maybe even the kind of moron who gets invited out by a guy (a date) and brings him dried fruit (not the same thing)?!

"A woman's hair is her life? Hmph, that's a fine saying. But words can't quite measure up to life. And I dare to throw mine in the gutter. I strive to shine like a beautiful gem even in the gutter, like my master exhorts me to."

"So it's this master's fault you turned out this way?!"

I knew it, I needed to pay a visit to that dojo! There were things we needed to discuss! Transforming my little sister into some human weapon... Was the place called Shocker by any chance?

"Ack, there's no going back... What now? I wonder what Tsukihi will say."

"Yeah, she might not like it," Karen muttered, (finally) looking concerned. Tsukihi's opinion was very important to her. "Urgh, I can't believe you made me do this."

"Don't blame it on me! She'll kill me!"

Well, either way, Karen's hair wasn't going to grow back by talking about it (or rather, I didn't want to anymore).

"Okay, Koyomi, time to get on my shoulders. Chicken walk, chicken walk ♪"

"What are you so perky about... Having to carry someone around on your shoulders excites you? You damn masochist. The only one being punished here is me. Uh, let's see…" Giving up, I started to get on Karen's shoulders, straddling her neck and wrapping my thighs on either side of the sad wreckage that was now her hair.

"Huh? Wait, are you getting on sitting up?"

"What do you mean?"

"It's just, don't people usually get on sideways?"

"Only in a judo throw!"

She'd look like a bandit abducting me. The normal way was at least a little better.

As we continued to banter, I straddled my sister's shoulders. Straddled.

……

Ooh…such a feeling of conquest.

The position really was like mounting. Not in the sense of getting on a horse, but as in what dogs did.

Thanks to her height and skill at martial arts, my sister maintained a perfectly subtle dynamic with me, where it was never quite clear who had the upper hand. At the moment, though, it was hard not to feel like I was on top.

I was overcome with an odd sense of superiority.

The moment, however, was fleeting.

"Okay, upsie-daisy!"

With that, Karen rose with my 125-pound frame on her shoulders as easily as if she were carrying nothing at all.

"Wh-Whoa, whoa, whoa! This is scary, this is damn scary! My eye level is so high, it's scary! Put me down! Put me down! Put me down right now!"

My vantage point was about equal to Karen's height, minus her head, plus my sitting height. Heck, even without doing the math, it was easily more than seven feet off the ground… Wow, some basketball players in America walked around like this every day?

My embarrassment at being carried around on my sister's shoulders vanished, overwritten like the ideology of the losing side in a war.

All that remained was the sheer terror of my vantage point.

"I'm sorry, please let me down! Uncle, uncle!"

Forget any sense of superiority, I was feeling like a loser now. I might actually grovel once she let me down. I'd do a handstand if that's what she wanted.

"Hmmm…" Paying no mind to my mangy yelps, Mistress Karen began walking at a brisk pace. In time, however, she stopped and tilted her head. "Koyomi, do you mind?"

"What is it?"

"Your crotch grinding into the back of my head feels gross."

"……"

Right, I knew we shouldn't be doing this at our age. It was a weird thing—

"Hey, I've got an idea," Karen suggested. "Since I cut off my ponytail, it's only fair if you cut off your thing."

"That's horrendous!"

This was all so frightening! The height, her inspiration! She deserved the Bram Stoker Award!

Besides, she decided to cut off her ponytail on her own, so how was that fair? Don't make it sound like it was merely my responsibility!

"Your hair might grow back, but if I cut off my thing, it's all over for me! In all kinds of ways."

Maybe back when I was a vampire! No, not even then!

Pain was still pain! Just thinking about it hurt!

"I see. Anyway, Koyomi, I can handle your weight but don't keep swaying like that or we'll lose our balance."

"Easy for you to say. I'm not you. How the heck am I supposed to balance myself stuck here like a giraffe?"

Giraffes have some amazing neck muscles, you know? If anyone's ever suggested that the Loch Ness Monster might actually be a giraffe, I for one lend my support to the theory.

"Fine," Karen conceded. "It will probably be a bit of a strain, but lean your upper body against my neck and head and shift the center of gravity forward. And then tuck your dangling legs under my armpits. That way I can hold you in place like the safety bar at an amusement park."

"Like this?"

"Clank," Karen added a sound effect. Instantly, not just my torso or my legs, but my entire body seemed to lock into place. It was less like a safety bar and more like a judo hold.

Like when they disable you by bending back just one thumb.

Or wait...that was aikido, wasn't it?

Either way, I'd yet to see Karen perform one normal, straightforward karate move.

What was up with her Shocker dojo?

"There, we're good," she said.

"Uh, I'm not sure I am. In fact, it's even less good? How much less good for me is this gonna get? I can't even move my fingertips. And I'm starting to feel pins and needles. Boss-lady, are you sure you're not cutting off my circulation?"

"Well, it's definitely better for me. Before, your calves kept chafing me right on the tip of my breasts and it was gross... I had your crotch on my head, and you're all up in my armpits now. Who knew carrying someone on your shoulders was so kinky?"

"Hmm... Usually, it'd be the guy carrying the girl."

It wasn't supposed to be a weird affair, but rather, cheerful and jaunty.

"Okay, Koyomi, let's get going. Tee-hee."

With that, Karen's legs, which had stood still, began to move again. Maybe that ponytail she cut off weighed as much as I do because her pace didn't even slow.

No, with each step she seemed to gain steam. You couldn't blame her. Considering our destination that summer vacation morning—you definitely couldn't blame Karen.

003

Just to be clear, let me take a moment to state that Karen and I aren't particularly close—she and my other sister, Tsukihi, the youngest child, were born a year apart and are pretty chummy-chummy, but I'm afraid the same cannot be said about my sisters and myself.

You might even say that we didn't get along. That there was hostility.

Karen and Tsukihi, for their part, never listened to me, while I, for my part, had it up to here with their infantilism—especially how they played at defenders of justice as the Fire Sisters. The recent encounter with Deishu Kaiki had fallen short of making them mend their ways.

Man, that Kaiki was so useless. In being a bother and nothing else, no other grownup came close.

So you see, it was rare for me and Karen to be out and about like this, just the two of us—almost as rare as it was for her to do anything at all without Tsukihi.

Which was why we tiptoed around each other when we spoke.

The fact that all the tiptoeing wound up with Karen cutting off her ponytail and me on her shoulders proved what a nuisance it was to be siblings.

It certainly wasn't like a manga or anime. That sort of affection for your little sister is as nonexistent as a unicorn. They say incest is the purview of the upper classes, so I suppose that makes sense. We Araragis are decidedly middle class.

So why today, Monday, August fourteenth? Why were Karen and I spending time together this day?

Relax, there's a perfectly good reason that isn't suddenly winning the lottery and ascending to the upper classes. A respectable reason, which I suppose I'd better give if there are to be no bizarre rumors about Koyomi Araragi getting along oh-so-well with his little sister.

Begin flashback.

Earlier that morning.

"Koyomi? Is there something you'd like me to do for you?"

I forgot to mention, but I'm a high school senior. In other words, I'm studying for entrance exams, so there's no vacationing in my summer vacation. It's just summer.

For everyone else, mid-August is the *Obon* holiday season, but sadly, as an exam taker, that passed me by, too. Actually, in the first place, our family doesn't pay much attention to old native customs.

Oshino would be furious if he knew.

So would Hanekawa, probably—then again, in her case, she'd scold me just as much if I used the holidays as an excuse not to study.

Well, getting scolded by Hanekawa only put a spring in my step, so she could go right ahead. I wish she'd get pissed off, her shoulders shaking, and her breasts, naturally, shaking as well.

Okay.

I'd woken up early once again and was working on my usual morning drills before breakfast when Karen suddenly (and without knocking) threw open the door and burst into my room.

My sister.

Karen Araragi.

The perpetually jersey-clad middle schooler.

"Not a thing…" I replied.

By the way, "throw open the door" doesn't entirely capture the reality of what she did. If this were a mystery that hinged on narrative devices, critics would call me out on it. In truth, like investigators rushing the culprit's hideout in a police drama, she didn't just throw the door open but kicked it open.

That was Karen's standard interaction with doors.

In her cultural milieu, they were always opened with the back of one's foot, whether it was a sliding Japanese one or a hinged Western one—

No… If it were a cultural thing, then Tsukihi and I, raised in the same milieu, would behave in the same manner, so scratch that.

"Whaaat? There must be something," Karen complained, approaching my desk (I didn't bother turning around) and throwing herself at me.

When I say she threw herself at me, I don't intend that as a figure of speech like "my legs are dead" or "his eyes popped out" or "walk through fire." I mean it literally. She approached me from behind and wrapped her arms around my neck like a scarf. She was glued to my back without a hint of hesitation. In that sense, she hadn't so much thrown herself at me, as on me.

Snap.

The No. 2 pencil in my right hand broke in half. My writing implement, pentagonal in shape to bring luck to the exam taker—what an ill omen.

I'm repeating myself here (as much as I'd rather not, given the shame and mortification), but my sister, Karen Araragi, is significantly taller than the average third-year middle school girl—and worse, is still growing. Taller today than yesterday, and taller still tomorrow than today, her height continues to increase.

Sure, she could measure as many feet and inches as she liked. That, in itself, was no skin off my back—the problem here was the lamentable fact that she was consequentially taller than me.

People of a certain size can't help intimidating the rest of us whether they mean to or not. On top of that, Karen did martial arts. She was a second-degree black belt.

In other words, having installed karate techniques on the hardware she'd been blessed with, namely her body, she possessed the fighting capabilities to easily take on some wild animals.

In fact, I had witnessed her putting her fist through a stucco wall like it was tofu. Afterward her arm had gotten stuck, and to free herself she'd bust down even more of the wall.

It was insane, a bonus round in an old-school fighting game.

Anyway, if you're wondering what the point is, I just thought you should know what kind of a grizzly-bear sister had thrown herself at, or rather, on me. Can you imagine my horror? I don't think you can, but I still wanted to put it into words.

"Come on, Koyomi, I want to help. Believe it or not, your sister is someone you can rely on. I'm your faithful little sister, you know? Your devoted little sister? Anything you want, just say the word and I'll do it. I am at your service, o-kay?"

"Nothing. There's absolutely nothing. What in the hell could I possibly want from my sister so early in the day? There is nothing I need, and there's nothing you can do. In the fifteen years since you were born, you haven't been of any help whatsoever to me, woman."

If anything, she could leave me be. I was busy memorizing vocabulary at the moment. With that implicit message, I brushed her arms from around my neck.

If she had a mind to, that is to say, if she lost it for a moment and squeezed those arms tighter, soon I'd be tilting my head, and not in the sense of feeling perplexed, but in the way of bidding this earthly plane a swift adieu. I didn't want her hanging off me any longer than necessary.

A bout against a legendary vampire. Mortal feline combat. The crab, the snail, the monkey, and the snake. And the bee.

After all those tribulations, it would be a shame if Koyomi Araragi, the battle-hardened veteran, were done in by his little sister's sleeper choke.

That aside, having my sister hanging all over me doesn't float my boat.

I was simply creeped out.

"Can't you see I'm trying to focus on my studies? I haven't the time to mess around with a lower life form, you amoeba. If you're bored why don't you go for a run? Feel free to never come...back..."

Assuming that all this nonsense was just her way of killing time, probably because her schedule didn't match up with Tsukihi's, I turned around, finally, to chase Karen away—and was left speechless by what I saw.

I had no words. I became acutely aware of humanity's state of mind before we acquired language. It hit me like a ton of bricks. I'd never have guessed that lacking the means to describe something in plain sight could inflict so much stress on an organism's psyche.

But if I must—

If I must, for the honor of the primate order, somehow put into words the uncanny sight—

"Let's see..."

Karen Araragi, my sister, was wearing a skirt.

......

So what, you might argue.

To convey if only a fifth of my shock, I might have put that in italics, like so: *My sister was wearing a skirt.*

But I'd even forgotten to italicize it. Italicization had been lost to me.

Like I said earlier, Karen always wore a jersey. To rephrase, she wore nothing else. Jerseys were her combat fatigues, or like the robes of a saint. Yet she had doffed the cloth and donned a skirt.

Her all-too-long legs were receiving undue emphasis.

A similar phenomenon was manifest, not just for her lower body, but from her waist up.

She wasn't wearing a sports top or a windbreaker. Not even a running dress.

Instead, she was attired in an entirely unsportsmanlike stole and sleeveless turtleneck.

Such long arms! So slender a neck!

And, and...

Who was this pretty girl?!

Napoleon I supposedly said, "The clothes make the man." If so, the Karen Araragi standing before me, in this room, in this house, was and was no longer Karen Araragi.

Well.

She was a middle school girl, after all.

It wasn't completely unheard of for her to wear the school-designated skirt and blouse (as for the likelihood, imagine glancing up at the sky and happening to spot a cascade of shooting stars, and you wouldn't be far off), but that was just her uniform.

If I took that into account, though, it was comprehensible. She was bending the rules, but she must have her reasons, and I could be magnanimous and let it slide.

Yet her current outfit looked bare to a degree that was unthinkable for school clothes.

It flaunted the edicts of nature.

She could...wear something other than a jersey?!

That was like Kiryl equipping the Zenithian Armor!

I gulped, hard. This took beating the summer heat to a new level.

They were probably Tsukihi's clothes. Her outfit looked like something you'd see on the pages of a fashion magazine, stylish and coordinated. Tsukihi, for her part, went for traditional Japanese clothing so hard that she joined her school's tea ceremony club just so she could wear kimonos, but she wasn't as much of a fanatic as Karen (in other words, didn't attach as much meaning to the way she dressed) and had plenty of ordinary clothes as well.

Still, Karen and Tsukihi possessed very different body types.

The turtleneck showed off Karen's contours as clearly as a form-fitting T-shirt, while the creased skirt, probably not designed to be very long in the first place, transformed into an extreme miniskirt.

She wasn't wearing stockings or even socks, and her long, bare legs jutting out from the hem of the skirt were enough to fill me with terror.

Terror.

A host of traumatic incidents came back to me. This and that and...

Hey, all of it happened in the past few months!

Seriously, how many brushes with death have I had in that time?!

But forget about my trauma... Right now, we're talking about Karen.

"Karen... If you're being bullied, you should have told me! Why didn't you come to me sooner, before things went so far?!"

"Nah, I'm not being bullied," Karen denied after I leapt irate from my swivel chair and grabbed and shook her by the shoulders, which she, with a tired look, let me do. "If anyone is bullying me, honestly, it's you."

"Urk."

"I can laugh about it now, but back in grade school, some of the heartless things you said made me want to kill myself."

"Urrk."

Deep.

Why was she confessing this to me now? Did I really say anything that mean?

"It's what inspired me to become a defender of justice—so you see, my hatred of evil actually stems from you."

"You don't say." What a thing to be responsible for, don't place that on me... "B-But, Karen, there's no way you'd dress like that unless somebody threatened you! Ah, you poor thing... Someone forced you to wear those silly clothes instead of your usual jersey and posted the pics on your school's secret student forum..."

Everything went black, and I cradled my head.

Unbelievable. Not even noticing that my sister was dealing with terrible stuff, I'd been studying for my sorry exams. Wrapped up in percentiles and the cult of academic merit, I'd lost sight of what matters most...

My conscience lashed at me like waves upon the shore. If I didn't get ahold of myself, I might go on some rampage. The only thing keeping me sane was my anger.

Anger at myself, and also against the world.

"Don't worry, Karen! I'll fix this somehow! I'm your brother, leave it to me! Just tell me the address and phone number of whoever's been bullying you, and the name of the homeroom teacher who turned a blind eye! I'll make them pay for what they've done!"

"Sometimes you're hotter than fire, big brother."

I'm crushing on you, Karen added with a smile.

It was a gentle smile.

Hmm. Judging from her reaction, I seemed to be on the wrong track.

But if she wasn't being bullied, what explanation was there? Didn't Sherlock Holmes say that when you've eliminated the logically untenable possibilities, whatever remains, however improbable, must be the truth?

Unless there was some possibility that I was missing?

Hrrm. Mr. Holmes' articulation of the process of elimination was kinda loose.

"Ahh, I got it! Cosplay!"

"Since when is a girl wearing a skirt cosplay?" Karen objected. "It's not like I never feel hurt, you know. That's the kind of stuff that made me want to die back in grade school."

"Oh, yeah? So you were pretty delicate once upon a time," I remarked as if it had nothing to do with me. I wasn't showing an ounce of remorse, if I do say so myself. "Well, if you're not being bullied and it's not cosplay, what the hell?"

"Oh, um, aren't I cute?"

With a husky moan, Karen struck an enticing pose with all the muscles in her body.

It was far from sexy. If anything, it was a superb martial arts stance. I guess that wasn't surprising since she'd rotated her hips while standing straight.

"I-I don't know about cute," I stuttered.

"Cute is the word," warned Karen, still in her enticing pose.

It was actually a fairly strained stance, and maintaining her balance couldn't have been easy, but she was indeed athletic.

By the way, while I'd rather not divulge a fact that touches on my dignity as an older brother, my sister is genuinely terrifying when she tries to intimidate me for real. According to legend, once, she even beat a lion at a staring contest at the zoo.

Looking away as casually as I could, I said, "C-Cute, yes."

N-No, I wasn't sucking up to my little sister on account of some unstated threat! *(Ex)cuse us,* is what I meant to say!

I just misspoke, like Hachikuji!

Sorry, a slip of the tongue!

"......"

Karen continued to intimidate me in the same pose. She was seriously scaring me.

The pain from when she beat the crap out of me the other day during the bee incident had to be engraved in my marrow as my latest trauma.

My body began trembling uncontrollably.

"Cute! Cute! Cuuute," I found myself repeating.

Clearly, I was just misspeaking serially here, and what I meant was, *Cut! Cut! Cut (your crap).* I'm sure Hachikuji's tongue would have slipped more elegantly, but I'm no Hachikuji. True, an elegant slip of the tongue is an odd metaphor.

"......"

We both fell silent. The awkwardness was palpable. Several seconds passed...

"Eheheh!"

...and, believe it or not, Karen hugged me.

A middle-school girl hugging you might sound adorable, but the facts on the ground belied that image.

That image is fake.

Going back to the lion at the zoo, and expanding on it, I imagine you've seen clips on TV and elsewhere of wild carnivores hunting in Africa and other places, right?

Karen's movements were analogous.

Swift and nimble. From her first step, she was already at top speed.

In traffic accidents and such, when humans are in imminent danger, we often mistakenly stiffen up. Well, even if I hadn't frozen, Karen's attacks were impossible to dodge—maybe during spring break, but not this summer vacation, not me.

Indeed, Karen was able to hug me head-on as if she were tackling me.

About a year ago, I'd witnessed her crashing through a steel girder at school with the same maneuver. It was already pretty deteriorated, but still—the scene flashed before my eyes.

Fortunately for me, I did not share in that steel girder's fate. The impact, however, was enough to knock the wind out of my guts.

My ribs, made of bone and not steel, creaked dangerously.

Karen, who had wrapped her arms around my back with no apparent concern for my lungs, now proceeded to slide them up around my neck and to pull herself close.

Total coverage. As in around-the-clock? No, twenty-four hours of this would be a little much. Actually, even one minute!

If she bear-hugged me with all her strength, she might split me right in half. Neither Shinobu over spring break nor the cat monster over Golden Week had done such a crazy thing to me.

If this wasn't horror, then what was?

"K-Karen?"

"Thank you! I'm so happy to hear my brother say that! So happy! Yay!" Still hugging me, squeezing even tighter, Karen let out a jubilant cry.

Yet another helping of horror…

This was all-you-can-eat horror.

"..........nkk!"

We had a serious situation here.

My sister…was being affectionate.

Well, maybe not a serious situation, but certainly an unfunny one. Honestly, she'd been weird from the beginning. Asking me if there was anything she could do for me, even if it was just to pass the time, was unlike Karen.

Can I make you pass out to pass the time? would have been more like her (which is scary enough coming from your little sister).

"Ahh, it's so relaxing hugging my big brother like this. It must be because you're so accepting. I bet this is what a Tempur-Pedic pillow feels like."

"Geez, stop, you're freaking me out. Yuck, yuck, yuck, let me go. I'm sorry, you really are." I thrashed around but couldn't pry myself loose. Physically, I was no match for Karen, but I'm not sure it was even her arm strength. It almost felt like some sort of structural restraint. "Seriously, what kind of prank is this? What's with your new character?"

She really wasn't being bullied? Then was it some kind of dare? In which case, I was the one getting mistreated here. What did I do to deserve to be picked on by a bunch of middle schoolers?

"Hey, be happy," Karen ordered. "Your cute little sister is bothering to act all cuddly."

"My cute little sister…"

"You just said I'm cute. Real men don't go back on their word."

"I haven't got any for you right now!"

Well, sure.

Maybe it was just the novelty of it, but she actually didn't look half bad in a skirt.

"Just, tell me what you're up to," I said. "Not just what you're doing, either. Explain in order, starting with what you think you are."

"Huh? Sure, I just thought…I'd turn over a new leaf and start pitching myself as the little sister who loves her brother and never disobeys him."

41

"Pitch all you want, I'm not buying it! Besides, you're stepping on Kanbaru's turf!"

Obviously she wasn't my little sister, but as my junior her position was similar.

"Kanbaru," Karen uttered—and suddenly let go of me.

The sense of freedom reminded me of being un-cuffed (something that actually happened to me late last month, the simile is based on experience)—and Karen took three steps back to put some space between us.

As though to avoid stepping on her master's shadow, as the saying goes.

Hm.

What now? Karen had a weird look on her face.

She'd been acting weird from the start, but this was straight-up weird (though "straight-up weird" is another odd turn of phrase).

As glad as I was to be free, she was acting very quiet all of a sudden. Maybe I'd surprised her by suddenly mentioning an unfamiliar name in the way of quipping.

"Umm, Karen. Don't let the 'baru' mislead you, it's got next to nothing to do with Bao the Visitor. Kanbaru is one grade under me at school, and…"

I figured this was my chance to change the topic, and if I was lucky, maybe Karen wearing a skirt could be consigned to the dustbin of history, so I proceeded to try to explain who Kanbaru was, but that was easier said than done.

My junior Kanbaru. A second-year student at Naoetsu High School, and a former ace basketball player.

In a sense, no one could be simpler to understand, but in a different sense, no one was as incomprehensible. How did I explain her?

It was almost like trying to explain how a centipede walks. Or like being asked how falling in love works.

If I just shared my plain, unadorned thoughts on her, it'd sound like I was badmouthing her. Her reputation would suffer, and I didn't want that at all.

My vocabulary sucked. No wonder I had so much trouble improving my composition scores.

"Let's see... Kanbaru is like an E5 series bullet train, one of those maglevs...or maybe a fighter jet...like the Phantom?"

As I babbled searching for the right analogy, Karen interrupted—and surprised me.

"Of course, Suruga Kanbaru."

Huh?

Wait, what? I'm pretty sure I hadn't said her full name yet.

"Karen?"

With a determined air, she yelled, "Big brother! I have a favor to ashk you!"

Suddenly raising her voice had made the end come off sounding babyish. The speed with which she followed up, however, cancelled out the trivial error.

Too fast for the eye to see, it was like a flash step. Or a full-body *Futae no Kiwami* double limit break.

Rapidly dropping to her knees, she planted her palms out in a forty-five-degree angle completely flush with the carpeted floor; bent her supple, lithe upper body forward as if it were an attachment designed for that purpose; and then smacked down her forehead, one of the hardest parts of the human body, as if in rebellion against Mother Earth.

Put simply, she prostrated herself in a *dogeza*.

Put simply or not, in fact.

"I beg you, please introduce your worthless little sister to Kanbaru-sensei!"

"........."

Ah. Right.

So that's what it was.

Karen's suspicious, totally uncharacteristic behavior, so suspicious that I might have called the police, the hospital, or maybe even a prison hospital if she weren't family, finally made sense.

Suruga Kanbaru—as I said, she was a former basketball ace, but that profile was far too commonplace to truly describe her. She was a phenomenon that transcended ordinary phenomena, the biggest star in our school's history.

Kanbaru was so talented that she led our sports-poor prep school's feeble basketball team all the way to the national finals. To say the least, how many girls could pull off a slam dunk?

She had to leave the team partway through her second year for certain reasons but never ceased to be a star. Even now she was quite popular, especially among the younger students.

Quite a few of her admirers were fanatical.

I don't even want to recall exactly when, but this one time, I got surrounded and mobbed by a throng of her fans, a terribly awkward and overwhelming experience. Fortunately, Hanekawa showed up with Kanbaru to break things up and I survived, but I'd feared for my life.

First Senjogahara's fan, Kanbaru, tried to kill me, and then Kanbaru's fans made their move. I sure had some luck. Maybe next time Kanbaru's fans' fans would try to kill me.

In any case, I was aware that her popularity, her power of attraction, exceeded the confines of Naoetsu High. Still, middle schoolers knew about her, too?

She really was something else.

Suruga Kanbaru.

"Well, come to think of it," I said, "since martial arts are a sport nowadays, you knowing about a national-level player who's a local star isn't weird at all."

Apparently it was the rule or custom or whatever at Karen's dojo not to participate in tournaments (Or rather, they couldn't. Their style was so focused on actual combat that they were forbidden from joining related clubs at school), but Karen being Karen, if she did enter into such competitions, then make no mistake—or mistake as you might—she'd get to the nationals.

Maybe she felt close to Kanbaru in some way.

Still, did my worthless sister just say "sensei"?

I didn't know about that.

"Please, Koyomi—oopsy, my dear big brother!!"

"'Oopsy'…"

"Daisy!"

"Great timing—but!"

In place of a verbal riposte, I stepped on Karen's head.

Yes, I'm the kind of older brother who grinds his younger sister's head beneath his foot as she lies prostrate.

Consider it payback for her scaring me earlier (not that I was scared!).

"Ahh, it's an honor to be stepped on by you, big brother," Karen dared to say, resilient, face down and unresisting.

Basically a jock, she aspired to fortitude of the mental variety as well, and if it was in the service of some goal, this degree of punishment and humiliation was, as expected, practically fun for her.

Hmph. If I do say so about my own sister, she was *M cool.*

"Actually," I told her, "I'm pretty tired of seeing you prostrate yourself. Quit flattening yourself for every little thing, or soon that's how you'll be saying good morning. Do I look like an imperial parade? What sort of lord am I? Let me tell you something, little miss Karen, *dogeza* is a form of violence in this day and age."

It was strong-arm blackmail.

Even if I was stepping on her head.

"Of course!" my sister agreed. "Then I'll lick your foot! Starting from the big toe and in descending order!"

"And I'm saying I've had enough of that!"

"Nrkk!"

Karen lifted her face slightly from her position on the floor to look up at me. A fire seemed to smolder in her eyes as if to welcome any obstacle standing in her way. It was quite a wonderful expression.

"Fine then!" she cried. "What about my virginity? You can take my virginity!"

"I don't want my little sister's virginity!"

I gave her a swift kick to her face.

Reality admits of certain situations where violence against your little sister, still in middle school, is warranted.

"Ghak!"

Dealt such a blow, you couldn't maintain a *dogeza* even if you were Karen. Yet if you were Karen, you instantly leapt backward on your knees to diffuse the impact.

She even transitioned into a backflip, a so-called moonsault (I don't know if it was to downplay her reflexes or what) in my hardly spacious room, brushing the ceiling but completing the remarkable maneuver.

10.00! 10.00! 10.00! 10.00! 10.00!

What an incredible athlete.

She landed on my bed. The springs creaked, loudly.

I'd be sleeping a little less comfortably from now on.

What did she have to do that for?

"Karen… I know you get carried away and it seems fine now, but in ten years' time, when you've matured physically and mentally into an adult, you're going to cringe when you remember how you prostrated yourself before me. Just so you know, I won't ever forget that you did."

"Hmph. This is about now, not ten years later. How can there be a tomorrow unless you survive today?"

"That's a great line and all…"

But it meant prostrating yourself?

How pathetic. What kind of tomorrow awaited someone performing a *dogeza* today?

"I'm still gonna ask you, though, just in case," I said. "You're not doing this kind of shit outside the house, are you? Like with your friends or classmates…or teachers at school?"

"Of course not! Everyone looks up to me."

"……"

I supposed that was true. She was one of the Fire Sisters of Tsuganoki

46

Second Middle School, after all. Plus, Karen was the enforcer of the pair, so she tended to stand out more than Tsukihi. Karen occupied the most dangerous, most conspicuous position as the hotshot.

"My rule is that I only bow down to my big brother!"

"Don't be singling me out."

It was a nuisance. Maybe she needed to go die once so she'd be cured of her stupidity. Or maybe she could just be stupid and go die once anyways.

True, partly on account of her popularity, I did think at some point that she "resembled" Kanbaru. Due to their different circumstances, there were various minor dissimilarities, of course, but they definitely had a lot in common. Karen hearing rumors abut Kanbaru and idolizing her wasn't unthinkable.

It wasn't, but...

As accustomed as I was to seeing her prostrate herself—it was pretty much an everyday sight—switching out her jersey for a skirt, which she usually detested (I guess she considered it the proper attire for a doting sister) was a first in the history of Karen Araragi.

Since, out of pride or self-respect or something, she usually hated asking me, her big brother, for help when there was something she needed to do, it had to have taken a lot of resolve on her part to beg this hard.

Hmm.

"I'm surprised Tsukihi was willing to lend you her clothes, though... They're probably going to get all stretched out on you."

"Yeah. That's why I borrowed them without asking."

"......"

She was gonna get chewed out. Tsukihi was even scarier than her.

"I know you praised me and all," noted Karen, "but skirts don't really suit me. I mean, 'suit' isn't even the right word because I'm flashing so much skin. This mini sure makes kicking easy, though."

"Well, I don't think it was designed to be *that* provocative."

You better not walk up any stairs, I cautioned, to which she retorted,

47

I'd never step out of the house in this embarrassing outfit.

Considering that she'd taken Tsukihi's clothes without asking, that didn't seem like a very nice thing to say. But I doubted Tsukihi would be too mad since it didn't pertain to her kimonos.

About only Level 2 on her anger scale.

"By the way, Karen, how did you know that Kanbaru and I are friends?"

I couldn't help it when it came to being a quipper and had uttered her name, but I'd been very careful to keep the fact under wraps. In general, I hid my socializing from my sisters because they were bound to make a big fuss. They knew what was up with Hanekawa and Sengoku, but that was pretty much it. I'd been particularly secretive about my relationship with Kanbaru...

"Oh, right," Karen explained, "you're half in-frame in an awful lot of the snapshots that come attached to her unofficial fan club *Kanbaru Seule*'s online newsletter..."

"They don't get her permission for those pics, do they!"

Unofficial fan club? *Kanbaru Seule*?!

Ah, of course, their cell phones! My parents decided to give both my sisters cell phones, at last, starting this summer, in light of the rash behavior that the "defenders of justice" get up to.

It was a bad idea.

Forget online newsletters, the amount of info the Fires Sisters got their hands on had increased drastically—the ruckus the other day with the bee was a case in point—and Karen also ended up finding out about me and Kanbaru (the pic attachments on their own probably weren't enough).

The information age was terrifying. The world was truly going to hell in a hand basket.

Maybe I needed to talk to my parents and have my sisters' cell phones taken away. Karen and Tsukihi were definitely less safe for having them.

"Whaaat? Koyomi, isn't that a pretty old-fashioned way of thinking?

Adults are always complaining about kids using phones during class, but back when they were kids, didn't they work on other stuff and pass notes and all that?"

"Well, true."

The tools change, but our behavior doesn't. People are people.

While griping that young folks don't read enough and are therefore ignorant, older generations can be clueless in turn about smartphones and the internet.

Kids who're unable to read classical literature and parents who're unable to read light novels might not be so different—put more extremely, Lady Murasaki may have been a brilliant woman of letters, but transported to the modern era, even a picture book would stump her.

Comparing a culture vertically is pointless.

Okay, that last line is Hanekawa's, verbatim.

"When I dug a little deeper," Karen reprised, "I found out that Kanbaru-sensei holds you in high esteem! I don't know what trick you used, but she looks up to you as some sort of mentor?"

"Well…that's not wrong." It wasn't wrong, but the way Karen put it sounded so off. I hadn't tricked Kanbaru or anything, but it was all in her head.

"And so, Koyomi, you've become a real person of interest among middle-school girls. 'Who's this short dude bossing Kanbaru-sensei around like some errand girl?'"

"Junior high kids I've never even met have got it out for me…" I wasn't bossing her around, and if anyone was being inconvenienced by her devotion, it was this guy, right here.

"No, they're all your fans. You're the burning focus of envious middle-school girls."

"So much charisma, without my even noticing…" It was unpleasant in its own way. There was such a thing as bad publicity.

"Obviously, I've kept it a secret that we're related, but this has got to mean something, right? I'm tied to her through you—it's like fate.

Like she and I were meant to meet. So please, couldn't you introduce me to Kanbaru-sensei?"

"Fate, eh…"

"I bet she and I would get along just swell, actually," Karen muttered as if she were just talking out loud, folding her hands behind her head, whistling, and casting furtive glances at me.

That was apparently her attempt at nonchalance.

What a pest. The fact that she was actually a good whistler only made it more aggravating.

Well, she and Kanbaru probably would get along—they were both jocks and tomboys.

All the same…

All the same, I didn't intend to introduce my sister to Kanbaru.

Not a chance in hell. I had my reasons.

Namely—I happened to be aware of the sportswoman and national-level athlete Kanbaru's little-known sexual proclivities.

"Karen."

"What is it, brother dear?"

"Give it up."

Szukk.

An unnatural sound emanated from my stomach. It almost sounded like a spade being buried into dirt.

Sister had resorted to violence against brother, and without a moment's hesitation.

A lightning-quick spearhand jab right between the ribs.

It felt like my liver was gone.

"Now, now, Koyomi. Let's talk this over."

"……"

Hold on, it was going to be a second before I could talk again.

It wasn't even a matter of pain. I simply couldn't speak.

"You're not ready to oblige your cute little sister? Fine, I've got some ideas."

"H-Hrk…"

Karen was sounding like a regular hoodlum. What she had weren't "ideas"; the gods had granted to someone they absolutely shouldn't have something they absolutely shouldn't have.

They could be a little too capricious.

If they were going to endow her with that option, equip her with some ideas first!

"Wh-Who ever heard of going straight from a *dogeza* to violence... Give me a break!" I was finally able to speak, but I could feel my diaphragm vibrating against my guts, and my voice came out too strained and plaintive to call it quipping. "What d'you mean?"

Trying to cover up how sorry I sounded, I attempted an allusion, but unfortunately, it sounded even sorrier.

I did like the first one best; I find it small-minded and limited of viewers to huff that only the initial series is truly *Gundam* or that they won't accept the new *Kamen Rider*, but when I consider the evolution of *Pretty Cure*, I kind of know how they feel.

"Give you a break? What am I to do, Koyomi? How else will you see my side of things if we don't talk this over?"

"Your idea of talking things over involves fists."

As Tsukihi once said to me, in the context of human culture, punching and kicking was actually a means of communication. I think that only applied, though, when the parties were evenly matched. One-sided violence didn't qualify.

Can we take a moment to recap?

Back in grade school, they taught me to be neat and tidy.

Let's try that now.

Karen Araragi's goal was to get me to introduce her to Suruga Kanbaru—or more accurately, to get me to introduce Suruga Kanbaru to her.

That seemed pretty set. Firmly, immovably.

Karen was the type to balk at nothing to reach her goal.

She wasn't above believing that with enough moxie even one plus one could equal three. Once she got going, there was nothing anyone could say to sway her.

But there was another side to it—Karen rarely pursued goals for her own sake. She was surprisingly selfless in that regard. While she never hesitated to act on someone else's behalf, her own will could be incredibly weak.

Even feeble.

That was one big reason I considered Karen a fake. I'd been telling her that justice for others' sake was only a flimsy imitation in face of justice for your own sake. That was exactly why…

When she did have a clear goal of her own like now, she was very insistent, and I, for my part, wanted to do everything I could to help her achieve it.

However.

This time—I just couldn't. I didn't want to introduce Kanbaru to her.

I absolutely did not want to introduce Kanbaru to Karen.

That was my standpoint, Koyomi Araragi's *objective*.

Experiencing the occasional setback built character. I didn't want Karen and Tsukihi to turn into people who're squashed by a setback—that was my stance.

There was no room for compromise between us. We were in total opposition on the matter.

It was a binary issue, all or nothing, and one of us had to completely give in to the other—and since I had no intention of doing so, my only option was for Karen to. How, though?

If it came to blows I'd lose.

No way I could beat Karen in a fight.

Well, if we're being precise, with full backup from Shinobu, I couldn't lose—but per human rules that was probably out of bounds.

I thought this staring down at my shadow.

We were indoors, so it was faint.

"Hrm…"

In any case, we weren't going to resolve this by talking things over or punching things out. Getting beaten up wasn't going to change my mind, if I do say so like it didn't concern myself.

I'm large enough to accept any amount of violence my sister can dish out—I'd like to think so, being her older brother and all.

Maybe not her "dear big brother," but still her big bro.

"I guess this calls for a match," I said.

"Huh?"

"When we disagree, we have a match. That's how it's been between us."

It won't be an even one, though, I added.

I returned to my desk and closed my drills. I had no choice but to cancel my early-morning study session. I'd make up for it later.

No English vocabulary word superseded family matters.

"You're making a unilateral request, Karen. In gaming terms, it's not a match between players. You're playing against the house."

"Ah…"

Glimmer.

Her tone shifted. She lit up, as they say. She was equipped with a vector-motion sensor that responded automatically to any mention of a serious match.

"All right, deal," she assented. "You get it, after all. Set any rules you like. I'll overcome any and all conditions to be acquainted with Kanbaru-sensei."

She was as dense as ever.

So dense that it sometimes made my skin crawl.

At this rate, she was going to grow up a catastrophe of a person—setbacks or otherwise, if she didn't learn better, she was going to be "at risk." So much so that I'd be worried even if she wasn't my sister. Seriously at risk, dangerously so.

Well.

I was about to teach her a lesson.

How to go about it? She said I could set any rules I want, but I couldn't make it too hard of a challenge.

My sister had a developed sense of distaste for cowardice and opportunism. Her "burning soul of justice" supposedly didn't tolerate it.

The line had to be just on this side of feasible rule-wise and just on the other side condition-wise—a seemingly fair and just setup.

That's what I needed, but I was drawing a blank.

While I didn't want to make it too hard, for Karen not many challenges fit that description to begin with.

I mean, she'd even undergone a hundred-man *kumite*—and come out with a winning record. She was a lot gutsier than your average person.

Once, with a hostage held against her, she was pummeled by a biker gang, but even then she never cried uncle—though, true, I did have to come to her aid on that occasion.

If I hadn't made it in time, it would have ended in tragedy...

How the heck did that happen to you in such a peaceful town?

In other words, excessive gutsiness was a problem. Too much could be worse than too little.

Even apart from the whole soul-of-justice issue.

If I wasn't careful and made it too hard, she might go overboard trying, and it wouldn't be just a setback, she might injure herself in some final manner.

She didn't know how to back down—so you had to back up. Miss Passionate was the type to confront an enemy even when she was ill.

In that sense, I was the one in a fix here... It'd have to be hard and great if I was going to force her to admit defeat.

In fact, just the other day, when I tried to stop Karen from confronting that adversary despite her illness, we got into a huge fight... Would I have to go that far again?

Pain didn't pain her, and shame couldn't shame her.

Okay, she was kind of incredible... Calling her M cool fell short.

Was she really my sister?

Maybe she was adopted?

Hey, that'd be kinda *moé*.

I shouldn't be getting cold feet even before settling on a match, but maybe it'd be faster if I just gave up now and introduced her to Kanbaru—hm?

Mmm, right. This was all because of Kanbaru. In which case, what if I followed Kanbaru's lead?

"Wait here a second," I said. "I'll go get what we need."

"What we need? Are you planning on having us play cards? No fair!"

"What a thing to be calling unfair…"

How bad did you have to be at games where you used your brains to think that?

Fear not, Karen, I won't go that route. You won't admit defeat if I did.

It had to be something that seemed possible but wasn't (though I honestly worried about my sister's future if a game of cards was too much for her).

Time to give her a glimpse of hell that rivaled the one I had over spring break!

I left Karen in my room and went down to the bathroom. I found what I was looking for right away and returned with the items.

Karen was sprawled out on the bed.

Talk about making yourself at home. Her legs were spread out audaciously, with her underwear clearly on display.

Apparently my idiot of a sister had even borrowed Tsukihi's underwear. I know they were both girls and all, but Karen was going a little too far.

"Ah, Koyomi. That was fast."

"Were you seriously trying to take a nap while I was gone? Are you Nobita or what?"

"'No better'? But I am, thanks to my beauty sleep."

"That wasn't even clever."

"Be nice or I'll start sulking 'Suneo' later," she shot back, working in another character from *Doraemon*.

"That was annoyingly clever!"

"Hm? Koyomi, what's that you're holding?"

With that observant remark, Karen sat up. The way she rubbed her eyes, she hadn't been just lying down but actually napping.

Was I dealing with a wild animal? Or some sort of grizzled soldier?

"That's my toothbrush," she said.

Indeed. I'd gone down to grab Karen's orange-handled, fine-bristled toothbrush. I also remembered to bring toothpaste, which I was holding in my other hand.

"Y-You don't mean..." Karen looked uncharacteristically afraid, even a little green around the gills.

Hm. She was quick on the uptake, all right. Being a wild-animal grizzled soldier, maybe she'd figured it out.

I was hoping to surprise her, so I felt a little let down until she pointed a shaky finger my way and accused, "You're planning on sticking it up my butt?!"

......

I was the one taken by surprise now. I felt like I'd grown some gills before going green around them.

What the hell went through that head of hers?

"I should have known any brother of mine would be capable of cooking up something truly fiendish!"

"Uh, this brother of yours wasn't thinking anything of the sort..." She was overestimating me. I was nowhere near that level as a man.

"Really? When some stalker was following around one of the girls in her class, Tsukihi came up with a similar punishment."

"I'm scared!"

My little sister was absolutely terrifying! Well, yes, it did sound like the sort of thing Tsukihi might come up with! Karen, herself, tended not to think along those lines.

"Not even Tsukihi struck on the idea of using toothpaste," she marveled. "I knew you were in a different league."

"Hey, don't lump me in with Tsukihi."

"I'm not. You're in a different league."

"I'm in a different everything from her."

I was a little aghast. Tsukihi was a worse punk than Karen and could join a women's biker gang. Her own brother certainly felt intimidated.

"Maybe she went too far, but a coward who stoops to stalking girls has it coming, don't you think?" asked Karen, her face somewhat serious.

Given the vibes I was getting, I probably shouldn't mention to her, for the time being, that Kanbaru used to stalk me.

I guess this was more of my sisters playing at defenders of justice. My saying so would only elicit the usual rebuttal that it wasn't make-believe, that they weren't its defenders but justice itself.

"A coward, huh? Yeah," I assented, "I'm not gonna stick up for a guy who chases middle-school girls' skirts."

"Oh, that reminds me. Tsukihi said she's investigating another rumor like that."

"A rumor?"

"Yup. Word is, some high school kid in our town likes to assault a little girl with pigtails from behind—he's more a pervert than a stalker because he hugs her and touches her all over. There haven't been a lot of eyewitnesses so who knows if it's true, but if it is, he's gonna pay for it."

"O-Oh."

Wh-Wh-Wh-What a pervert, I agreed, averting my eyes with all I had.

Sometimes I forget that Mayoi Hachikuji isn't some kind of otherworldly fairy that only Hanekawa and I can see.

So there were eyewitnesses, if not many.

Terrifying—our information society.

Ubiquitous.

"If some scumbag out there is sexually harassing innocent little girls," Karen fumed, "I won't leave it up to Tsukihi. I'll get in on the action and rearrange the guy's face."

"Ha…hahahaha. You two sure keep busy, huh? Tell you what, if you find out anything else, come straight to me. You won't regret it."

"Look at you, getting involved for a change. I guess there's a righteous heart beating somewhere in your chest, after all."

"But of course. Hahahaha."

"We're getting off topic, though, aren't we? If you're not sticking it in my butt, then what the heck is that toothbrush for? What else would anyone do with a toothbrush?"

"……"

That was some kind of question. If we took it out of context, she was the real pervert. She'd have a lot to discuss with Kanbaru.

However!

Believe it or not, Kanbaru's perverse imagination soared even higher! The spirit of that woman far outstripped pale words like "stalker" and "pervert"!

Which is why I didn't want to introduce them!

"Karen, you mean you didn't know? A toothbrush is a tool that many people use to brush their teeth."

"A-Ah. That does ring a bell."

"Of course, if we're being sticklers, it's also used to clean other things. Great for getting at those hard-to-reach crevices around the sink or tub, it…"

Ack. I was getting off topic again. Since we were talking about Kanbaru, I couldn't help but think of cleaning. Tomorrow was the fifteenth, so I needed to go help with her room as usual.

"Koyomi, maybe a toothbrush is a tool you use to brush your teeth, but what's your point? You're not going to make me brush my teeth, are you?"

"Right. I'm not." I nodded. "I'm not making you…because I'll do the brushing."

"…?" Karen cocked her head. The gravity of the situation still eluded her. "Um, I don't get it… You're gonna brush my teeth for me? Why? I mean, if you want to, I don't mind…but how is that any sort

58

of match?"

She looked so dumbfounded.

Heheheh. Knowing that her aloof expression wouldn't be on her face for much longer filled my heart with joy.

"You and Tsukihi both get your hair cut at a salon, don't you? Me, I get queasy about it. Having some stranger touch my head makes me weirdly tense."

"Well, I see what you mean. I wouldn't want to get my hair cut by a stylist that I don't know."

"Psychologically, people aren't comfortable having their hair touched by anyone not close to them. I bet some girls would even rather be touched on their bodies than on their hair."

Hachikuji was like that.

Once, when I grabbed her pigtails and pretended I was steering them like a Harley Davidson, she got really angry at me, even dropping her usual polite diction. I'd never seen her in such a rage… My regrets were still a fresh memory.

"Yeah…so?" asked Karen, a touch of wariness in her voice. Unable to see where this was going, she was feeling anxious. Her vigilance was second to none.

"It's a matter of touch—a haircut is the simplest example, but I could give others. Would you ever trust a non-professional to perform a full-body massage on you? It's that sort of thing."

"That sort of thing…"

"Brushing one's teeth is that sort of thing," I said, though I didn't know why I was speaking deliberately like I was giving a lecture. "You seem unperturbed, but having someone brush your teeth isn't a common experience. Unlike a haircut or a massage, it's something you can usually manage yourself and do take care of on your own."

I was saying this to someone who'd be chopping off her own ponytail a few hours later, but obviously I had no way of knowing. How could I have seen that coming?

"Let me break it down, Karen—getting your teeth brushed by

another person is going to feel incredibly creepy. If you can keep yourself from freaking out for five minutes, you win. I'll introduce you to Kanbaru. But if you make a peep before the five minutes are up, I win, and I won't introduce you to her."

"Haha!"

Faced with the rules and conditions, the match that I laid out, Karen laughed—like she was relieved. Actually, it was more of a snort, as if the wind had just been let out of her sails.

"Wow," she said, "the way you were making such a big deal of this, I was starting to get scared. Now I'm kind of disappointed."

"Are you?"

"Yeah, bring it on. I don't want to imagine having my teeth brushed by a total stranger, but my own brother? I can do this. Are you sure you won't be the one to give in first, humiliated that you're brushing your sister's teeth? I gotta say, there's nothing you could do to me that I'd find embarrassing."

Well, lookee here. She thought she was dealing with an amateur.

"……"

Keheheh! She'd fallen into my trap! Even her arrogant tone was music to my ears.

I knew full well that she was impervious to shame. How many years did she think I'd been her big brother?

In fact, I became her big brother before she was even born!

"Sure," I consented, "if I break first you win."

"Yeah? I don't know, it seems like a really easy challenge for getting to meet Kanbaru-sensei. I almost feel bad. You could've picked a bigger hurdle. You're so KY."

"KY?"

"You can't read the air."

"Ah"—*kuuki yomenai*—"I've heard that one before."

"How about SF for 'a bit mysterious'? I wonder why."

"What a grandmaster...so far ahead of his times."

That wordplay, *sukoshi fushigi*, belonged to Fujio Fujiko. It was more than a bit mysterious, but enough of that.

"Let's begin," I said. "Sit there."

"Aye, aye."

Karen plopped herself down on the bed willy-nilly, sending her skirt flipping up in a mess. Maybe she wasn't used to wearing one, and the hem was also too short, but clearly skirts weren't meant for her, I thought as I sat down next to her.

Like best friends.

I added a small amount of toothpaste to the brush, twisted my body in her direction, and placed my left hand behind her head.

"Say 'ahh.'"

"Ahh."

I had her open her mouth and inserted the toothbrush.

Now then.

Time to experience the terror that was Kanbaru-sensei.

Take comfort in knowing that none other than Kanbaru's fetishistic sensibility was your downfall!

"Gh...mphh?!"

Karen finally seemed to grasp the danger she had stumbled into approximately a minute into the match.

Her expression shifted. Well, make that quaked.

I'd never seen a face look so alarmed—and ecstatic.

"Mm...mmph, g-grk?!"

Now she understood.

Too late, Karen-chan.

The match was on.

Yes. My talk of hair salons and massages had been misdirection. Getting your teeth brushed is on a different plane.

We're talking about fiddling around *in your mouth*.

Not outside, but inside your body. Not the surface, but underneath.

Let's not sugarcoat it. The truth is that it generates *pleasure*.

In other words, it feels good.

Brushing your teeth is such an everyday act that you become

accustomed to it and don't notice—I hadn't thought about it, either, until Kanbaru pointed it out to me.

Yet it's a stern fact.

Caressing a delicate part of your body with fine bristles can only feel good. When it's someone else doing it to boot, can anyone possibly keep it together?

Karen had guts. She didn't bend to pain or humiliation.

She was a masochist, you could say. A total, utter masochist.

Which is exactly what made pleasing her, *indulging* her in this way such an effective means of breaking her spirit.

Tenacity felled by pleasure! Pride bowing to indolence!

"Ng-gh…nmmphh!"

As I focused on a spot behind her molars and scrubbed where tooth met gum, Karen reacted in a most sensitive manner. Her body started to twitch and convulse.

Her eyes seemed about to roll back.

This was getting scary in its own way…

It was my first time trying this, but the great Kanbaru-sensei certainly lived up to her name.

Don't hate me, Karen. I'm doing this for your own good!

You don't want to meet the woman who came up with this crazy idea!

"Ng-gh…huph, huph, huph. N…gh, ahh, ahhh…"

Unfortunately—I had miscalculated.

I'd failed to account for just how gutsy Karen Araragi was. Not even pleasure could break this Gutsy Frog.

I thought she wouldn't last two minutes, but she was gritting her teeth—well, she couldn't since I was brushing them (another reason your body went limp), but she withstood my strikes, my strokes, my pampering.

This whole girls' manga-like situation of being pleasured by her older brother must have felt really naughty to her, and yet… Hmph, not bad, Karen. Not bad at all.

She was inspiring me to try harder.

I (even though it was a little out of bounds) began brushing her tongue.

The underside of her tongue, to be precise—that part of the body was pretty much exposed muscle.

"Karen, you'll feel so much better if you just gave up—correction! Give up and it won't feel so good anymore!"

She was in tickling hell. There was no way she could endure this.

Another minute was the most she could take!

"Uh oh... Hold on?!"

In fact, the one who couldn't take another minute—was me.

I guess Kanbaru figured it was too obvious to mention, but there was a serious pitfall in this match (which probably wasn't how she thought of it in the first place).

I'd focused on the psyche of the *brushee* and rushed into this without stopping to consider the very important matter of how I, the *brusher*, would feel.

It was a huge blunder. One I wouldn't, couldn't recover from.

"Aaah... Pheuuu. H-Hnkk!"

......

Holy shit!

Karen's moaning gasps were making me feel all funny inside!

My heart was thumping faster!

Her every reaction was getting me worked up!

What was this complex feeling, like we were breaking a taboo?!

Knowing that I was pleasuring my own sister felt so immoral!

Each audible scrape of the toothbrush, every frothing of paste in her mouth, began to feel less like cleaning Karen's teeth and more like polishing my own soul.

Was I satisfying myself the most by brushing someone else's teeth rather than mine?!

Was I so happy to be of use?!

Is this what my schoolteachers call "service"?!

Okay, probably not!

This was bad. Even the streak of drool spilling from the corner of Karen's mouth, something I would usually just find gross, was instilling a strange sense of affection!

If I didn't stop working the brush immediately, something terrible might happen—but even though I knew that, knew that this was wrong, my hand seemed to have a mind of its own. Like some sort of automated machine (an electric toothbrush, even), it refused to stop.

If anything, its movements grew more ferocious. The more I focused, the worse it got.

Karen's convulsions, likewise, intensified—she was clutching the bed sheet firmly in her hands, I guess because she couldn't grit her teeth, but that still wasn't enough to keep her body in check.

And her face had turned crimson red, like it was about to burst into flame.

"Holy…" I said, without meaning to. I managed to swallow the words just in time—but the ones that almost escaped my mouth surprised even myself.

Holy. She looked so cute.

I've fulfilled my position as Karen's older brother for some sixteen years now (The number includes the time she was in our mother's womb, by the way. That's what I was getting at when I said I've been her brother since before she was born—I wasn't being rhetorical), but I never found her so cute before.

Earlier, it was only because she'd been threatening me that I praised how she looked in a skirt. No, I mean, it was just a slip of the tongue, and I sure as hell wasn't going to tell her she was cute now—but I couldn't retract having thought so.

Once the data leaked, you couldn't retrieve it.

Holy.

Holy, holy, holy.

This was insane.

Was Karen always this cute?

Wait… Wait a sec…

Was my little sister actually the cutest girl in the world?

Until now, I'd considered my ideal woman to be Tsubasa Hanekawa, but had I been mistaken? Even if she didn't top Hanekawa, did Karen give her a good run for her money?

Whoa, whoa, hold up!

Koyomi Araragi, stop right there! Do you hear what you're saying?! What mortal could possibly compete with Tsubasa Hanekawa?!

This was an illusion, all an illusion! I was just drunk on the bizarre situation!

I saw that, knew it was true!

A-And yet…

"N-Nuhhh…" I moaned as if joining Karen in chorus.

There was some kind of synergy. I lost sight of myself.

My mental circuitry even entertained the possibility that I'd been born into this world just to brush Karen's teeth.

What an idiotic mental circuitry mine was.

How could brushing someone's teeth backfire so horrendously? I had stumbled into dealing with dark, forbidden arts.

But it was far too late for regret.

Ignorance was no defense. Ignorance would be my undoing.

This was beyond my control. My only choice was to let the pieces fall where they may.

"K-Karen…"

You know—like cigarettes?

That stuff people stick in their mouths and light up to breathe the smoke? Those super dangerous cancer sticks or whatever that are so terrible for you?

Imagine if they were some stupendous health supplement that made you better the more you smoked.

Would they ever have gotten as popular?

Well, I'm still a minor, and I don't intend to pick up the habit even when I get older, but that guy Oshino constantly letting a cigarette dangle between his lips (not that he ever lit it) had left a strong impression on me.

You couldn't help wondering.

Maybe it's precisely because it's bad for you—because you shouldn't—that so many people smoke. That so many don't stop even now.

It's wrong, you're not supposed to do it. Precisely for that reason—

It's terribly attractive.

It's terribly enticing.

It's terribly numbing.

By the time you realize…

By the time I realized—I'd pushed Karen down onto my bed.

With my left hand still cradling her head, I'd leaned over her and pinned her down.

She was bigger than me, but I only had to use a fraction of my weight—and she went down smoothly, not resisting.

I looked at Karen. Gazed at her.

She was swooning, melting into puddles.

She was in heaven.

"Karen, Karen. Karen…"

I repeated her name, over and over. Every time I spoke it, a fever flared up from deep inside me.

Karen's body, too, was hot.

"B-Big bwother…"

Thanks to the toothbrush inserted in her mouth—well, probably even if it hadn't been there—she was lisping, her pupils unfocused.

Yet she said—bravely, she said:

"B-Big bwother… Go ahead."

Ahead?!

Ahead to where?!

That's how I'd wisecrack under normal circumstances, but I was feeling all sloppy as well.

Sloppy. Slippery.

Syrupy. Seeping.
Woolly. Woozy.
Wobbly. Worming.

I, Koyomi Araragi, gently removed my left hand from behind Karen Araragi's head and slowly extended it toward her breasts—

"What in tarnation?"

That was when a boorish, insensitive, deflating—no, a saving voice cut in.

When I turned to look at the doorway that I had apparently left open, my other sibling, my littler little sister, that is to say Tsukihi, dressed in her traditional Japanese clothing, stood there awestruck.

Her eyes wide as saucers, her mouth circular, she looked like one of those ancient *dogu* statuettes. More dumbstruck than awestruck, she might have clenched her jaw if it weren't on the floor.

"Koyomi? Karen? What in tarnation?"

For some reason Tsukihi was speaking with a Kyoto accent. It fact, it sounded a little like the Gion courtesan variant.

I guess she was confused.

"W-Wait, Tsukihi," I shouted, "don't get us wrong!"

Well, shout as I might, there was nothing to misconstrue here. This was, in fact, exactly what it looked like. The situation was pretty hard to misread.

"Koyomi, why are you brushing Karen's teeth and pushing her down on your bed with loving kindness written all over your face? And Karen, why are you dressed in my clothes with a swoon in your eyes when Koyomi is pinning you on his bed?"

Tsukihi had recovered her senses enough to drop her accent, but the question she posed wasn't as easy to dismiss.

Her wide-open eyes regained their normal shape to a degree—but only because she was narrowing them in reproach. We'd gone from circles to triangles.

The cold stare, coming from Tsukihi, was enough to shock me and Karen back to our senses.

Once I snapped out of it—

It was just as Tsukihi said. In other words, her question couldn't be dismissed.

"Gosh! Why am I brushing Karen's teeth and pushing her down on my bed with loving kindness written all over my face?!"

"Whaaat? Why am I dressed in your clothes with a swoon in my eyes when Koyomi is pinning me on his bed?!"

"Unbelievable!"

"Unbelievable!"

It was unbelievable. I'd never been so shocked in my life.

That...was...close!

Now there was a line you didn't cross!

Taboo, too taboo!

"Y-You saved us, Tsukihi! Thank you!"

"Y-You saved us, Tsukihi! Thank you!"

Said Karen and I, in unison.

It wasn't just our voices that were in synch. We whipped our bodies in Tsukihi's direction and thrust a finger at her, our movements perfectly identical.

If this were synchronized swimming, we were golden.

Under the circumstances, though, our synchronicity only worsened the impression we made on Tsukihi. There was no upside.

A tin medal at the arcade was all we were going to win.

I mean, I was still propped on top of Karen as we spoke.

"Huh... Huh."

Indeed, what Tsukihi did next was to nod with great interest.

Her eyes were no longer even narrowed, but shut tight, and her face was expressionless.

Karen and I were breathing hard, for an entirely different reason this time.

We were awaiting judgment, anxiously.

Viscous beads of sweat slithered across my skin.

"Yup..."

When Tsukihi raised her head, her face was cheerful and bright.

It looked like we were going to receive a sympathetic verdict. Maybe allowances would be made for extenuating circumstances, or at the least we would get a suspended sentence. Karen and I perked up.

"Would you two mind staying right there?" requested Tsukihi. "I'm going to pop over to the convenience store to buy myself an awl."

Swoosh, went the rug out from under our feet.

A death sentence.

Man, an awl...

With a grin frozen on her face yet unsmiling, Tsukihi, at anger level 99, went out into the hall. *Wham,* she slammed the door behind her with withering force.

"Tsukihi," Karen shouted after her, "I don't think they sell awls at the convenience store! You're going to have to go to a dedicated hardware store!"

The comment seemed a little misguided. Tsukihi ignored it completely.

Her feet went pounding down the stairs, and then soon all was quiet.

Yikes. What had just happened?

This was pure pandemonium. Even if she couldn't buy an awl at a convenience store, with the mood she was in, she'd find one somewhere.

What to do?

Well, the more pressing issue was probably what was going to be done to us.

"Koyomi, you're crushing me," Karen complained as I wracked my head.

"Oh, sorry."

I got off of her. She sat up as well and rearranged her disheveled *de facto* miniskirt. She seemed a little self-conscious.

A shy Karen was a rare sight. Usually, nothing embarrassed her.

"Koyomi, about our match?"

"Huh?"

Match? Was that word supposed to mean something to me? Was it the name of some plant? One of the vocabulary words I'd memorized that morning?

When I cocked my head in confusion, she added, "It's been way more than five minutes."

Ah, right. Now that she mentioned it, this whole incident had started as a match between us. Finally remembering, I glanced up at the clock.

Indeed, the five minutes were up. Or rather, fifteen minutes had passed.

No wonder Tsukihi stumbled on us like that.

"Aw, shucks..."

Ouch. I'd lost.

Actually, putting aside having lost, I had to give props to Karen for her tenacity. It was time for me to cede her the respect she was owed.

I may have forgotten myself partway through, but anyone who could withstand such extreme punishment deserved kudos.

For fifteen minutes, too. She was a monster.

"Ha, I guess you got me... A promise is a promise. Okay, okay, Karen, I'll introduce you to Kanbaru."

That didn't mean I liked it one bit, but if Karen really wanted to meet Kanbaru, I didn't have any reason to interfere. Or at least no right.

I did suspect they would get along. They were two of a kind, after all.

"You did well, Karen. Victory is yours. Yup, I guess today was my turn to lose. I give."

"Mm-m..."

Despite my congratulations, her response seemed lukewarm.

Ahem, she cleared her throat loudly as I wondered what was up. *Ahem, ah-h-hem.*

She coughed several times, apparently on purpose—and then hunched her large frame into a coy ball.

70

"K-Koyomi."

"Yeah?"

"W-Well, if you want, I mean only if you insist, I guess we could go for two out of three."

"......"

"S-See, Tsukihi interrupted us before we were done, so usually it wouldn't count. B-Besides, we've got plenty of time to kill until she gets back. I wouldn't mind keeping you company for a few more rounds..."

Feigning extreme nonchalance, her cheeks flushing red as she made her proposal, Karen glanced at me bashfully.

"Well..." I—quietly gripped the toothbrush, which was still in my hand. "I-In that case, I'll request a rematch...maybe?"

"O-Of course. I wouldn't want to r-run...from a challenge... I accept!"

"Sh-Should we switch dealers?"

"Okay. Th-That only sounds fair!"

Neither of us meeting the other's eyes—we plunged into a best-of-three match.

Which is how, as of that morning...

Karen and I began to get along just a little better.

004

Thus ends the flashback.

And so I was currently heading to Kanbaru's with Karen.

A promise may have been a promise, but considering nothing was written down, I was under no obligation to keep it. Still, a promise is a promise is a promise.

I would accept my role as their mediator, their go-between. With that decision made, my one condition for Karen was that she change immediately—which is why she was now dressed in a jersey.

Of course, since she was about to meet the great Kanbaru-sensei, it was no ordinary jersey. It was her best outfit, the lucky one she only wore on special occasions: a loud and flashy, fluorescent bicycle-racing jersey finished off on the bottom with a smart set of cycling shorts.

I guess no one asked for that info…

But why did my sister own a bicycle-racing jersey when she didn't even own a bicycle? It seemed bizarre.

I did own a bicycle, by the way, but wasn't riding it.

Although I wouldn't go so far as to say that Kanbaru's house was isolated, it was a bit far to walk. Nevertheless, I decided to hoof it because I wanted to avoid riding two on a bike (not on principle, just with my sister).

She'd been walking on her hands instead of her hooves.

Now I was riding on her shoulders.

You know, once you got used to it, it was actually kind of fun being up so high.

Well, my reluctance to ride two to a bicycle with my little sister leading to me riding on her shoulders proved how halting and awkward our conversations were, even if we were getting along a little better.

As for Karen, she usually wasn't quite this much of a dunderhead, but I guess she was so worked up or worked over at the thought of meeting Kanbaru that her brain had plain stopped working.

However.

What I hadn't expected was Kanbaru's response.

Introducing them hardly qualified as a good deed and it didn't have to be today, but I figured if I was going to keep my promise, I might as well do it soon. Immediately afterward (as in immediately after escaping, by the skin of our teeth, the demonic glint of Tsukihi's awl, a part of the story that is too realistic to be funny and that I therefore omit), I rang Kanbaru's cell phone.

As I mentioned earlier, it was the middle of summer, during the *Obon* holidays. Since Kanbaru already lived with her grandfather and grandmother, there was no need for her to go away to visit her country home.

The call did connect, but her reaction surprised me.

"I don't know, my senior Araragi. That doesn't sound like a very good idea. I did express my interest in your little sister, but it was just a joke. I wasn't being serious."

That didn't sound like Kanbaru at all. Perverted fool or not, she was just about the most big-hearted person of anyone I knew. She definitely wasn't the type to act shy.

When I pressed her, she seemed genuinely distressed.

"As grateful as I am that you would think of me, I wouldn't feel right taking your sister's virginity."

"Who said you could?!" I'd rather take it myself in that case! Drop dead!

"I do appreciate the thought."

"You can't have the thought either! There's nothing about my sister you can have!"

And so.

Kanbaru's unexpected response just meant she was the same wonderful woman I'd come to know and expect. Eventually, after a little pushing, I was able to successfully arrange a noontime visit to her house with Karen.

"Sure thing," Kanbaru said. "I'll put on clothes and wait for you."

"Why is nudity the default..."

I nearly changed my mind again about introducing them, but after coming this far, it wouldn't be right.

Karen would beat the crap out of me. I wouldn't like that.

"Koyomi," Karen asked suddenly from below, "you know how the number for ambulance services and fire fighters is the same? 119. Why is that? Isn't that a little confusing? Does a fire truck ever show up when someone meant to call an ambulance, and vice versa?"

......

What a silly question. What even made her think of that? I'm pretty sure we hadn't passed any emergency vehicles.

"Maybe it does happen once in a while," I answered. "But if there were three emergency numbers, for the police, ambulances, and the fire department, and they were all different, won't people have trouble remembering them all?"

"All? It's only three numbers. And they're three digits each. How could anyone have trouble remembering that much?"

"Well, just think about it. Have you ever meant to call the weather forecast and gotten the current time instead?"

"Never."

"Oh."

"I've called for the time and gotten the weather forecast instead, though."

"Same thing."

Never underestimate the challenges posed by simplicity. It's precisely because the numbers are only three digits that people sometimes mix them up in a panic.

"Of the ten numbers beginning with two ones," I continued, "1-1-0 and 1-1-9 are the easiest to remember. That must be why they took the three most urgent services and shoehorned them into two numbers. The scenario you mentioned is probably a lot better than a police car showing up when you meant to call for an ambulance or a fire truck."

"Really? If someone's injured the police could arrest the assailant, and if there's a fire they could arrest the arsonist."

"Why do injuries and fires have to be crime-related for you?" Her idea of justice was dangerous. Her premise was criminal behavior.

"But then, if you were injured and a fire truck showed up, you'd get angry and yell, 'What are you gonna do, hose me better?!'"

"I'd never yell that even if I got angry."

"If an ambulance came to a fire, you'd get angry too. 'What, did you just *assume* that I got burned?!'"

"That sounds like a reasonable assumption."

"It'd be different if a police car showed up. You wouldn't get angry. They'd arrest you."

"For a defender of justice, you bend pretty quickly to the state."

"Don't get me wrong, I was just talking in general. Tsukihi and I never bow to authority. The Fire Sisters have clashed with the police plenty of times."

"Yeah... I'm the one who always has to pick you up from the station."

Geez, I didn't want to be reminded. I'd ended up befriending a female officer for no reason.

"But Karen, aren't you forgetting something? What if a fire truck or an ambulance showed up in the middle of a crime? Wouldn't people get really mad then?"

"Hmm, you can't win them all. It's so hard to make everyone happy. Well, the perp would get scared off by the sound of the sirens, so I guess it's okay?"

"Like a panic buzzer?"

"Like a panic buzzer. So yeah, they should separate ambulances and fires. You're right that 110 and 119 are easy to remember, but what about 111? That's pretty handy, isn't it? Why don't we make that for fire?"

"'We'? I don't have that kind of power. Besides, I'm not sure, but isn't 111 probably already assigned to something? Come to think of it, all the numbers starting with '1-1' must be taken."

"Maybe, but I bet 111 is just the number for some lottery. I don't see why they shouldn't have to give it up."

"If you're playing on 'one' and 'won,' you've got the mind of a grade school kid."

Give me a break.

Our banter would sound hopelessly moronic to someone like Hanekawa, who no doubt knew the answer to all this.

This conversation went beyond halting. We were headed straight into the bushes.

"What they usually say," I went on, "is that 110 and 119 were chosen to help people calm down since they tend to be in a panic and can hardly think straight when they're calling those numbers."

"Huh? What do you mean? Quit talking nonsense or I'll punch you."

"Aren't you being a little too impatient with your older brother?!"

"I am?"

"I don't deserve a knuckle sandwich for explaining things in order… Anyway, this is from before cell phones and touch-tone phones, way back in the day. Apparently there used to be these artifacts called rotary phones. Maybe you've seen them on TV?"

"Ah, rotary. I might have, I'm not sure. That word 'rotary' does sound pretty retro, though."

"Right. And on rotary phones, dialing the numbers '0' and '9' took time. They were set up so you had to rotate a dial." Not that I'd ever seen one in person, either, but apparently the "0" and "9" were placed at the end of the dial.

"What about '1'?"

"Hm?"

"If the '0' and '9' took time to dial, what about the '1'? Did that take time to dial, too?"

"No, the '1'…was on the other end, I think." Meaning it actually took the least amount of time to turn. Hrrm.

"Shouldn't they have made the emergency numbers 009 and 000 in that case?"

"Well, 009 sounds like you're calling for a cyborg… The fact that it's an emergency only makes the situation feel less serious."

"I get that. I totally get that."

"You do? You actually do?"

"What about 000?"

"Everyone knows you can't use one number in a row for your PIN. There are too many people out to scam you these days. You gotta watch out, okay?"

"We were talking about phone numbers."

"That reminds me, Karen-chan, I have something interesting to share with you about three-digit numbers."

"If it's not interesting, I'm going to punch you."

"How about a less scary rejoinder!"

"Get on with it."

"Actually, it's just some math trivia I learned from Hanekawa. Think of a three-digit number. Any, including 110 or 119. Now repeat it."

"Okey dokey."

"The six-digit number you end up with will always be divisible by seven. 110110 or 119119, it doesn't matter. Give it a try."

Seven was a solitary number, but since it was solitary, nothing remained—when you put it that way it sounded pretty deep. But honestly, it was just a mathematical trick.

"Huh," Karen grunted. "Let me give it a try... Uh, wait...I've got three left over."

"How can you mess up single-digit division? What a waste of a neat piece of trivia."

And so on.

And so forth.

As described above, around noon on August fourteenth, on our way to the Kanbaru residence, I was engaged in an unproductive, harmless, and not particularly interesting conversation with Karen, on whose shoulders I sat—

When at the same vantage point more than seven feet off the ground—

Another point of view suddenly presented itself before me.

"You, fiendish young man—there's something I'm keen to ask. Can you spare a moment?"

The tallest person I've ever met, it goes without saying, is Dramaturgy, the vampire hunter. In addition to his seven feet, thanks to the traumatically terrible impression he left, I recall him as being closer to eight or even ten feet tall.

To be precise, whether or not Dramaturgy qualifies as a person is open to debate...

In any case, if you're wondering if *she*, who had appeared before my eyes, rivaled even Dramaturgy in height, that is not in fact the case. Purely in terms of stature, she didn't look much taller or shorter than me.

She was merely propped on top of something that added to her natural height—just as I was propped atop Karen's shoulders.

This person was—standing on a mailbox.

"I'm fixing to get to Eikow Cram School. Can you tell a body how to get there?"

Kyoto dialect—and not the pidgin accent my sister Tsukihi slipped into, confused, in the morning. From what I could tell, it was the genuine article.

The shorthaired woman wore a cool, detached expression.

She looked to be about in her late twenties. She was clothed in a muted pants and top, with a striped inner and a pair of classy, heelless shoes. Overall her outfit was clean and prim, like something a grade school teacher might wear—there was nothing particularly unusual about her.

That is, of course, if you ignored the fact that she was standing on a mailbox.

"Umm…"

I wasn't sure how to respond. For some reason, I sensed that the comic-relief stretch was coming to an end.

Enough fun and games?

Was playtime over?

Well, after more than a hundred manuscript pages of goofing off, even I was starting to feel a little full.

"Hey, fiendish young man," the woman said. Still in Kyoto dialect, her words sounded pushy, but her expression was laidback. "Didn't your folk rear you to be kind to a body in trouble?"

"Um, well…"

I was at a loss for words. Of course, I had been taught to be nice to people in trouble, but the lady didn't really look to be in trouble. And I certainly wasn't taught to be nice to people who stand on mailboxes.

If anything, I needed to tell her to stop that.

On the other hand, though I wasn't standing on a mailbox, I was perched on the shoulders of my sister, a middle schooler. It was the fair outcome of a fair match, but the unlikely situation was hard to justify. To an objective observer, at least, treating a mailbox as a stepping-stone was somewhat preferable to putting your little sister to like use.

You couldn't fault the woman for calling me fiendish. In fact, it was sort of impressive that she'd asked me for directions.

"I'm Yozuru Kagenui—have you heard of me?" the lady introduced herself out of the blue.

Usually, you didn't introduce yourself just to ask directions (nor did you stand on a mailbox—but maybe neither was as unusual as making your little sister carry you around). Was this lady famous enough to receive special treatment when she gave her name?

If she was, her fame rivaled an actress or politician's.

She didn't look like either.

Being pretty clueless about both celebrities and politics, however, I didn't have much faith in my judgment. Maybe I was facing a VIP.

I glanced down at Karen to check her reaction.

"......"

A blank slate.

Hmm. Come to think of it, Karen was just as clueless when it came to celebrities and politics.

Tsukihi would have been a different story. She was practically glued to the TV—though your middle-school sister being familiar with the ins and outs of politics in addition to show business would be less endearing than freaky.

I took another glance at the lady—at Yozuru Kagenui.

She did have a pretty face.

Was she a pop star known for her Kyoto dialect?

Or maybe a politician known for her Kyoto dialect? Well, most politicians from there probably spoke that way, so there'd be nothing unique about that.

It wouldn't do not to introduce myself in turn.

"I'm Koyomi Araragi," I replied for the time being.

"I'm Karen Araragi," my sister followed suit. Just when I thought she was a good girl who knew her manners, she continued, "Some folks choose to call me one of the Fire Sisters, but what can I say."

To my great dismay, my sister was the sort of oaf who shared her nickname with a complete stranger. The fact that she worded it like it was gossip made it even more cringeworthy. To begin with, it was mostly just my sisters calling themselves that.

"Hmm... A fiendish older brother—and the little sister a hornet. Amusing."

"......"

Huh? Did she just say—hornet?

"Hyahaha. But that looks to be settled now, so I'll not stir that pot. Well? I hate to keep jawing on about this, but do you know where Eikow Cram School is, or not?"

"Oh, uh..."

Ei...kow... Eikow Cram School...

Unfortunately, I'd never heard of it... There were a few cram schools near the train station, maybe it was one of those. Should I just point her in that direction?

She did look like she was traveling.

On closer inspection, her hair appeared to be lightened slightly, so at the very least she didn't seem to be a local.

No one in our town dyed our hair. I doubt you could even buy hair dye around here.

When Karen turned hers pink on a lark way back when, apparently she'd done it with regular paint. It was colored over with India ink, so it must have been a crazy marbled mess right afterwards.

As middle-school debuts go, it was a straightforward blunder, and I imagine she still winces at the memory—unless she's forgotten about it completely.

Dying her hair on a whim, chopping it off on another. My sister loves to trash her equivalent of life.

"Let me see, just a second," I muttered.

There was no reason for me to go to too much trouble just because I was asked for directions—she was an adult, after all. Wouldn't it actually be rude if a kid like me acted like she was helpless? I mean, she could just use the GPS on her cell phone.

But perhaps, like a certain someone who used to live in our town, Kagenui sucked at anything tech. Perhaps she belonged to the rotary-phone generation (←a most definitely rude thought).

I glanced down at Karen again, but she was keeping quiet, happy to let me deal with the situation all on my own. While she was very much the philanthropic type and didn't begrudge an act of kindness to a stranger, this wasn't the kind of issue that could be solved through violence, which rendered her useless.

Sheesh, what sort of defender of justice did that make her...

"Just a second," I said. "One of my friends is a wondergirl who knows where all the cram schools in the country are located."

At the end of the day, I was about as useless as Karen.

When in trouble, rely on Hanekawa.

Tsubasa Hanekawa, my classmate and our class president. A model student among model students boasting top scores in the national mock exams—no, who didn't even boast about it because she was in a league of her own.

She'd helped me in all sorts of ways since I met her during spring break. In fact, this summer vacation too, she was helping me all the time, in the progressive tense, as my tutor for college entrance exams—from dawn to dusk, good morning to good night, even in my dreams.

I did ask her to take *Obon* off, though.

Still, like Kanbaru, although for entirely different reasons, Hanekawa had no hometown to return to—and was probably at the library focusing on her own studies at the moment.

It was time for a phone call!

A phone call to Miss Hanekawa!

Oh lucky day!

You might consider me a nuisance for calling my savior, Tsubasa Hanekawa, over such a trivial matter, but trivial matters are what I want to discuss most with Hanekawa!

At least...

At least it was better than getting her embroiled in something serious like what happened last time.

That said, I needed to keep the call brief today and cut out the chitchat. This part of the story didn't feel like a comic-relief sequence.

I just had to ask where Eikow Cram School was, and frankly, to hear her voice.

"Yes, this is Hanekawa. Araragi? Are you studying like you're supposed to? You're not slacking off? Ah, good. Me? Of course. I'm just doing some light lunchtime learning."

Lunchtime learning... It sounded like a segment on a TV show.

Despite her nation-leading scores, Hanekawa had no intention of applying to college, so these were probably private studies.

"Private studies" was some phrase when I thought about it...

Hmm. It was noon, the hottest time of day. Was Miss Hanekawa only wearing a single, thin layer without a bra for her private studies? Maybe she just got out of the shower, and her hair was all wet and slick—

"Araragi, you're not thinking dirty thoughts, are you?" she quipped on cue. I swear, she had ESP. I couldn't even fantasize safely. "Also, it sounds like you're outside. Are you sure you're studying?"

So sharp.

Well, I wasn't slacking off, though. I made sure to finish my morning drills before leaving, and I meant to get back home and study once I dropped Karen off at Kanbaru's.

"Also, Araragi, it sounds like you're speaking from a position about three feet higher than usual. Please tell me you're not making Karen carry you on her shoulders?"

Too sharp!

This was getting into horror territory!

I mean, hold on. Did a few feet really change how your voice sounded? It wasn't like I was talking to her face to face, so my voice wasn't coming from overhead or anything... Sure, voice is sound, and since sound is vibrating air, I guess a change in air pressure would alter your voice... But did another person's worth of height make for such a drastic change?

Come on. That made it seem like I'm super-short...

"In fact, Araragi, I have this nagging suspicion that you're toying with Karen and shoving your crotch into the back of her head…"

What a way to put it. Some pervert she was making me out to be.

No, I wasn't bullying or toying with Karen… But now that Hanekawa put it so matter-of-factly, I had to wonder what the heck I was doing on my little sister's shoulders.

Uh-uh, I couldn't be so matter-of-fact. This was no time to come to my senses. I had to embrace the fever and forget myself!

"Eikow Cram School? Yes, I do know it," Hanekawa said.

She did know. She really did…

I'd hyped her to the lady, but Hanekawa was the self-educated variety of genius. Though I hadn't really expected her to know where all the cram schools in the country are, now I half-believed it.

Like always, I told Hanekawa that she knew everything. Like always, she responded, "I don't know everything. I only know what I know."

How wonderful.

Every time I heard her say it, I was reminded that I had lived another day.

……

Well, I made her say it so often, lately I had a distinct feeling that she was just humoring me with that reply. She'd look a bit put-upon half of the time.

But how I loved the face she made!

"Araragi, you're not having naughty thoughts again, are you?"

Wow. That was beyond sharp. That was pointed.

Piercing.

"You know," she lamented, "I'm beginning to give up on making you turn over a new leaf."

Don't give up, Hanekawa! Don't abandon me!

"Too bad," she said, "since Senjogahara did mend her ways—humph. Well, all right. It sounds like you're in a hurry, so I'll save the lecture for next time."

I had a lecture to look forward to.

A part of me thought, *Crap, now I've done it, I'm gonna get scolded by Hanekawa!* But another part of me couldn't help but feel excited at the prospect, so I guess I was Karen's brother after all.

The Araragi siblings. We were M cool.

"Besides, Araragi, you ought to know where Eikow Cram School is—because, you see, it's those ruins where Mister Oshino and Shinobu lived for all that time. It's the name of the cram school that used to be in that building."

Hanekawa didn't make too much of it, but when I heard her answer, I was both surprised and persuaded.

I was surprised to learn that the place I knew so well, the cram school in those memorable ruins where I spent most of spring break, (obviously) had a name.

I was persuaded—for the lady's sake. A newfangled feature like GPS was worse than helpless when you were dealing with a school that had gone out of business years ago.

Eikow Cram School, huh? That place had such a smart-sounding name? Given that they once took up a whole building, I did figure they were fairly big even if they weren't a famous chain.

Well, smart-sounding or not, it had since been turned into a squat by a scruffy aloha shirt-wearing geezer and served in the abduction of an innocent high-school boy, so I guess it had come down hard in the world. *Sic transit*, and all that.

Humph…

But I could think about that later. I didn't want to keep the lady waiting or interfere with Hanekawa's studies.

I didn't mind Karen having to stand still with me on her shoulders—not one bit, I'm proud to say!

When I thanked Hanekawa, she replied, "No need to thank me, that was nothing. Okay, Araragi. Say hello to Kanbaru for me. Bye-bye."

I hung up.

Wait a sec… I never said a word about going to see Kanbaru…

There must have been some clue in our exchange (for Hanekawa it was probably self-evident and hardly worth a remark), but still, she wasn't just off the charts, I was using the wrong units.

All I meant to do was ask for directions real quick, and I'd surrendered my privacy.

What a terrible deal.

Now Hanekawa thought of me as a guy who fantasized about the class president and enjoyed shoving his crotch into the back of his little sister's head as he headed to a female schoolmate's house...

If I ever ran into a pervert like that, I'd punch first and ask questions later.

"Any progress, fiendish young man?"

I was starting to feel a little cobalt and a little blue (in other words, I was feeling cobalt blue), but the lady's voice brought me back to Earth.

"Ah, yes... Let's see..."

I may not have known the name, but explaining how to get to that ruined building was even easier for me than pointing the way to the station. Obviously my trips had decreased in frequency since Oshino's departure, but I'd trekked out there countless times.

Yet three or so problems remained.

One: that building was off the beaten track, so explaining the way step by step didn't mean that she'd get it right—it was easy to explain but hard to understand.

The barrier or whatever that Oshino had set up was long gone, but that didn't alter the geographical conditions.

That worry, however, proved unfounded. Despite her funky, acrobatic entry atop a mailbox, Ms. Kagneui seemed to possess a decent head on her shoulders. I only had to explain once for her to get it.

"A-ha. Hm, I see, that way."

It didn't sound like she was pretending to understand out of vanity because I was a kid and a younger person. From her response, I got the impression that she already had a general idea of the route to her destination prior to asking for my help.

As for the second problem:

"It's pretty far, though… Will you be all right?"

"Don't fuss yourself about me. I got from home to here on foot fair enough. Anything up to fifty miles is just a daunder in my mind."

From home… Kyoto? Somewhere in the region, at least.

Amazing. That was even more amazing than anything up to four hundred pounds not counting as weight for Karen.

Oh, uh, was it just a joke?

But if she said she was fine, then I guess she was. I decided to put that aside and move on—to the third problem.

"That cram school has gone under, though. Ms. Kagenui, what do you want to go there for?"

The last problem—which maybe it wasn't my place to address.

I'd simply been asked for directions and had no cause to pry. Whatever she wanted to do there was her own business. I didn't need to know.

Maybe there were reasons to visit a cram school that had gone bankrupt. Those reasons surely had nothing to do with me.

Still, try to see where I was coming from.

That abandoned building didn't just hold memories for us, it also really meant something—and hearing that some stranger was on her way there was making me feel a little stressed.

Not so much that it was worth mentioning. But mention it I had.

"Eh, what do I want to gang there for? For starters, I might set up base there," Kagenui deflected with a vague answer, just as you might expect.

I could hardly blame her. She was under no obligation to report her goals to me.

All I'd done was give her directions. It had given me the opportunity to talk to Hanekawa when she wasn't tutoring me, so in any case, as far as I was concerned, I'd been paid back any debt in kind.

We were even.

"Thank you kindly, fiendish young man. Oh, by the by. If you happen across a waif this tall with the same question, show her the same generosity you did to me?"

With that—Kagenui leapt from atop the mailbox.

And onto a nearby concrete block wall—that is to say, to a more elevated point of view than my own—before strutting away like a gymnast traversing a balance beam, as if it were the most natural thing in the world.

Until she was lost from sight, Kagenui never once touched the ground—skipping from concrete wall to guard rail, and so on and so forth, as she went.

Ahh...of course.

She was playing that game. The ground was a shark-infested ocean, and she'd get eaten if she descended too low... Well, I did play it, too—when I was a kid.

That's why she'd been standing on a mailbox...

"Hm? Hey, Karen, you've been awfully quiet." I conked my sister on the head like I was checking to make sure she was in working order. "What's the big idea anyway, leaving me to deal with a weirdo all by myself? It's your fault I'm getting scolded by Hanekawa."

"Ah, sorry," apologized Karen, not noticing my subtle diversion of blame, my elegant pass. "It's just, I don't know—she seemed really strong. I was on guard."

"Strong?"

Huh? Since this was Karen, didn't she mean strong in the sense of combat proficiency?

"Oh yeah? Not to me," I disagreed. "Putting aside her speech and behavior, she seemed like a pretty lady you'd find anywhere."

"While she was talking to you, the axis of her body didn't bend even an inch. She has a figure skater's sense of balance."

"Huh..." True, even if it was a childish game, at grownup size and weight, walking along a block wall was quite a feat. "You do it all the time, though. Upside down on your hands, too."

"Uhh, sure… But she was really built. Her fists were the perfect shape for beating the crap out of people."

"Th-They were?"

"Yeah. At her level, if she punched a car on its bumper, she'd set off the airbag."

"Hmph."

Traffic-accident level.

I found that hard to believe… Astonishing if true.

Karen was in no way a good judge of character, but she did have a keen eye for physical prowess.

Barking dogs seldom bite, and perhaps the opposite was also true.

"Well, come to think of it," I admitted, "she did seem pretty relaxed and confident—intrepid, or indomitable. She had the kind of vibe that only people who're sure of their fighting abilities do."

In fact, her vibe resembled Dramaturgy's. It overwhelmed everyone and was the hardest to deal with for timid people like Sengoku.

In terms of civilians, Kanbaru, whom we were on our way to see, had a bit of that going. Or Karen, I suppose, for that matter.

They were the same breed.

"My master might be an even match," my sister commented. "I wouldn't be able to beat her, to say the least."

"Oh my," I answered teasingly, but Karen, who belonged to the same breed, speaking in such a way was quite surprising to me. "Why so humble?"

"I know when I'm out of my depths—as long as the opponent isn't evil."

"I see."

In other words, if the opponent was evil, she couldn't tell anymore and charged in whether she was dealing with a monster or at her worst condition.

What a dangerous little sister. She and Tsukihi shouldn't be the Fire Sisters but the Danger Sisters.

"Not that we're sure," Karen went on, her head moving just a little as she glanced somewhat disgustedly in the direction of Kagenui's exit, "that she isn't evil."

0 0 5

That reminds me, I have some good news.

Rejoice.

A few of the more overenthusiastic fans might be disappointed, but the vast majority of people, I'm sure, will consider it a positive development.

Hanekawa touched on it during our conversation—but Hitagi Senjogahara.

A fellow third-year and classmate at Naoetsu High, the school that Hanekawa and I attend, and my so-called girlfriend, she turned over a whole new leaf.

Yes, the happy news I have to share is that the woman known for catchphrases like "Roll over and play dead, doggy" or even "Roll over dead and play, doggy"—the second coming of Tiger Jeet Singh, the fierce tiger—was reborn.

From a naughty girl into a good girl.

How could I not feel happy even if it makes me a happy fool?

It goes without saying that a grand banquet was held among friends, but I will leave it to another time to regale you with stories of those raucous celebrations, and for now relate the rebirth itself.

The events leading up to it were as follows:

You're all aware of Senjogahara's vicious personality—or perhaps I should say, the almost otherworldly effrontery and despotism with which she indulged herself. It hardly bears mentioning at this point. But her venom was not a wanton quality that she displayed from birth. There was, in fact, a perfectly good reason for her maliciousness.

She had been emotionally traumatized.

Put that way it might sound trite, but it was pressing for her.

Nothing is more pressing in this world than the trite stuff.

We might all bear scars pertaining to our birth or upbringing, but the main reason that Senjogahara's axle snapped in the way it did was that she *tried too hard*, in my opinion.

Trying hard can be a sin, for which you are punished.

A crab.

She met—encountered a crab.

Met with and robbed, she lost it.

In the end, I can only vaguely imagine what high school must have been like for her—vaguely imagine, despite being classmates our first and second years as well...

Those two years would have been more than enough to close her heart. Let alone a couple of years, one day—might have done it.

Rejecting anyone who approached her.

Viewing generosity as aggression.

Opening her heart to no one.

Allowing no one into her heart.

Making no friends, barely speaking to her classmates, always answering teachers who called on her with a cold and curt "I don't know"—

Withdrawn.

Distrustful.

Aloof.

As a sort of joke behind her back, she was dubbed the cloistered princess—but for those who knew the truth, that nickname sounded terribly ironic.

Discovering her secret entirely by accident, I found myself serving as an intermediary between her and Oshino due to that knowledge. As a result, for better or worse, we were at least able to resolve her problem with the aberration.

But so what?

Even with the aberration resolved, even liberated from the crab.

Though released from turmoil and parted from her troubles.

While she opened her heart and let people in...

That didn't mean—her broken heart had been mended.

Her wounds could heal in time. The scars, too, might fade, in time—but that didn't erase the fact that she'd borne them. Old wounds could still be fresh memories.

Her manners and person, covered all over in bristles like a cactus, touchy from head to toe, couldn't easily return to normal—or rather, it was her new normal.

The touchiness was now her.

The venom and malice, the withdrawal and distrust and aloofness, and even her hostile nature were her actual personality—a troublesome situation.

Scales might fall from one's eyes, but the ones coating Senjogahara didn't.

Even after she began dating me, and even after she reconciled with Kanbaru, her personality didn't experience any essential or fundamental transformation.

That said, only ever showing her true colors to me and Kanbaru, she continued to act like a shy kitty at school—but after the crab issue was solved, maybe her motivation to play the part was beginning to wane, and her "actual personality" became known to our cat specialist Tsubasa Hanekawa.

Since then, unbeknownst to me, Senjogahara had been subjected to Hanekawa's personality rehabilitation program (supposedly an enhanced version of the one administered to me since April, the mere thought of it makes my hair stand on end), but with all due respect to

Hanekawa, this rebirth I'm talking about had nothing to do with it.

Deishu Kaiki.

A colleague, so to speak, of Oshino—and a competitor.

A conman.

Senjogahara's reunion with him played a big part.

In fact, it's the only cause, really.

All there is to it.

Kaiki was a useless fraud and a terrible nuisance—but a chance encounter with the man who had swindled her family served as wonderful shock treatment a few years later.

It wasn't good fortune, nor was it a miracle. According to Hitagi Senjogahara's own words, thanks to her reunion, her rematch, with Deishu Kaiki, she—settled it.

She must've expelled all the poison in her on that occasion.

A detox.

The venom festering in her system for two years—was countered.

It probably isn't necessary for me to say this, but just in case, I want to state in no uncertain terms that it wasn't thanks to Kaiki—he doesn't deserve a single ounce of gratitude.

He didn't do a damn thing.

To borrow a phrase from Oshino, Senjogahara got saved all on her own. Not thanks to Kaiki.

Of course, it isn't thanks to Koyomi Araragi or Tsubasa Hanekawa, either—this is a triumphant rehabilitation that Hitagi Senjogahara wrested from a loathsome con artist through her own will and action.

And thus, in that manner, she became sweet and affectionate— totally the *dere* in *tsundere*, so to speak.

Karen this morning didn't hold a candle to her.

Color me surprised, for my part, that Miss 'Gahara actually included the non-dismissive mode.

If I told you that it affected her ability to tutor me for college exams, and that Hanekawa and I, after serious deliberation, dismissed her before the holidays (hence Senjogahara was currently away visiting her father's family), maybe you'd get a picture of just how fawning she became.

But you'd be picturing it wrong, or should I say, insufficiently.

Her sweetness exceeded those dimensions.

Calling me for no reason (before, she even blocked me some days), sending texts with emoji (she used to forward spam to me), and giving me cute pet names (instead of making do with belittlement) was just the beginning.

She no longer tore off flowers.

She no longer squashed insects.

She didn't initiate conversations by bitching.

She spoke frank words of praise where they were due.

She reserved stationery for its intended uses.

This wasn't limited to stationery, so using a potato peeler to julienne off my skin if I said anything remotely negative about her cooking was a thing of the past, too.

So was her threat to perform amputations if her bare legs were ever witnessed (meaning, of course, the viewer's legs). No longer so reluctant to expose her skin, she wore shorter skirts (the hem moving from below to above her knees) and lighter clothes that were decently appropriate for midsummer.

Even her expressionless iron mask was gone, her once monotone and mechanical speech featured a certain amount of intonation, and, more than anything, she laughed often. Laughed pleasantly.

In other words—she'd become an ordinary girl.

It was such a drastic shift in personality that I wondered if someone had taken her place while I wasn't looking.

It wasn't a polite front, either.

Not a cloistered princess, not a shy kitty, but a normal, cute high-school girl acting her age.

Neither risqué nor outré, neither weirdly closed off nor combative, reacting normally to normal events, she was a normal high-school girl.

Back in junior high, she'd been a track-and-field ace, respected and popular, and thinking that maybe this was what she'd been like, and that Hanekawa and Kanbaru had gotten to spend their middle-school years near such a beautiful presence, I sulked, *You cheaters, I am so, so disappointed in you,* but according to them—

"This goes beyond the way she was then."

Senjogahara was being so sugary sweet that even Kanbaru, who revered her as a goddess and fully accepted even her most biting remarks, was a little taken aback.

I don't know, I'm not sure "tsundere" described it anymore.

Tsunderrhage, maybe?

The genre was niche to begin with, so why was Senjogahara striving to break new ground?

......

Tsunderrhage makes it sound like an official medical emergency, and I suppose in a way that was how it felt to me. Well, not official, maybe, but personally alarming. That's because I was worried that all of it might be an unbelievably long setup. In fact, her rehabilitation and sweetness being an epic prank was an easier idea to swallow for me.

If that was it, though, she was taking the joke too far.

Even for a nasty prank.

If she was being malicious, then she wasn't just trying to make me fidget. I was being shaken down.

After all—as part of her sickly sweet offensive, Senjogahara had cut her straight black hair, which she'd grown out for ages.

From what I've heard, she'd worn the same hairstyle since grade school, like Karen—though, of course, unlike with my sister's ponytail, Senjogahara didn't hack her own hair off impulsively, not being a moron.

She made a decision and an appointment and went to a hair salon. She paid the appropriate price—and came out of it with short hair.

She'd even gotten rid of her straight bangs, replacing them with an exaggerated shag that looked like a saw.

Tsubasa Hanekawa, Suruga Kanbaru, and now Hitagi Senjogahara—not one of the Naoetsu High straight-bangs sisterhood remained.

That was just sad. Not being able to call Senjogahara "the last line of defense" anymore fills me with regret.

Since Kanbaru was growing her hair out (by the way, hers now hung down in two bunches, i.e. low pigtails, a tantalizing contrast with her boyish speech), Senjogahara's hair was even shorter than Kanbaru's.

Since some girls cut their hair out of heartache, why shouldn't other girls do it out of love? That was Senjogahara's own take. The former must have been a reference to Hanekawa, who changed her hairstyle after the culture festival.

She, too, broke with the past that way. She'd always been overly serious but was taking it easier since then, relaxing her draconian measures against herself.

I guess you could say Hanekawa had become a normal girl as well. Perhaps, in the same way that Hanekawa was my role model, she was also Senjogahara's.

Normal.

For people who had led their kinds of lives, whether for a long or brief while, those two syllables were in no way business as usual.

Because it was too lofty an ambition—to say they yearned for it didn't come close.

That's why.

In any case, my significant other insisting that she was going to cut her hair out of love didn't feel all that bad (in fact, any rhetoric that it was just sad or that I was filled with regret to the contrary, as a matter of taste, I rather like it when girls change their hairstyles), but I can't help but conjecture that it was really her way of finding closure.

A clean break of a haircut, not setting but resetting.

Especially because long hair with straight bangs—a "princess" cut sounds nice and all, but the old-fashioned, doll-like style, rare these days—had been chosen for Senjogahara when she was little, by her estranged mother, who said it looked good on her daughter.

It had occurred to me before that despite her grownup visuals, her hairstyle was pretty Lolita, and it was in fact a holdover from her Lolita days.

From a certain perspective, the style wasn't just a sentimental issue but, if I may exaggerate, one of identity. It might sound silly to make so much of hair—but what else was there for Senjogahara to rely on?

She didn't mess with it throughout middle school and practically forgot to in high school.

For her, it meant more than a style update or wanting to try something different, but a turning point.

Neither forgetting it, nor carrying it as a burden, but accepting it was what made it the past.

In that sense, Hitagi Senjogahara didn't change or turn a new leaf, didn't revert or redeem—let alone become oversweet.

She overcame a complex.

She managed to grow up, that's what we ought to say.

……………

Maybe, along with the fizz, she'd lost a great deal of charm as a character, but she also acquired more depth as a person, so that's that.

That goes for Hanekawa, too. Being asked to maintain such an extreme personality indefinitely is nothing if not a nightmare. Being flexible and growing as they did is necessary.

It's not like they can't die or age.

In practice, unless you're Deishu Kaiki—no one would say that Senjogahara's growth made her a boring woman.

To begin with, I'd hate to share the opinion of someone whose last name reads like you typed it out by mistake.

Speaking of which, Hanekawa once noted that Senjogahara seemed prettier and more evanescent than she was in middle school—but recently expanded on that by adding, "This Senjogahara is the best so far."

Yup.

I knew this day would come.

I'd wished for the day.

I'd believed in the day.

Congratulations, Hitagi Senjogahara.

Congratulations to me, too.

Even putting aside my personal relief that I was no longer in mortal danger, when I took in all this, I was simply glad, as someone close to Senjogahara, and I also felt inspired to truly live.

Not that I was dead, or anything.

I had yet to do a pinky's worth of lifting my own complex regarding aberrations, though.

That's too serious a matter to say *enough small talk*, but let's put it aside for now and get back to the story at hand.

Afterwards, I (still riding on her shoulders) safely dropped Karen off at Kanbaru's house and introduced both parties at the gate.

"Karen, meet Suruga Kanbaru, a junior at Naoetsu High. Be careful, she's a pervert. This is Karen Araragi, in her last year at Tsuganoki Second Middle School. Be careful, she's stupid."

After much fretting, I'd given up and decided to go the honest route.

You just don't tell lies that aren't gonna hold up. No point in upselling.

I didn't want them demanding a cooling-off period because I'd omitted important details.

I had a strict no-returns policy in place.

"Aww."

"Aww."

. . . .

Why were they blushing in unison?

I wasn't complimenting them!

That was something of a digression, or a joke session, but having introduced them, and trusting that Kanbaru wouldn't actually try to put the moves on my little sister (any lapse of self-control would be resisted by Karen's combat skills), I figured that I was done and decided to go home. That was when Kanbaru invited Karen in of all things, a barbaric deed that I promptly thwarted with a flying dropkick to Kanbaru's back.

Out of concern not for Karen's chastity but for Kanbaru's good name.

I hadn't been over to tidy up since the end of July, and the next visit was scheduled for the fifteenth, in other words, tomorrow, which meant that Kanbaru's room was at its most festering state of disarray at the moment. So you see, it was a drop kick of love.

"What do you think you're doing to Kanbaru-sensei?!"

Exploding in a fury the way I might if someone slandered Hanekawa, Karen slammed me with her knee before I could even land.

Talk about a burst of speed.

I did not stick my landing.

"What do you think you're doing to my senior Araragi?!"

Fearing a follow-up attack if I lay there sprawled, I quickly righted myself just in time to catch sight of Kanbaru rushing in to berate Karen.

Uh, so my flying drop kick had done absolutely zero damage… What had I been kneed for?

Hmm. Some weird love triangle was forming here.

Or should I say a three-way standoff?

How about an unlovely triangle?

At any rate, as I headed home alone, walking neither on my hands nor carried on anyone's shoulders, at last—

Mayoi Hachikuji made her appearance.

About halfway between my house and Kanbaru's—on a street corner a little past the mailbox where Kagenui had asked me for directions.

I spotted a fifth grader with pigtails and a knapsack. Hachikuji.

Enter Mayoi Hachikuji.

She had yet to notice me in turn.

"……"

I fell silent. And then exhaled a long, slow breath.

Now, now… I'm sure you're all expecting me to make a big scene and run up and tackle her. A little girl standing there obliviously like a fawn that knows not the meaning of danger—I bet you think I'm going to hug her from behind and rub my cheeks all over her face, or something.

Please.

Fine. I admit that there was a time when I would have.

It's true.

But that's such a long time ago. Ancient history, as they say.

As a person, I was still a work in progress back then. I hadn't grown up yet. They're episodes from a bygone era when I was a boy, and emotionally immature.

As much as I'd like to summon and unspool some of those memories now, um, I honestly don't remember much of it.

Understand if I don't exactly welcome people digging up every little thing that may or may not have happened back in those days.

Does that make me small?

If you dredge up stories about when I was a brat every time I see your face, I might start to avoid you. Who wouldn't be baffled if, say, your first crush was your teacher in kindergarten, and people brought it up after you've become an adult?

I'm an adult now, okay? Those days are over.

Biologically speaking, the past Koyomi Araragi and the present Koyomi Araragi are practically different people. After all, the cells in my body are constantly being replaced.

No one stays the same forever.

That time in my life was fun while it lasted, but everyone has to graduate from kindergarten at some point.

Yeah, that happened, didn't it?

That's the only impression that the remembrance sequence requires.

That's what living means.

Sad or not, it can't be helped.

Because there's no life without growth, is there?

Hitagi Senjogahara grew up.

Tsubasa Hanekawa grew up.

Now I had to as well. Didn't I just say so?

Complexes are meant to be overcome.

Lolicon included.

During our elementary-school safety drills, they taught us not to SDT (shove, dash, or talk), and I somehow came to think of that as Small Darling Tweens, but that, too, is only a fond memory.

Yes, our interests and tastes keep changing, shifting.

No child plays with transformer robots or Barbie dolls forever.

Moving on is almost a duty.

In the first place, who gets excited over grade schoolers with pigtails in this day and age?

Pigtails? Grade schoolers?

A bit dated, no? May I say, out of touch?

I, for one, have lost all interest in this girl Mayoi Hachikuji. Sure, depending on your perspective, long ago there might have been a time when I really liked her. Even if there had been, in the grand scheme of things, that past is so long gone as to be B.C. It's *passé*, as the French would say.

Currently, I'm only interested in, you know, Sima Qian. Great historian.

That's right, I'm moé for Sima Qian.

Yup.

Well…

Well, well.

Well, well, well, well, that said, precisely because I had lost interest in Hachikuji, maybe there was no reason to ignore her now.

I didn't care enough about her to ignore her.

In fact, if I did ignore her, wouldn't people make the outlandish, uncalled-for assumption that I was trying to overcompensate?

You could say ignoring someone was a backhanded compliment.

Given the case.

Given the case, all right?

Maybe the sensible thing to do was to call out to her casually, to offer clear proof that Hachikuji meant nothing to me, the way you might attend a class reunion just to demonstrate that you weren't hung up on whatever.

You had to honor the past for what it was. Growth and change were important, but yeah, something taking you back was a valid emotion, and keeping in touch wasn't a bad thing.

Nostalgia.

Who hasn't thumbed through a photo album? Perused old memories?

People talk about learning from the past. Sometimes that's how you take a new step in life.

It's not like always looking ahead lets you see the future.

You could say that real spiritual growth comes not from neglecting the past but from valuing it.

There. I couldn't argue with a conclusion like that. Why resist or have any misgivings? If I didn't get home soon and start studying, Hanekawa would scold me, but that didn't mean I couldn't spare a minute for Hachikuji.

"Now then."

No more preliminaries. It was time for the drama to begin.

I was getting impatient too, I can assure you.

As if to make up for the time I spent on those preliminaries, I sped forth like the howling wind.

I couldn't break the light-speed barrier, but I could have broken through a speedway barrier.

Okay!

I'll grab her tight!

I'll rub my cheeks all over her!

Touch and fondle her!

Love her to my heart's content!

Today is the day I embrace Hachikuji!

"Hachikujiiiiiiiiiiiiiiiiiiiiiiiiiiiiiiiiiiiiiiiiiiiiiiiiiiiiiiiiiiiiiiiiiiiii iiiiiiiiiiiiiiiiiiiiiiiiiiiiiiiiiiiiiiiiiiiiiiiiiiiiiiiiiiiiiiiiiiiiiiiiiiiiiiiiii iiiiiiiiiiiiiiiiiiiiiiiiiiiiiiiiiiiiiiiiiiiiiiiiiiiiiiiiiiiiiiiiiiiiiiiiiiiiiiiiii iiiiiiiiiiiiiiiiiiiiiiiiiiiiiiiiiiiiiiiiiiiiiiiiiiiiiiiiiiiiiiiiiiiii…gahhh!!"

Just as I was about to bury my talons into her, my feet tripped on something, and I splattered against the asphalt like a rotten apple against a grater.

Zlik zlik zlik.

The amazing sound came from my skin.

Or more like my flesh.

"A-Ack?! Mister Araragi?!"

Turning around at the noise, Hachikuji yelped in surprise.

It was the most surprised I'd ever seen her.

And she'd noticed me…

Now I wasn't going to get to grab her. Or rub my cheeks on her.

Touch or fondle her.

Love her, or embrace her.

Oh, the despair… That my great fortune, running into Hachikuji, should end so ignominiously!

They say to seize opportunity by the forelock, and the expression seemed meant for the situation.

Dammit. What kind of bizarre haircut was that anyway?

Opportunity was so high fashion.

Crushed more by my disappointment than the pain of having my skin scraped off, I was unable to get up for a while.

My clothes were in tatters to match my body and soul, but I couldn't care less.

It was my heartache that consumed me.

It hurt.

Oh, I felt so alone it hurt.

Then I noticed something else.

Amidst the pain that afflicted my whole being, there was a different sensation against my skin, something that wasn't quite pain.

It was my ankle.

A small hand was gripping my ankle firmly, sock and all.

I caught just the briefest glimpse, but the small hand, so pale it didn't look Japanese, immediately sank into the ground—no, not into the ground.

It sank into shadow.

My shadow.

My shade.

"Hey, Shinobu! You did that?!"

I'd begun to think that I was pasted onto the ground and might never get up again, that the Creeping Chaos was none other than me, but buoyed by anger, I sprang to my feet and madly stamped on my own shadow like I was dancing the Twist.

Not that it would do any damage to Shinobu, but I had to vent somehow.

"Shit! You! You! How dare you? How dare you get in my way? In the way of my biggest goal in life! No more blood for you, you golden-eyed blond! I should've just abandoned you!"

I couldn't snap out of bizarre antics that any bystander would have found completely mystifying and unhinged. Meanwhile, there was no reaction from my shadow—I looked like a total lunatic.

Urk.

She was going to play dumb.

What an inconsiderate jerk

"U-Umm," a voice called from behind me, "Mister Kikirara?"

It was Hachikuji.

How rare, she was addressing my back instead of the other way around—obviously, she didn't try to hug me. If anything, she seemed to be keeping her distance.

"There's so little of it left that I'm not even sure you're mispronouncing my name," I answered, "but don't be referring to me like I'm a Little Twin Stars collectible figurine. I'll keep telling you until you remember, my name is Araragi."

As I spoke, I turned around. Cutting short my impotent Twist.

"Besides, when I fell down just now and surprised you, you said it perfectly fine."

"Sorry, a slip of the tongue."

"No, it was on purpose."

"Smile of the month. Tee-hee!"

"That's so adorable!"

Now it was my turn to be surprised.

What was this? She'd switched up her usual routine.

While I stood there unable to respond to my unexpected cue—

"Hah. Mister Araragi, you're still so bad at improvising."

She turned on her heel and began to walk away.

W-Wait!

She couldn't flash a smile like that and just leave me!

Dammit, lately she was setting the bar way too high for our exchanges.

Just what did she expect from me?

What kind of guy did she want me to be?

It probably took someone of Hanekawa's caliber to come up with a proper reaction to that on the spot.

Hachikuji could try to leave, but she had the gait of a grade schooler. I caught up with her right away.

I thought about yanking on her pigtails, but that would be like bullying so I decided not to. She'd flipped out on me once for it, too.

Hmm. Come to think of it, of all the people I knew, she was the only one who hadn't changed her hairstyle from the initial setup. As I said earlier, Senjogahara now wore her hair boldly short, and after this and that, Kanbaru had hers down in two strands. Sengoku often pulled her overly long bangs back with a headband these days, and Hanekawa ditched not only her braids but also her glasses.

Karen also cut her ponytail off this morning on the spur of the moment, and that reminds me, at the beginning of August, Tsukihi also changed her hairstyle—though in her case she always is so I didn't make much of it.

Well, I'll come back to Tsukihi's image change later.

As for me, I'd been growing my hair out ever since spring break, while Shinobu didn't have a hairstyle in the usual sense.

In this regard, too, Mayoi Hachikuji was a precious character.

Although…that lack of change—that stasis—was far from a good thing for her.

In fact, it was sort of tragic.

Always the same, down the road.

Incapable of alteration or transformation, eternally unchanging.

A snail.

A snail, spiraling like a vortex.

"Hey, Hachikuji, you want a ride on my shoulders?"

"Excuse me?"

"Come on, it's perfectly normal. A high-school boy giving a grade-school acquaintance of his a fun ride on his shoulders."

"It'd only be fun for you…" grimaced Hachikuji.

My attempt to support and console had fallen flat. I don't think even the sentiment got across to her. If anything, she resented it.

"With times being what they are," she warned, "please be more careful about what you say. You're really starting to come off as some sort of sex offender in your dealings with me."

"True, the word on the street is that my love approaches criminal proportions. You can't blame them. At its most potent, love has brought kingdoms to their knees. But unlike the statesmen of yore, I'd never lay the blame on a ruinous beauty. I'd take responsibility as the ruinous dude."

"Ahaha. How annoying."

Hachikuji laughed merrily at me.

Well, at least I made her laugh.

I guess she didn't need any support or consolation from me regarding her circumstances. It was none of my business and maybe only puzzling for her.

Man, my own characterization was so ad hoc. Bullshitting about Sima Qian had come back to bite me.

"Anyway, Mister Charabuki...."

"Ugh, Hachikuji. Please don't mispronounce my name like I'm a veggie ingredient simmered in soy sauce for true connoisseurs. It's Araragi."

"Sorry, smile of the month. Tee-hee!"

"You skipped a step!"

Why was I getting the abridged version?

Yet when she smiled like that, it was hard not to let it slide.

"Hmm," she pondered, "if I wanted it to be food-based, maybe I should have gone with Arrabiata."

"You're very strict on yourself..."

Not that she was lenient with me.

"Anyway, Mister Araragi, you seem pretty fancy-free today, strolling around town in the middle of the day. Did you give up on studying for your exams?"

"Fancy-free strolling..."

"Have you gotten tired of trying to impress Miss Hanekawa by pretending to be serious?"

"That's defamation!"

"If this were a twelve-step plan, she wouldn't be taken in by your act forever. Let me guess, did she catch on to how you were gazing at her in her camisole in the name of entrance exams? Half your motivation has to do with her breasts, anyway."

"What do you take me for?!"

"The other half owes to my bodacious body, if I do say so myself."

"Exactly what part of your body is bodacious? I'd say it's chunky, like a nice beef stew."

She was developing nicely enough for an elementary schoolgirl, but only for an elementary schoolgirl.

Also.

Hanekawa still wore her uniform even outside of school, despite her image change.

Let alone a camisole, her everyday clothes remained an enigma. Really, what did she wear?

......

In the first place...

I don't know. Did she own any? Her home situation was complicated, but the neglect couldn't be that severe...

Hmm. A bit of mysterious darkness?

"Um, Mister Araragi, I'd like to talk to you about serious stuff for a moment," Hachikuji said with a serious, stuffy look.

I smelled a setup. These expressions of intent had never once led to a serious conversation.

"People not sticking to their fashion and hairstyle choices is hardly helpful," she grumbled, "for the anime adaptation."

"Again with the anime!"

"They won't be able to reuse those cells."

"Why is reusing them the premise?! Don't make it so low-budget!"

"Good grief. The only part they'll be able to recycle now is my transformation scene."

Yeah, like there'd be any.

Since when was she the magical girl?

"Well, true," I admitted, "anime characters' clothes and hair and stuff do stay the same. Sometimes you even see them going to bed with their hair up."

"That's partly for the studio's convenience, but apparently it's also for the viewers' sake."

"Oh?"

"When the design changes, you honestly can't tell who's who anymore."

"......"

Baloney, I wanted to say.

But to the uninitiated, all of the Gundam designs supposedly look the same. Or all the girls tend to look the same—you hear that a lot.

111

"My goodness," sighed Hachikuji. "Thanks to everyone just fooling around, I have to sound like a spoil sport. Please, give these matters some thought. What about the second and third seasons? If a character nobody recognizes starts cavorting across the screen, they'll just turn the channel to something else."

"Nope. No second or third season. First time's the charm, and that's it."

It was icky to plan so far ahead.

And "turn" the channel? That was some musty diction.

Did she have a rotary phone at home, or what?

"But I guess Senjogahara is the worst offender," I pointed out. "It's not just her recent haircut, she was always tying it up and letting it down and arranging it all sorts of ways."

"It's going to be difficult to reproduce that in the anime."

"Yep."

"To begin with, though, do you think it's okay to broadcast a character like her?"

"Uhh…"

I couldn't reply straightaway.

Her successful rehabilitation made it all the more clear how flat-out bonkers Miss 'Gahara used to be. Without her, though, the story wouldn't make much sense.

"Fine, then what about this," Hachikuji suggested. "In the anime version, I could play the heroine for you."

"Ambitious, much?"

"Why not? Time to forget that woman who's the heroine in name only."

"Don't be so harsh to somehow who just turned over a new leaf!"

"That's my point. Getting reborn turned her into a completely uninteresting character. Am I right?"

"You sound like Kaiki!!"

"Tee-hee. I'd wear a camisole, you know? I totally would."

"Is there any demand out there for you in a camisole?"

"Maybe a bra top?"

"Bra top… Putting aside the demand issue, wearing something so provocative in my presence would not end well for you."

"I'd strip if it's necessary!"

"You're not safe for broadcast, either."

What a dangerous grade schooler.

I'm begging you, show a little moderation before the sponsors start to pull out.

"Et tu, Brute? Right in my flat chest!"

"Sorry, Hachikuji, I can't bring myself to laugh at that. Remember, you're a girl. Stay away from smutty jokes."

"Did you tune out at the mere of mention of my flat chest?!"

"Well, Hachikuji. You know I love you, but it's not because boobless Lolitas are my type."

People get me wrong on this. My preference is actually for busty, bodacious bodies.

"I only spare time for you," I explained, "because you have large breasts for your age. It's just that I have high expectations for their future, as nearly nonexistent as they may be today."

"Did a human being just say that?"

"You know, though, Hachikuji. While I'm dating Senjogahara and totally love Hanekawa, I can't picture myself marrying anyone other than you."

"My precious first time getting proposed to isn't something you, Mister Araragi, ought to snatch away from me."

In fact, it's best if you didn't propose to anyone still in grade school, chided Hachikuji, shaking her head.

Urk.

She wasn't giving me the time of day.

How might I transmit the passion overflowing in my chest to hers? Maybe if I touched hers directly? Or massaged it, to increase conductivity?

"Uh oh," she muttered, "I'm getting a bad feeling."

"Stay vigilant, Hachikuji. I've been casing your breasts for ages, waiting for the slightest opportunity to touch."

"I thought you said you didn't care for flat chests. In fact you've been mapping every nook and cranny."

"Assume that every male in this country is after your nearly nonexistent breasts."

"I can't ever step outside…"

Actually, that country is doomed, Hachikuji noted.

My favorability rating probably was, our country's fate aside.

Were there at least some percentage points left? Where did I stand if we took a poll?

"When we come down to it," Hachikuji lamented, "Miss Kanbaru, Sengoku, and Shinobu are also quite problematic in terms of broadcast standards."

"Yeah…"

It was the quiet Sengoku who might pose the greatest issue.

You just didn't visit a shrine in your school bathing suit.

What kind of centerfold photo shoot was that?

When I stopped to think about it, all of the members were pretty awful. There wasn't a single decent character among us.

"Only Hanekawa will survive," I predicted.

"But in her case, her upbringing is way too out there in being so dark and gloomy."

"Yeah…more like pitch-black."

Did this story only feature dark pasts, black hearts, and murky libidos?

"As far as Hanekawa goes," I remarked, "there's also the cat problem."

"Ahh, Miss Toyama Black."

"You mean Miss Black Hanekawa."

Not only did it sound completely different, Toyama Black was no household name. Unless you were from Toyama Prefecture or a ramen aficionado, you could only scratch your head at the farfetched reference.

"Ah, speaking of which," Hachikuji said, "I saw the design for the anime version of your character the other day."

"What?"

"They made you handsome. For my own part I find that kind of disappointing and boring, but you should be glad. It looks like you dodged the bullet on this one."

"Huh…"

I wasn't sure how to respond.

I hadn't seen it.

Made me handsome…

"You know," she went on, "not like Sengoku back in the day, but your hair was hiding your left eye. Kind of a nihilistic vibe."

"Nihilistic? Ah, come to think of it, that was my characterization at the outset…"

An acerbic wiseass. You'd never know it now.

I feel like I abandoned that side of my personality pretty early on. I guess once I started hanging out with Hachikuji.

An elementary-school temptress.

"Your nickname is going to be Kitaro without a doubt," she declared.

"Without a doubt…"

Our tale did have to do with *yokai*. I could see that happening. Hanekawa would be Cat Girl, then. And Senjogahara

……

Would she be the human heroine Yumeko?

Are we sure about that?

"It really does suit you almost like it was custom tailored," Hachikuji remarked. "I mean that tiger-print geezer house vest of yours."

"I'm not wearing one!"

What kind of teenager would that make me?

I wasn't wearing remote-control clogs, either! My hair didn't stand like an antenna in the presence of monsters, for that matter!

115

"Mister Araragi, you need to be more faithful to the concept. Don't be so obstinate."

"The real me has to adapt my design to some anime?!"

"It's known as the law of 'When the Adaptation Begins, the Original Suffers.'"

"What a scary law!"

"Well, I suppose it's not so much the original, but the original creator, who suffers."

"Way too scary!"

"Hey, Koyomi!"

"You sound just like him!"

In print, though, you couldn't even tell it was an impression. She was just being overfriendly for all you knew.

"It's impossible," she observed, "to do a bad impression of his Eyeball father."

"True... Anyway, I like Kitaro and all, but I'm not sure how I feel about it being my nickname."

"Is that so."

"Anyway, putting aside whether they made my character handsome, the height, what about the height? What did they do with my height?"

"Mm. They stayed faithful to the original."

"Nkk..."

Okay.

Okay, then.

I knew this day would come, when my height (or lack thereof) would be exposed to the world... They say you have to know when to throw in the towel, but I was crestfallen.

Sigh.

Maybe I should spend the rest of my days riding around on Karen's shoulders.

When it came to overcoming complexes, aberrations were one thing, but I didn't see how I'd ever get over how I felt about my height.

I could just stop caring so much, I know.

"Because you're no stranger to me, Mister Araragi, I tried talking them into changing your height to seven feet, but no luck. The truth is the truth, they told me."

"Now I'm more worried that you have such a say in how the anime turns out."

Was she the producer or what?

Hachikuji Pro?

"Well, my only real concern," she confessed, "is what kind of dance we'll be doing for the ending theme."

"You really are fixated on that."

"Usually I might go for something like break dancing, but what if we went really out of the box and did the Awa Dance?"

"How avant-garde…" Traditional yet funky moves. But we'd probably made enough meta-comments. We were trying some people's patience at this point.

"Ahaha! It's written into my character. I'm allowed to get meta."

"I suppose." She really was like a producer. I envied her, but I couldn't leave it at that. What to do with this girl? "You know, you spouted some pretty foreboding stuff, but you're still hanging around town. In fact, I'm running into you more often now. Since August started, I feel like I've been bumping into you everywhere."

"Yes, you're right. I dropped a foreshadowing bomb on a whim, but I have no idea where to take it from there."

"Like a newspaper serialization in its last gasps…"

Why draw it out at all, then? Could she stop being so misleading?

"Well, I tried negotiating with the director of programming," she shared. "No good ever comes of dragging out the original on account of the anime. No good, plus it's just unnecessary. There's always room for an anime even if you're finished with the original."

"You make it sound like you're ordering dessert."

"They didn't listen, though. My opinion fell on deaf ears. Needled from above and prodded from below. I tell you, the TV business is rough."

"So you let them gang up on Hachikuji Pro."

"Go big or go home. The only option left is to put out another sequel...from a different publisher."

"From a different publisher?!"

"You see, the original suffered."

"No, it didn't! It did not!"

"How about from ███████ Paperbacks?"

"Why black it out?! That only gives off an air of impropriety!"

"How about from Fujimi Fantasia Paperbacks?"

"For the love of God, do censor it, actually!"

"By the way, Mister Dusteragi..."

"While I indeed have plans to go clean up Kanbaru's room tomorrow, don't make it sound like I'm some cleaning aficionado who just loves to clean and consistently opts for a method that doesn't involve any moisture. It's Araragi."

"Sorry, a slip of the tongue."

"No, it was on purpose..."

"A slip of the teeth. Chomp!"

"That better be a love bite?!"

Yes! I managed to keep up with the adlibbing!

I wasn't the type to be outwitted at every turn!

You've grown, Koyomi Araragi!

"To change the subject," Hachikuji continued without pausing to praise me. I seemed to have a producer who believed in negative reinforcement. "Are you familiar with the urban legend about the Rolls Royce?"

"Huh? Rolls Royce... You mean the car?"

"Yes. Um, judging from your reaction, you've never heard it?"

"Nope. Well, not that I'm aware of."

"Ahh. I'm not surprised. I bet the only urban legend you do know is the one about the axe-man."

"You think I'm that pathetic?"

Urban legends. Whispers on the street. Secondhand gossip.

Sure, I was nowhere as knowledgeable of such things as Oshino.

"Don't put on a front, Mister Araragi. Trying to act smart will only embarrass you later. Quoting game theory like a know-it-all when you've only heard of the Prisoner's Dilemma is just painful."

"I know the Rational Pigs, too!"

It was only because Hanekawa talked about it once, though. I'd already forgotten the details. All I remembered was getting flustered at the prim Miss Hanekawa going, "Pig… Pig… Big pig… Little pig… Pig eats… Pig wants to eat… Pig wants to eat and presses lever."

What an unfortunate memory I had.

"A Rolls Royce breaks down in the middle of a desert road," Hachikuji backtracked and started telling me the so-called urban legend. "With no solution in sight and at his wits' end, the driver decides to call the manufacturer for repairs. Unexpectedly, despite being in the middle of the desert, an aircraft soon delivers a brand-new Rolls Royce of the same model."

"Wow, that's amazing."

"No, the amazing part is yet to come. The driver gets home safely, but after waiting and waiting, no bill arrives from the manufacturer for services rendered. Since it's a luxury car, he wants to be clear about the cost, grows impatient, and calls the manufacturer again. But the company says it doesn't know what he's talking about."

"Doesn't know? After delivering a friggin' Rolls Royce by air? Or did some other company send the new car?"

"Naturally, the driver has the same question. Confused, he begins to explain, 'But the other day, when my Rolls Royce broke down in the desert…' The representative curtly interrupts, 'Rolls Royces don't break down, sir.'"

"So cool!"

Wow.

The customer support for fancy companies was on a different level!

"No, Mister Araragi. It's just an urban legend."

"Oh…right." She'd told me so at the start, but I'd gotten too wrapped up in the story. "And? It was pretty interesting and all, but why bring it up now?"

"No reason. I thought it'd make for good small talk."

"You… Don't introduce random bits just so you can mispronounce my name." Maybe a rival company like Rolls Royce was on the mind of a Harley Davidson like her.

"Well, if you don't care for small talk, then how about a riddle, Mister Doalagi."

"Let me resist the urge to point out that I was right and you clearly just want to mispronounce my name and instead ask you not to make it sound like I'm the Chunichi Dragons' mascot! It's Araragi!"

"It wasn't a slip of the tongue. You're Mister Doalagi."

"You sound so sure!" Another curveball! It broke so hard I was ducking!

"The only person who thinks your name is Araragi is you. Everyone else thinks you're Mister Doalagi."

"Huh. They do?"

"Don't go around thinking you own your name just because it's your name. Ninety-nine out of a hundred people are saying that it's Doalagi, so don't be obtuse and insist that it's Araragi."

"Uh, umm…"

When she put it that way, I started doubting myself.

Weird, was I mispronouncing my name all this time? Wasn't Araragi—

"You're very popular in Nagoya," Hachikuji assured me.

"Like a hometown idol…"

"If I mispronounced it as Ayaragi, you'd be very popular in Yamaguchi Prefecture."

"That minor place name at least sounds more similar, but Hachikuji, what about the riddle? If you aren't just out to mangle my name, then get on with it already."

"Hm? Oh, uh…"

"You're clearly trying to think of something only now."

"Ah, there's a good one." *Pam,* she struck her palm with her fist. "Hmm, you might know this one already. It appeared in *Die Hard 3*."

"*Die Hard 3*. Yeah, I've seen it so I probably do. The villain poses all sorts of mean riddles to the cop who's the hero, right?"

"I'm not sure if I remember it right, but I think this is how it goes. 'Imagine a dog enters a forest. How far can that dog walk into the forest?'"

"......"

Hold on, was that in the movie? Honestly, I hadn't experienced that masterpiece since it was on TV when I was in middle school, so I didn't remember very well, either.

"Oh, I forgot to tell you," Hachikuji apologized. "This riddle only appears in the novelization."

"Then how'd I possibly know?! You think I've checked out the novelization of a movie from more than ten years ago?!"

The riddle itself was the blind spot! Most people in Japan didn't even know that the first two *Die Hard* movies were based on novels!

"Oh, but this might spoil it for people," Hachikuji cautioned. "Anyone who doesn't want to know the answer should skip ahead a few pages."

"How thoughtful of you..." That is, if the book could still be hunted down in the first place. "What are you a buff of, anyway? Well, fine. And the answer is?"

"Don't be so impatient. Try thinking for yourself a little."

"The truth is, I'm not good at riddles. I'm not very witty."

"I wouldn't say that...but okay, in that case, time's up. The answer is that the dog can walk halfway into the forest."

"Huh. Why?"

"Because for the remaining half, he's walking out of the forest."

"A-ha!"

It was a pretty neat answer. You could even say witty.

I let myself feel impressed. Yes, old movies had a thing or two to teach us, this was how culture got carried down from one generation to the next—

"Right, it was pretty interesting and all, Hachikuji, but why bring it up now?"

"Please don't repeat yourself. When you do that, you're forcing me to do it again." If you were going to repeat a gag, up to three times was the iron rule. "I promise to make it seem like it was actually foreshadowing in the guise of small talk, so could you let me off the hook just this once?"

"How could that riddle possibly turn out to be foreshadowing?"

"Let's see. Here, how about this. On the road of life, you're living for the first half, but proceeding toward death for the second half—that makes sense, doesn't it?"

"Sort of..." Framing it as a life lesson was so phony, though. She was starting to sound like a conman I knew. "But that doesn't apply to immortal beings, like vampires."

"Right. There's no beginning or end for immortals."

And they obviously don't break down, tied in Hachikuji.

True. Going on living and going on dying being synonymous—that defined immortality. No breakdowns, no replacements, and needless to say, no guarantees.

"Still," Hachikuji said, "if I don't mix in a little nonsense, everything would be foreshadowing, and that could spoil the second half."

"What an icky kind of foresight..."

If she was going to be so mindful, she might have directed the scene differently. What an amateur. For all her strategizing, who was ever going to suspect that a Rolls Royce in the desert and a dog wandering in the forest were clues?

"Well, Mister Araragi, why am I the only one with anything to say? It's your turn now. Initiate some interesting small talk, please."

"Geez, get off my back. I'm out of fun trivia."

"Whaaat?" Hachikuji looked displeased. "Don't be such a stick in the mud. Educate me. Something math-related, your forte, would do nicely."

"I tried that with my sister this morning and bombed."

"Ah, say no more." Hachikuji's grumpy expression turned smug. "Since you'll be getting more attention thanks to the anime, you're distancing yourself from all the anarchic banter. Basically, you're selling out."

"What a nasty way to put it!"

"Hey, why not, right? If that's what you want, then by all means, go ahead. Excuse me for getting in your way. Here, I'll butt out, so why don't you continue with the plot? You're through with any kind of silly banter if it's not foreshadowing anything, yes? Go on, practice your oh-so-lofty craft and fashion your noble, moving masterpiece, if that's what interests you."

"What did I say to deserve all that?!"

I was being subjected to such a tongue lashing just because I couldn't think of a good math story to share?

Hmm, knowledge—so important. Maybe I should have discussed root numbers.

"But Hachikuji, trying to be clever can backfire. You don't want to get too convoluted in your approach."

"I suppose you have a point. But if small talk and riddles are off the table—hmmm. Okay, how about this?"

Hachikuji suddenly straightened up. She looked serious, the smile disappearing from her face. With a vulnerable, lonely, and yet fulfilled air, she nodded.

"Mister Araragi. I came here today to say goodbye."

"You're gonna make me cry!"

That line, alone, almost made me bawl reflexively like a little mallet testing my nerves!

"You know, Mister Araragi... I always liked that side of you."

"My tear ducts! They're going to burst!"

"The truth is, I was supposed to go back to my town a long time ago. I was so worried about you that I ended up staying this long... But it's fine now. You'll be fine on your own, now."

"No! You mean it was all for me?!"

"Please find happiness with Miss Senjogahara. And don't be such a burden on Miss Hanekawa, okay? And…every now and then, could you please think of me? Don't forget that you once knew a little girl named Mayoi Hachikuji—who was a very good friend."

"You might as well kill me!!"

I was past tearing up and sobbing my heart out now.

Yeah, forget it!

That bit of foreshadowing could remain a loose end!

Or else, even if there were a million of me, I'd die a million sobbing deaths.

She could go on making small talk as an excuse to mispronounce my name.

"Hey, Hachikuji, now that it's come to this, why don't you just live in my shadow with Shinobu? That way, you'll never get lost again."

"Living face to face with her sounds pretty nerve-wracking…"

Then—

And then.

Like always, just like always, it was right in the middle of such lax, nonsense banter with Hachikuji, in the midst of a silly, fun chat that could go on for a thousand more manuscript sheets—

Like eight trumpets announcing the end of comic relief, another voice inserted itself, as if it had found an opening.

"Hello, kind monster sir. Do you know how to get where I'm going? Tell me if you do—he said with a dashing look."

The speaker wasn't standing on a mailbox or speaking in Kyoto dialect, but I immediately sensed that the kid, who looked about Hachikuji's age, was *something* to that lady, Kagenui, from earlier.

"There's supposed to be an Eikow Cram School that shut down… You don't happen to know where it is, do you, kind monster sir?—he said with a dashing look."

"……"

Despite the last bit, the kid's face was expressionless. It was a flat, inanimate, and inorganic expressionless that reminded me of how Senjogahara used to be.

And despite the choice of pronoun, the child was dressed in an orange drawstring blouse paired with a cute tiered skirt.

A girl who used the male pronoun!

So they really existed!

I'd thought it was an anime invention!

Once I recognized her as such, her colored-tights-and-mules combination filled my heart with joy.

Next to me Hachikuji muttered, "Seeing you dance on your heels at the sight of a little girl makes it hard to put much stock in your assertion that you're not a loli-lover..."

Be quiet!

Hmm? Huh?

When it came to shyness, Hachikuji gave even Sengoku and pre-change Senjogahara a decent run for their money. The fact that she was still standing next to me instead of running off after being accosted by a stranger was pretty unique.

Did Hachikuji know this girl? No, that didn't make sense.

"My name is Yotsugi Ononoki," the kid went on to introduce herself.

Doing so without being asked was another thing she shared in common with Kagenui.

Maybe they were together after all—in fact, didn't the lady mention something about a little girl in parting?

Ononoki?

That was an odd name...and pretty stalwart sounding. *Ono* meant axe, and as with the axe-man that had just come up—it had a ferocious or virile ring to it.

On the other hand, Hachikuji might mispronounce my name that way.

Ononoki, huh?

"—he said with a dashing look."

"......"

What an obnoxious verbal tic.

It was way too long for rounding out a sentence.

And where was the dashing look, anyway?

It made for a pretty lackluster performance.

"I see. I'm Koyomi Araragi."

"Nice to meet you, kind monster sir—he said with a dashing look."

"Uh, same here."

She didn't get it, did she?

And why was she referring to me like I was a character from some children's show?

Unlike the time with Kagenui, I wasn't riding on my sister's shoulders or anything, so why call me that?

I was pretty sure "monster" wasn't one of my nicknames.

Unless Ononoki had witnessed my failed attempt to sexually harass Hachikuji as per my usual custom?

"Let's see, Eikow Cram School..."

I'd explained how to get there just a while ago, so I barely needed to think.

Too bad. If I didn't remember, I could call Hanekawa again.

Yozuru and Yotsugi.

Their first names sounded similar. Maybe she and Kagenui were sisters on vacation somewhere nearby, and they got separated and were meeting up at an abandoned building?

That seemed pretty improbable.

Unlike their first names, their last names were just different, and they didn't look like each other, either. Furthermore, our town wasn't exactly a popular vacation spot, and what sort of travelers chose school ruins as a rendezvous point for when they got separated?

Kagenui, herself, had said something about setting up base.

In any case.

It wasn't my place to pry.

I just needed to answer her question.

When Kagenui stopped me it had resulted in a lucky accident, namely an unplanned exchange with Hanekawa, but right now I was having a fun chat with Hachikuji. Maybe it was rude, but you could say I wanted Ononoki to move along.

Besides.

Although her blank face made it difficult to tell if she was really in trouble, she wasn't standing on a mailbox or anything, and I had no reason to think twice about helping her.

I could dismiss her weird verbal tic as just a juvenile attempt to stand out.

Not that I thought it was working out for her, but it was hardly my responsibility to dispense such advice.

In fact, I didn't even need to ascertain if she and Kagenui were really together.

Coming to deeply regret not finding out their relationship while I had the chance—didn't seem like a possibility.

"Hmm, I see. You saved me, thank you, kind monster sir. You too, li'l miss snail—he said with a dashing look."

Apparently having understood the complicated directions on her first try like Kagenui, Ononoki spoke those words quietly in response to my explanation. Then she turned her back on us in a fairly cold manner. Her words of thanks were accompanied with a deep bow of her head but came off sounding perfunctory, and she barely said goodbye.

She somehow didn't strike me as disagreeable, though.

How to put it—what she seemed to be lacking weren't mere manners, but on a larger scale, any sense of culture.

She wasn't a stranger to feelings, but rather, to means of conveying them—that was the vibe.

In that sense, the kid really did resemble the old Senjogahara. In Senjogahara's case, the traits had been acquired, but I got the feeling that Ononoki's personality was innate.

To tell the truth.

She didn't seem human—or even biological.

A chunk of iron imbued with personhood.

Or maybe even a blade that was a person—a little girl.

Wait.

"Huh?" A question floated into my mind only now that Ononoki was gone. "Hachikuji... Didn't she refer to you as 'li'l miss snail'?"

"Hm? Ah, yes, she did." Hachikuji nodded, so I hadn't simply misheard. "What's the matter? You shouldn't be so petty, Mister Araragi. Don't you know by now that jealousy leads nowhere? As grateful as I am for the inimitable love you shower on this puny, that is to say, lolacious body of mine, is a little girl my age talking to me any reason to scowl?"

"Well, I do find it unforgivable... But that's not what I meant."

Hmm. It was weird, wasn't it?

Kagenui—Yozuru Kagenui—had called me "fiendish" as well and added something about Karen.

Something about bees or hornets.

"Monster? Fiendish?"

A fiend.

Monstrous bloodsucker—vampire.

I couldn't help but glance down at the shadow the summer sun cast—as usual, as ever, there was no response.

"Mister Araragi, as far as I could tell, though, that girl looked really competent. My master might be an even match."

"Except you don't have a master."

006

Later, after returning home: "I've something urgent to discuss with thee. Can we parley for a moment?"

I'd actually already eaten at Kanbaru's—I meant to head straight home after dropping Karen off, but before I could leave, Kanbaru's grandmother propositioned me.

To stay for lunch, I mean.

Kanbaru lived with her grandfather and grandmother. It was just the three of them—as you would expect from the impressive mansion where they lived, her grandfather, the breadwinner of the family, had the type of job with no mandatory retirement age, and he was rarely in the house during the day.

Today's "matchmaking" had been so sudden that it hadn't occurred to me, but when I stopped to think about it, noon meant lunchtime. Kanbaru's grandmother had already prepared extra meals in addition to her granddaughter's.

Which is how I wound up being invited to partake.

I figured since I had come all this way, I might as well be polite and stay for a little while. Maybe I'd troubled them, though, like a guest who didn't know that it was time to leave. But Kanbaru's grandmother was an iron chef in the kitchen, and I couldn't quite resist the temptation.

Because it was still *Obon*, I guess, it looked like she'd put more effort into it than usual. My stomach certainly appreciated the proper, home-cooked traditional Japanese repast.

While I ate, I couldn't help wondering when Kanbaru's grandmother had grown to trust me so much. Maybe she just couldn't neglect a strange older boy who came over twice a month to clean up her granddaughter's room…

Still, though. I knew she was my younger schoolmate's grandmother and was pushing well past sixty, but my heart skipped a beat over the fact that I was eating alone with a woman, just the two of us.

Putting that aside.

I imagined she was worried about Kanbaru's left arm—about her granddaughter.

But as Kanbaru said the other day, her grandmother…and grandfather couldn't poke in their noses too far. Thanks to all the business with Kanbaru's mother.

If Grandma Kanbaru felt beholden to me somehow on that score… I'm afraid her gratitude was misplaced. Like Senjogahara, Kanbaru— got saved all on her own. There was nothing I could do, or did do, in the matter.

So let's just assume that she'd invited me to lunch simply to be welcoming.

Just in case, I exchanged phone numbers and email addresses with her (unlike Kanbaru, she was a whirling dervish with her phone, a regular Cyberspace Granny) before heading home—which is when I had my hanky-panky with Hachikuji and that girl Ononoki asked me for directions.

Thus, walking through our front door, I went straight upstairs to my room to change, ready to study with renewed vigor without dallying. As soon as I sat down at my desk, however, a budding young girl with golden eyes and hair emerged from my shadow.

"……"

Shinobu Oshino.

A vampire who had lived for five hundred years—the aberration who had died for as long.

Ironblooded, hotblooded, yet coldblooded.

She was also the monster who, over spring break, plunged me, an ordinary high school loser, into the deepest depths of hell and ruthlessly forced me to writhe there on my belly—or rather, the husk and dregs of that monster.

She was my former master—and my current servant.

Koyomi Araragi became a vampire from being attacked by Shinobu Oshino, and Shinobu Oshino ceased to be a vampire for attacking Koyomi Araragi. Much transpired, and much was lost. Indeed, all was lost. There wasn't a lot more to say about it.

These days, Shinobu was sealed in my shadow. In turn, so long as she remained there, she could utilize her vampiric skills to a certain extent.

Shinobu was also free to enter and leave my shadow as she pleased.

She had no problem ignoring me when I wanted a reaction out of her, but now that I was trying to study, lo and behold, she dares to show up.

"Hmph…"

I swiveled my chair and faced my desk.

Hm? Where was my pencil?

Ah, right, Karen had made me break my five-sided pencil. I'd just have to use a mechanical one for now. I could buy a new lucky charm for myself another day.

"Are ye deaf, ye clotpole?!"

Shinobu grabbed me from behind in a sleep choke and began relentlessly crushing my windpipe with her wan, thin arms… Hey, I thought vampires used striking techniques!

"I give, I give, I give! Let go, let go, let go! We can talk this outch!"

Shouting the famous line from the May 15 Incident (I had all the studying to thank for that, but having messed up a word, I didn't get full points), I desperately tapped Shinobu's elbow. *Ah, of course, I* realized, *this morning Shinobu must have watched from my shadow while Karen "draped herself over" me.*

While my sister hadn't meant it as a chokehold but was probably just being playful (to butter me up so I'd introduce her to Kanbaru), all I could think about on the receiving end was whether she was going to break my neck. That concern, or rather panic, must have been transmitted to Shinobu via my shadow. That explained why she was doing this now.

Yet by that logic, if we were connected by my shadow, when Shinobu choked me she was choking herself as well. She probably just hadn't thought that far ahead. Removing her arms from around my neck, she began coughing and hacking a little, in pain.

Talk about dumb.

By the way, our shared sensations only went one way, from me to Shinobu. It didn't work in the other direction. If Karen kneed me, the damage was reflected on Shinobu, but if I caressed Shinobu's flat chest, there'd be no feedback.

An awful example, but ease of understanding is the priority here.

"What? Parley? You're always doing this," I complained. "Whenever I want you to come out you never show, but as soon as you see me starting to do something, you decide to pop out. Who are you, the reverse Bob in a Bottle? 'You don't sneeze, I don't please, that's the way it goes'?"

"I think I'd be Illana," Shinobu said, finally recovering. For a former aristocratic vampire, she was oddly steeped in Japanese culture.

Oshino's elite tutoring had produced dramatic results in a very short period of time, but a slight imbalance was observable due to the forced cultivation.

"My lord and master, 'tis only natural that I do not appear at the hour of thy choosing. Our daily cycles are opposite."

"Oh yeah, you're a night person."

That was a funny concept to apply to a vampire, but they hated the sun and loved the moon. It was ingrained behavior, a survival instinct that she couldn't help but maintain even after ceasing to be a vampire.

Just the way humans fear fire.

A phony term like "night person" that belonged to human culture was far too paltry to describe a true creature of the night.

"Aye, I am a night person."

"……"

Shinobu, where is your vampire pride?

Says the guy who took it away from her.

"But what about now?" I asked her. "It's broad daylight. Heck, this is probably the time of day when the sun is strongest."

"Aye. I would appreciate a little sunscreen. And mayhap a pair of sunglasses. My eyes blister."

"Okay…" I don't know, lately Shinobu seemed to be turning into a sad-sack cartoon vampire. Before long she'd be drinking tomato juice instead of blood.

"I obviously have a fair reason for dragging myself awake at this hour."

"A fair reason? I don't know what that might be, but I recall you interfering with my perfectly innocent attempt to canoodle with Hachikuji. Why should I parley with you about anything?"

"Hmph. As someone in the same category, I could not look the other way. Maybe while I sleep, but I was awake."

The same category.

Was that the Lolita category?

"Can't it wait until later?" I requested. "Until after I get a little studying done?"

"'Tis a thorny matter. It importunes fast action."

"What… Fine, tell me."

I was such a softy.

I wasn't even pouncing on an excuse to slack off… I was actually beginning to enjoy studying (Hanekawa's doing).

But I guess Shinobu was my weak point.

My biggest complex, you might say.

Though it was in my shadow, we were basically together around the clock. We had to get along going forward, so it was important to meet each other half way.

I swiveled my chair back around and faced Shinobu, who now spoke in a grave tone.

"According to intelligence I have become privy to through channels most secret, Mister Donut is holding a hundred-yen sale this very moment."

"……"

Hey. Her secret channel was clearly just the ad that came with the paper. I'd seen it too.

"My lord and master, pray let us depart immediately before they sell out."

"Calm down, those kind of stores don't sell out so easily…"

I couldn't believe she was interfering with my studies for this. Shinobu's love for Mister was a tradition that stemmed from her days in the abandoned building with Oshino, but she was graduating from passive waiting and getting proactive about it.

She sure had gotten lowbrow, fast. At least seek blood instead of donuts.

I'd often used them as bait to lure her out like a crawdad on a fishing pole when she'd sunk into my shadow and refused to come out, but all that over-fishing was taking its toll.

She'd become picky about food.

"The talk in certain quarters," she informed me, "is that there are new specials. We must make forth on this."

"Certain quarters… This source of yours just consists of store flyers. Quit pretending like you've got some vast network. Did you drag yourself awake just to tell me that? It couldn't wait until tonight?"

She'd even obstructed my rendezvous with Hachikuji.

That was her fair reason? Then my best guess as to why there'd been no reaction from my shadow after Ononoki left was that the former vampire had simply been dozing off.

True, when I thought about it, Mister Donut was already closed during Shinobu's regular waking hours.

"Fine, fine, I get it," I said. "I'll go buy you some before dinner. It'll be a nice break for me. You like the golden chocolate flavor, right?"

"Nay."

Shinobu shook her head emphatically, obstinately.

Hmm?

I could have sworn that's what she told me—was I mistaken? I remembered thinking *golden like her hair*, so I was almost positive it was golden chocolate...unless there were others in the golden line at Mister Donut that I just wasn't aware of?

But that wasn't why Shinobu had shaken her head. She had a terrible request to make of me.

"Ye can take me to the store. I wish to see them with my own eyes and choose for myself."

"......"

Right, if she just wanted me to buy them, she could have left a note. She'd fought off her drowsiness to appear in the middle of the day because she hoped to make a personal visit.

"It's pretty bright outside," I warned. "Are you sure you can handle it?"

"Perhaps my eyes sting a little. But I am hardly a proper vampire now—not even sunscreen, but a simple bonnet, should be more than adequate."

"Huh..."

Maybe for her, but not for me—well, I say that, but I suspected Shinobu might request something like this soon. I guess the day had come.

Parley my ass, baby girl. She just wanted to be spoiled.

Like I said, I knew Mister Donut was hosting a hundred-yen sale—I'd seen the same ad that Shinobu had. I actually meant to pick some up soon.

Shinobu was probably pestering me like this right now because this morning, just in time (a late "night" for her), she'd witnessed me giving in to my usually hostile sister.

Just as she'd imitated the sleeper hold, she must have figured I was an easy mark. *The fool,* she must have thought, *he is in a happy dream and his guard is down just because his sister was affectionate to him.*

Shinobu was a crafty one.

Hrmm.

Perhaps as an act of largesse to commemorate Senjogahara's rebirth, I could honor such a minor request.

But Shinobu stood out, so I didn't like to take her outside. On top of her blondness and foreignness drawing attention, she was as pretty as a doll. In a way it was worse than chatting with Hachikuji.

In all honesty, if we're being truthful, turning down her bratty request was a simple matter... We had a strange master-servant relationship where each of us was simultaneously the other's master and slave, but strictly in terms of the chain of command, I stood on top.

That authority was unimaginably coercive. I'd experimented in a variety of ways, but at present, it seemed that Shinobu Oshino was well and truly subservient to Koyomi Araragi.

It was more than just a right of command but a wholesale transfer of rights. Vampire rules were frightening.

So if I answered her with a flat-out no, Shinobu had no choice but to back down. My potent authority, however, meant that I shouldn't wield it casually, and I couldn't brush away her requests. In a way, power that was too powerful was vulnerable. Strength could be weakness.

"It would behoove thee to grant my suit, would it not? Ye may not want me to meddle always in your trysts with the pigtailed maidling."

"Hah, you're taking her hostage?! My beloved Hachikuji?! You scoundrel!" Well, actually, she wasn't taking her hostage but into protective custody. "But you forget... I usually run into Hachikuji during the day. Do you think you can stay up forever? Two or three days maybe, but always?"

136

"Hmph, ye have a point." Shinobu folded her arms. Vampire appetites were fierce, and that extended to sleep. Desire came first for them.

"Besides, you're underestimating me. I'm not the kind of guy to bow to threats."

"Fine, then I have another notion for thee. With my unstinting aid, thou could have thy way with the little maidling."

"Urk. That's a pretty attractive offer."

A little girl's human rights were being trampled on with relish in a nondescript room in an ordinary house. It was a horror story. Or did Hachikuji have no human rights?

"Keheheh. 'Tis a sweet thought, is it not? Abetted by my special power, thou could fulfill thy erotic urges with all the maids of the land, her included."

"Nrk... You're tempting me."

Right, Shinobu looked like a little girl, but she was Draculina underneath. There was a succubus element to her, and she didn't particularly balk at sexual topics. If her appetite for food and sleep were so strong, that only made sense.

Dammit... I was kind of all over the place at the time, but why hadn't I noticed over spring break when she was her adult version and in grownup mode?!

I would never stop lamenting that bitter past, that grave misstep.

"Hm? But Shinobu, you've lost most of your vampiric skills. What could you possibly do? In general you can't use your 'special powers,' can you?"

Energy drain and not much else, wasn't it?

In a broad sense, that was just her version of eating.

I wasn't going to let her snack on Hachikuji, my forever-preserved rations.

"Let us see..." Shinobu knitted her brow.

She looked perplexed. Once upon a time she'd been a legendary vampire capable of extraordinary, omnipotent feats. She seemed overwhelmed in the face of her current powerlessness.

"I could conceal myself in thy shadow…and peep up her skirt from the ground to spy out the color of her underwear," she suggested feebly, and it was indeed a shabby plan.

The whole thing stank of small potatoes and was beginning to make me sad.

"Aye, call it underpants transparency!"

"Using administrative lingo doesn't make it any more persuasive, okay?" I sighed. "Enough already, I get it. The stars just have it out for me today. I'll take you to Mister Donut."

I was probably wasting way more time arguing with her like this, anyway—and it wasn't just that it was getting too sad for me, although that was of course the main reason. Now that I thought about it, I had something I wanted to ask Shinobu, myself.

She'd ignored me earlier—but Yotsugi Ononoki. And Yozuru Kagenui. I wanted to ask her about them.

Even if she'd been half-asleep, if those two were *somebody*, then Shinobu would have sensed *something*.

As an aberration among aberrations, the king of aberrations—the aberration slayer that she was.

"Fool, ye fell for my gilded words!"

"Geez, tell me how you really feel, why don't you? Anyway, I'll signal for you once I'm outside the store. I'm gonna go by bike so you can stay in my shadow until we get there. You probably don't want to be out in the sun any longer than you have to, right?"

"Aye, the sun is my enemy."

"Your enemy."

"One day I shall vanquish it."

"……"

She may have been small potatoes, but she still thought big for sure.

"It should only take me about half an hour to get there, so try and stay up that long."

138

"Fret not. While I wait, I shall play my Nintendo DS in thy shadow."

"......"

She had a Nintendo DS in there? I didn't realize my shadow came equipped with a four-dimensional pocket. Think of all the extra storage space.

"Nay, I cannot bring in any material items. The only substance that can enter thy shadow is my own flesh."

"So how do you have a DS in there?"

"I have the ability to create matter, so a game device is simple enough. For my model, I used the one ye borrowed from the maiden with the forelocks like Yo Nihiruda."

"How do you even know the leader in that program?"

Sengoku, she meant.

Anyways, now it made sense... Shinobu could create clothes for herself. A game device should be easy enough, and in fact, Sengoku had lent me her DS a little while back.

When I went to her place before to hang out, she only had old consoles like the MSX 2 and the MZ-721, so I assumed she wasn't interested in more recent games. I happened to mention, though, that I wanted to try out the Nintendo DS because I heard there was a lot of educational software for it. The very next day she lent me her DS along with the software.

So you had one all along, I thought.

It did bother me how it looked strangely new and sparkling, as if it had been bought just the day before. In any case, I used it to study for a little while afterward.

I'd already returned it, but it had been such a huge help that as a thank-you I promised to take her to the pool someday soon.

Cute, wasn't it? That's where she begged me to take her. She was still just a kid, I guess.

Oh yeah, she also asked me to be her acting coach for the class play they were putting on for her school talent show. I'd have to do that for her over summer vacation, too.

......

You know, I'm not sure why, but sometimes I got this feeling that enemies were pressing close to the gates—this creeping feeling that something was hot on my heels, driving me into a corner. Like a forest of established facts was rising around me...

All I did was borrow a DS from one of my sister's friends, but from a distance, did I look like I was in danger?

"Alas, it is only in thy shadow that I can play with the concocted DS—I still cannot draw my powers while outside. Until later."

With that, Shinobu dove into my shadow.

Honestly, if she could make a gaming device, couldn't she make herself Mister Donut snacks as well?

I guess it just didn't work that way. Self-sufficiency might be the cornerstone of life, but sometimes food only tasted good because someone else prepared it for you.

In any case, off I go.

I'd be lying if I said I didn't feel abused, but since I wasn't being subjected to domestic violence from Senjogahara anymore, all things considered, I hadn't met much misfortune lately. If I didn't strike a balance like this, I'd be a no-goodnik who spent all his time harassing gargantuan little sisters and lost little girls.

I had to shore up my favorability rating. I could certainly chauffeur a vampire.

I got out of my seat, changed from my around-the-house clothes back into my outside clothes, grabbed the key to my bicycle lock, left my room, and went down the stairs—and bumped into Tsukihi walking down the hallway.

Hrmph. Bad timing. I was hoping to sneak out without her seeing me.

She'd just bathed.

The heat must have been too much for her, and she'd decided to take a shower after lunch—Tsukihi had a strong metabolism and tended to sweat easily.

Incidentally, both our parents worked, even over *Obon* and New Year's, so during summer vacation my sisters and I had to make our own lunch. I'd wedded Karen off to Kanbaru and also had my fill there, so Tsukihi had managed on her own, cooking and then cleaning up all by herself. Self-sufficiency, indeed. As a member of her school's tea ceremony club (?), cooking and housework came easily to her.

If you thought, *That's par for the course for the Fire Sisters*, however, you lose... The other half of the duo, Karen, is as horrendous a cook as you might expect (her cleaning skills are okay).

Anyway, Tsukihi must have headed for the shower after doing the dishes.

Talk about relaxed.

A fan of traditional Japanese attire, she was dressed in a *yukata* and holding a washcloth in one hand, her skin supple and faintly rosy from the hot water. She was plodding along her house's hallway like she was at some kind of hot springs.

This wasn't Hanekawa—Tsukihi with her hair all wet and slick left me cold.

"Ah, Koyomi. Are you heading out again?"

"Yup, again."

"What happened to studying?"

"God has other plans for me today."

Well, not God but a certain demon.

Uh huh, Tsukihi nodded as if she didn't quite understand.

Hmph, she looked so laidback and carefree as she stood inclining her head.

Her droopy eyes, slack expression, sloping shoulders, and hunched posture reminded me of a certain lazy-panda mascot.

But appearances were deceiving. Tsukihi Araragi, who had tried to make shish kabobs out of Karen and me with an awl this morning, was anything but laidback, carefree, or lazy.

She was a non-lazy panda. In other words, she was a bear.

Tsukihi didn't have Karen's fighting skills and was the Fire Sisters' strategist, but her hysterical, moody aggressiveness was almost freakish, even if I shouldn't say that about my own sibling.

My honest-to-goodness view was that Karen, the hotheaded type of moron, was at least manageable, while Tsukihi, a twisted and devious sort of stupid, was beyond me.

If Karen was a red flame, Tsukihi was a blue flame. If you drew too close, you might get burned, and it wouldn't just be your skin.

Now that we had smoothed over the sharp edges of the fierce tiger, Hitagi Senjogahara, the biggest task on my plate was how best to civilize my middle-school sister.

I'd have to discuss it with Hanekawa next time.

An even more extensive therapy course might be necessary.

"Koyomi, do you think Karen will be late coming home today?"

"Maybe. Dunno."

I'd told her to be back by dinner, but she was so elated to meet the great Kanbaru-sensei that she might not have heard me. Worst case, she might even stay the night.

Hey, maybe she was becoming a woman tonight—or at least, a young lady. In which case, I washed my hands of the whole thing.

I didn't know and I didn't care.

"Huh, I see," Tsukihi said. "When Karen gets worked up about something, she loses sight of everything else."

"Like you're one to talk," I quipped.

Tsukihi puffed her cheeks out as if that was uncalled for.

She had no self-awareness. That was what made her so scary. The fact that puffing her cheeks out made her even more like a lazy panda was also scary.

"What," I asked, "did you need something from Karen? I thought you were done for now with your Fire Sisters defenders of justice make-believe, including the follow-up."

"No. I don't need anything. It's just that…" The expression on her face was complicated—like she didn't really want to finish her sentence.

"It seems Karen's been doing a lot more stuff without me."

"Hm?"

Was she? As far as I could tell, they were together around the clock like always. Joined at the hip. Fellow pilgrims.

Well, they were my family and all, but maybe that was just the view from outside. Maybe Karen and Tsukihi felt some disconnect— some harbinger of change.

"Are you two fighting? Have things been awkward?"

"Nah, not at all, not at all," my sister replied. "I've no better friend, or *Ribbon*."

"Ciao?"

"Chu Chu!"

The secret language of siblings.

Anyone overhearing us would have no idea what the heck we were talking about. The fact that we were able to communicate like this proved just how scary siblinghood is—unless, well, we didn't know what the heck we were saying, either.

A total communication breakdown.

"Still, I guess I'm starting to think we can't go around calling ourselves the Fire Sisters forever."

"Hah," a laugh half-escaped my lips. *I'm not surprised,* part of me wanted to say, but the other part was pretty surprised to hear her say that.

"When you think about it, you used to be BFFs with me and Karen, too. We even called you Homie Koyomi, remember?"

"Never once."

We did all play together, though, with Sengoku in the mix, for example.

We might not have been on best terms as siblings, but we weren't born with bad blood between us—I guess we'd started to grow apart around the time I began middle school?

I think my sisters suddenly felt like little kids to me. Looking back on that time now, it seems pretty selfish and egotistical of me.

I wasn't the best older brother, and Karen and Tsukihi were fairly unorthodox little sisters, so maybe I shouldn't generalize about brothers and sisters.

"Well, when all's said and done, Karen will be starting high school soon," I reminded. "I know you guys go to an escalator school, but the high school is on a different campus, right? You'll be on different schedules, too…"

I glanced down at my own shadow as I spoke—it was vague and indistinct since we were in the hallway and the lights were off. Although Karen wasn't going to start staying up all night and sleeping all day, I thought about the vampire playing with a Nintendo DS in there.

"Your lives will branch apart in various ways. That's probably not something you're real happy about, nor Karen for that matter."

"Yeah. And once we hit our late teens, the police will probably stop overlooking stuff."

"……"

She appeared to lack even a moment's compunction over using her gender and age as a weapon.

Scary girl.

If you asked me, it was just make-believe, but the Fire Sisters playing at defenders of justice was probably helpful according to society. That said, I doubted Karen's and Tsukihi's idea of justice were even the same.

Working tirelessly for the sake of others without expecting anything in return—if that qualified as justice, then in Karen's case, justice was her *goal*.

It was an extremely straightforward conception—straightforward and juvenile. Obvious, upright, no one could ever misinterpret her intentions. That was Karen Araragi.

However, in Tsukihi's case—justice was her *hobby*.

Something to do.

It was harder to brand as juvenile—because plenty of adults out there were like that, too.

Both versions of justice reeked of fakeness, but their natures were actually diametrically opposed.

There was diversity in fakeness.

Though they accommodated each other well, Karen believed that the end justified the means, while Tsukihi believed that the means justified the end.

If Karen was a masochist—then Tsukihi was a sadist.

If Tsukihi was true south—then Karen was true north.

They weren't identical like twins.

They were compatible only when all their bumps and sockets fit together.

An older sister always eager to go on a rampage and a younger sister always able to ferret out a reason to do so—the Fire Sisters of Tsuganoki Second Middle School.

Red flame, blue flame.

"Koyomi, you've probably figured this out already..." I doubted she'd read the flow of my argument, but Tsukihi turned to exactly what I was thinking about. "I don't think I'm as passionate a believer in justice as Karen is."

"Okay..." Another surprising remark. That was pretty clear to me, but Tsukihi's self-awareness left me totally flabbergasted.

"I love justice, I think it's great and all, but I don't think there's any firm core of justice in me. Karen's always saying that the justice coursing through her veins won't allow it or that the spirit of justice flares up in her."

"She is." Such embarrassing words, and with a straight face.

"But I've never felt like that. There's justice in Karen, but not in me. The justice that I believe in—is Karen's justice, and yours."

"Mine?" Huh, what was that supposed to mean?

"I might be the strategist of the Fire Sisters, but in the end the Fire Sisters is all about Karen. I'm just support, a helping hand. If she didn't believe so strongly in justice, I probably wouldn't believe in such a shaky thing," Tsukihi stated impassively. "In that sense you're right, Koyomi. When it comes to me, at least—my justice is a fake. I'm too easily swayed by other people's views to be able to claim that mantle."

"......"

Hrrm. When she said it outright like that, I wasn't sure how to respond—I felt like she'd chosen me as her audience for a guilt-free admission.

It was so contrary to the stuff she usually spouted. If this was what she thought about when she was alone, that really was surprising to me.

Whenever the Fire Sisters disagreed, Karen's opinion took precedence—I'd always assumed that was because Karen was older, but I guess there'd been another reason.

And here I thought I knew everything there was to know about my sisters. Even as I struggled to mask my confusion, Tsukihi spoke again.

"If Karen is someone who carries out justice for others, then I'm someone who does it influenced by others. We were facing in different directions from the start—so you see, I've started to suspect, more and more these days, that the Fire Sisters might be past its prime. Just look at what happened last time, when you put yourself on the line to stop her. Karen acted alone, didn't she?"

"Yeah, now that you mention it..."

Karen had pretty much acted alone. I'd seen it as yet another one of her trademark rampages, but now that Tsukihi said so—maybe it was a clear and present indication of coming change.

A sign that Karen Araragi—was graduating from the Fire Sisters.

"But so what? It's no big deal," I commented. "Look at it this way instead... Up until now, you guys were just way too close."

When I began middle school, my attitude toward my sisters changed. When Karen entered middle school, however, for better or for worse, her attitude toward Tsukihi remained the same.

That probably owed to Karen's clear-cut and simple personality—but even she couldn't stay a kid forever.

She couldn't.

She couldn't!

Please tell me she couldn't!

Ahem… I just want that to be true so bad that I got carried away—but anyway.

Once Karen entered high school, her world would expand again. Sure, she might change—and in an entirely different manner from how I became a loser in high school.

She might end up changing. Growing.

She was still only fifteen—there was plenty of room for her to mature.

"I understand that's just how things are," Tsukihi said. "But still. Once she's in high school, is she going to start teasing me the way you do?" She let out an exaggerated sigh. "Two against one would hardly be fair. A one-sided match, a power play! The game balance we managed to preserve for so long would come tumbling down. I'll be crying into my pillow every night before I go to sleep."

"You're making me sound bad. I see myself as your dependable big brother, always taking care of you guys."

"Taking care. What, you mean by brushing our teeth while you grab our tits?"

"Ahahaha," the dependable big brother tried to laugh that scene away.

Tsukihi was being open with me, but unfortunately she hadn't forgotten about this morning—that was asking for too much. Stumbling upon your older brother and sister making out in bed was generally the kind of trauma that lasted a lifetime.

"All right, I've decided." Tsukihi balled her hand into a tight fist as if to indicate some inner resolve. "When Karen comes home today, I'll have a talk with her. A serious conversation about the future of the Fire Sisters."

"Really? You mean you might split up?"

"It's possible! Her music and mine just don't mesh! If Karen wants to go solo, I won't hold her back! I'll swallow my tears and send her off with a smile!"

I was partly (okay, totally) teasing her when I mentioned splitting, but as she spoke, Tsukihi pointed her finger at me as if I'd hit the nail on the head.

She looked like an idiot.

I was hopeful about the likelihood of Karen growing up once she began high school, but I couldn't help thinking that the day Tsukihi finally grows up was still a long, long way off.

You'd think she was smarter from the way she'd been talking.

"Koyomi, you have to come to the wrap-up party! There'll be lots of middle-school girls!"

"If you insist. I'll free up enough time and show my face, at least," I answered indifferently.

The bit about lots of middle-school girls had nothing to do with it, of course.

Well, regardless of her resolve, I doubted my little sisters would actually be having that discussion tonight. Tsukihi was going to be sidetracked by a most infuriating surprise: the loss of Karen's precious ponytail.

That awl was going to be wielded against me once more, that was guaranteed.

Hmm. Just to be safe, maybe I should have Shinobu drink a little of my blood in advance.

Ah, I almost forgot. Having brought up Karen's ponytail, I need to tell you about Tsukihi's hairstyle.

This morning I was so busy trying to dodge an awl that I lacked the peace of mind to go into any detail, but she, too, had changed her hair at the start of August.

Unlike Hanekawa, Senjogahara, or Karen, however, Tsukihi changed her hairstyle as easily as you changed clothes, so it wasn't surprising. But the Dutch bob must have not pleased her because she kept it for less than a month, a particularly brief cycle.

As of today, August fourteenth, Tsukihi Araragi had her hair in a refined, single-length shoulder cut. It was hard to tell since she'd just come out of the shower, but I noticed a slight inward curl. Whatever it was that she did, it was a glossy styling that made her cuticles sparkle even though there was barely any light in the hallway.

If I could stop being her brother for a moment and give an objective appraisal, the cut made her look somewhat grown up in contrast to what she was really like on the inside.

Still, long and straight, Dutch bob—her hairstyle was all over the place… Were cornrows next?

Now that was where I put my foot down.

Anyway, new hair, new girl, I suppose. Although I said "in contrast," I felt like Tsukihi was acting a little less childish after switching to this new single-length style. Maybe I was just imagining things, but the possibility filled me with hope—take this morning, for instance. Looking back on it now, an awl might actually signify moderation. Back when she still had the bob, she could easily have grabbed an electric drill from the shed instead.

Not that any of this really matters. I just thought you might like to know.

By the way, since I'd been growing my hair out to hide the kiss mark Shinobu had left at the base of my neck during spring break and missed my chance to get it trimmed up, I was sporting quite the mop by this point.

Less like Kitaro, and more like Misery from *Outer Zone*.

Okay, that was an exaggeration.

"Well, dependable big brother? Weren't you headed out somewhere?"

"Ah, that's right."

I'd gotten wrapped up in our conversation. I may not have been able to feel what Shinobu was feeling, but she was probably starting to lose her patience inside my shadow. For all I knew, there were tears of bitterness streaming down her face as she played with her DS.

"Well then, mind the fort," I said. "I should be back soon. I'll head to the store while I'm out, too. Do you need anything?"

"I'm fine. Have funs."

"Funs I will have. Now hurry up and get back to your room. I can't open the front door while you're standing half-naked in the hallway."

"Hrn?"

"I'm telling you not to walk around in such a loose getup. No being provocative unprovoked."

Japanese clothing was all fine and dandy, but she had to do it right. What an amateur. Her *obi* was wrapped around her waist in slapdash fashion, so her tits and legs were practically on display... She had the body of a kid, so it wasn't even sexy.

If anything, the sight was a turn-off.

Hm? Wait a second...

"Tsukihi."

"Yeah?"

"Prepare to be undressed," I announced, reaching for the knot on her obi.

"Wha? What? Koyomi, stop, what are you doing?! Aieee!!"

Tsukihi tried to resist me, but it was the other sister who was the fighter. My littler little sister's resistance meant little to me. Believe it or not, I had seen my fair share of battle.

I wasn't quite the dastardly magistrate in a period piece, but I did grab the sash and spin her round and round, faster and faster, until it was completely unraveled. I mercilessly peeled away her yukata, tied her hands together with the now-free obi, and shoved her down onto the hallway floor and straddled her.

Seriously, if the front door opened now and someone caught a glimpse of this, I was finished in all sorts of ways.

If it was Karen, that would be one thing, but if it was my mom and dad, then more than finished, it would be the end.

The series would end with this paragraph.

The worst possible conclusion... We'd really regret that the story had continued.

Today wasn't looking good for my favorability rating. It wasn't just falling but freefalling, in practically a straight line, with no sign of bottoming out.

And thus.

"Hmm? Just as I thought," I said.

"What, what, what? What just happened? What's going on? Can someone please tell me why my brother just stripped me, tied me up, and shoved me down?"

"Well, Tsukihi. Didn't you use to have a scar right around here?"

I pointed at a spot near her chest.

Usually it would be hidden by her underwear, but she'd just gotten out of the shower and wasn't wearing a bra (one of her sports bras made out of soft material), leaving the area completely exposed.

I caught a brief glimpse through the opening of her flimsy yukata and thought that something seemed off—and I was right.

The scar that should have been there—was gone.

The event that left that scar had created such a strong impression that I still remembered it. In fact, it was impossible to forget. It was more an incident than an event.

The scar.

Back when Tsukihi was in elementary school, she got herself wrapped up in trouble for reasons that weren't entirely clear—and as the result of that trouble, she jumped off the roof of the school building and got that scar.

She didn't hit the ground. As luck would have it, or maybe like in a kung-fu movie, she landed on the canopy of a truck that just happened to be parked underneath, and thereby managed to escape with her life—but the injuries she suffered were obviously pretty grave.

In particular, the scar on her chest, where a piece of the canopy's frame stabbed her, had been guaranteed in no uncertain terms by the doctor to remain for the rest of her life.

Hm?

"Wait, wait," I said. "Actually, you don't have any scars on your body at all."

Now that I looked closer, it wasn't just the wounds from then. As a Fire Sister and defender of justice who lacked the impressive fighting skills of her partner, Tsukihi was constantly acquiring new scrapes and bruises.

Okay, I'll level with you, I may have been behind some of those scrapes and bruises—but all of them had vanished.

Not a trace of them, her skin was smooth and clean.

Faintly rosy from bathing—supple, lustrous, like a drop of water would just bounce off.

"Wounds heal, you know. I'm a human being."

"Hrm? Yeah, I guess that makes sense."

It made sense. It did.

Still, something seemed strange. I mean, why hadn't I noticed before? I'm not always ogling my sister's skin (what kind of pervert do you take me for) so I couldn't say for sure… But was it because she was still young?

Part of the metabolic process? Hrrm…

"Um, would you mind getting off me now, Koyomi? Taking my clothes off is one thing, but if all you wanted to do was check for scars, I don't see why you had to tie my hands up or straddle me."

"No, I suppose that was unnecessary."

I'd gotten carried away.

In the course of one day, I'd straddled both of my sisters. What kind of brother was I?

Hmph. Well, I guess this was a good thing. Better less scars than more scars. She was a girl, after all, and "battle scars" only sounded cool.

Satisfied (it probably wasn't that big of a deal in the first place), I touched Tsukihi's breast once and let her go.

"Why did you grab my breast before getting off?!"

"No reason, really."

Why not, as long as it was there?

On a whim, to put it succinctly.

"It caught my eye so I just wondered what it felt like."

"That casually?!" cried Tsukihi.

"Yeah. Here. *Puyo-puyo. Puyo-puyo.*"

"Don't poke them with your feet! And stop making goofy sound effects like some puzzle game."

"Fire!"

"Don't make a chain!"

"Ice Storm! Diacute! Brain Dumbed! Jugem! Bayoe-n!"

"Zonked!"

No garbage puyo fell on my side—though I felt like there might be a disastrous number of nuisance puyo in the queue (hard puyo, at that).

Honestly, as a fan since *Story of Sorcery*, I wanted to get off a real seven-hit chain at least once, while I lived.

"Hey, stop touching your little sister's breasts so much!"

"I'd seem like a very, very incredible character if someone heard that out of context…"

There wouldn't be a speck of favorability to him, and words like "fiendish" and "monster" would be too tame.

That guy was an evil *rakshasa*.

"We'll use that on the in-store displays!" recommended Tsukihi.

"What bookstore would want to put that up?"

"Brave ones, let's hope."

"Don't go stirring up trouble."

Talk about interference with business.

"Cripes…" Grumbling, Tsukihi stood up from the floor and hurriedly put on the yukata that I'd removed. "If you keep doing stuff like this, Karen and I are gonna have to squeal on you to Miss Hanekawa."

"No, not that."

I could only imagine how angry she'd get.

Be that as it may, I was pretty aboveboard as to where I drew the line, to turn a calm gaze on it. There were people whom it was all right to touch, and people whom it wasn't all right to touch, a clear difference.

"Cripes. Cripes and criminy," muttered Tsukihi. "After all the trouble Karen and I go through to keep our relationships with our boyfriends so pure, why should we have to subject ourselves to such a deep relationship with our own brother?"

"Quit your complaining. Chances are Karen is going through something similar at this very moment."

A deep, or as they put it, a Teens' Love relationship—courtesy of the wicked clutches of my junior. When you thought about it that way, maybe the Fire Sisters did share a connection on some unseen level.

Anyway, boyfriends. That's right, they did have those.

"Ah, let's see. Was your boyfriend's name Rosokuzawa? You still haven't broken up with him?"

"I hate to disappoint you, but we are head over heels in love. Call us love bombers. As for Karen's boyfriend, Mizudori, I understand there's been some discord…but I think they're still getting on well, overall. Of course, if they found out the kind of stuff our brother does to us, we'd have to break up right away."

"Hmph."

That got on my nerves.

As their older brother, the mere fact that they had boyfriends was unforgivable. Dating while they were still in middle school? It made me resentful.

I wish they'd break up.

Of course, for my own part, if Senjogahara ever found out how I behaved with my sisters, she might hit me with her own set of divorce papers.

In that regard, it was still probably too early to introduce Senjogahara, reborn or not, as my girlfriend. I was already in enough trouble on account of my sisters using the Tsubasa Hanekawa card. When it came to this stuff, Hanekawa wasn't exactly on my side.

"Anyway, I'm really going this time," I declared.

"Don't come back! You're not welcome in this house anymore!"

"Oh, but I will always return...to your heart!"

And so, after our spontaneous exchange in sibling-speak, I waited until Tsukihi ascended to the second floor and finally opened the front door and stepped outside.

Naturally, I had no way of knowing.

No way of knowing, at that point in time—that I would never place my hands on that front door again.

0 0 7

"Flocky choux? What is this? How can this be? Have they taken a pon de-ring and a French cruller and united them? What a surfeit of wonder! Old-fashioned! I hanker at the very sight of them! The very sight, I tell thee! I need not even sample one morsel to comprehend the daintiness of their flavor…but sample, I shall! And tofu donuts? The mere name rouses me! Look at these muffins, lined up like fat, glittering jewels! Why have they been hiding the existence of muffins from me for so long?! Ah, fie on thee, villain. And what is this? The golden chocolate, the many other donuts I have eaten in the past, like chosen ones, displayed in such teeming mounds? Magnificence! For reals?! My lord, can I eat them all?"

"Of course not."

Did she expect me to buy so many donuts that we racked up enough points on one visit to order the giant Pon de Lion stuffed animal from their gift catalog?

You know what? Not a shred of her character from the beginning of the series remained. Or from the middle.

Wasn't she ditching her traits a little too soon?

If she was going to change so much, she could quit talking like a geezer while she was at it.

Especially if she was also gonna say, "For reals?!"

Even when they actually existed, aberrations ultimately lacked substance, so the surrounding environment influenced them in an undiluted fashion—Black Hanekawa was a perfect example.

Between her first appearance and her second, the monster cat's character had changed significantly—as a direct reflection of the changes in Hanekawa's heart and mind.

I could only conclude, then, that much of the responsibility for Shinobu turning into such an idiot fell on my doorstep...

I see. Was that the impression I gave, objectively speaking (for instance, to Hachikuji or Hanekawa)?

For reals?

And so.

I, Koyomi Araragi, granted the wish of a Lolita and former vampire, Shinobu Oshino, by escorting her to Mister Donut.

As the lone Mister Donut franchise in the area, it was an extremely valuable location.

Though a chain store, this was the only Mister Donut I had ever seen, so if you were to tell me that it was the flagship store or even the only one in all of Japan, I might just believe you. Considering the dearth of convenience stores and fast-food restaurants, it was something of a miracle that the franchise was in our area.

Which I suppose is why it wasn't a very large Mister Donut (they didn't offer the meat buns, broth noodles, or other dim sum that the larger stores carried), but Shinobu's eyes still sparkled with delight as if she were in a wonderland out of one of her finest dreams.

Even her blond hair seemed to glitter with an extra shine. Kind of like a Super Saiyan.

As you may guess from all that sparkling, and from her outburst when we entered the store, she was inordinately excited.

I don't think I had ever seen the little girl version of Shinobu show such unalloyed excitement over anything. That said, I could hardly get worked up with her.

As a pretty little blond girl, she was already drawing enough attention for the both of us. The more nuts Shinobu got, the calmer I had to be.

"Nrrr," she growled, "I cannot have them all? No, I suppose not—I gave it an assay but knew it wouldn't bode even as I said it. Worry not, I too have learned the customs of the human world. I shan't overshoot, the opportunity to eat at Mister Donut, alone, contents me. Verily then, what would ye say to one of each flavor?"

"I don't know where you get your concept of money from, but I'm begging you, cut me some slack. I'd go bankrupt in no time."

I lived off an allowance. It's not like I had a part-time job. We were so far out in the sticks that there was nowhere to work in the first place.

"Eh? What? Art thou suggesting that I must choose, cruelly enough, from amongst these great, heaping mounds of donuts?"

Shinobu went pale with sudden disappointment.

Over mere donuts.

I felt sorry for her from a different angle.

"I'll bring you back here once a month," I promised, "so exercise some restraint for today. Stop being such a greedy pig and display some of that class of yours. You do still have some, right? Class? Let's just see what you can handle and start with maybe three. Reasonable, yes?"

"Now, now, my lord and master, must thou be so barren-spirited? 'Greedy'! What a cankerous thing to say. After all, we are only talking about coin. Would it not be wiser for thee to consider this an investment, say a down-payment, to buy my favor?"

"What good would it do me for you to owe me favors?"

"We spoke of the contents of maidens' skirts."

"I'll find out what's up a girl's skirt on my own. I don't need your illegal leaks."

"Nrrr. My lord appears to be a man among men."

"Tsk. It's about time you noticed. Every day for breakfast, I have croque-monsieur."

"The breakfast of gentlemen!"

"And I'm also punctual!"

We were having a stupid conversation, just a stupid conversation, okay?

"Ahh, enough. Fine," I relented, "how about you and I each choose five? That'll be ten total, which we can share."

I suppose it was a hundred-yen sale. I could spare a thousand yen. I didn't need any favors, but it wouldn't hurt to put her in a good mood. To keep the lines of communication smooth between us—I doubted I'd be asking her for any help, but I still didn't want her getting in the way of my canoodling with Hachikuji.

"But in return, no muffins or pies," I laid down. "Those aren't included in the sale."

"Argh... I'll bear it, if I must."

Shinobu nodded in the most reluctant fashion you can imagine.

What a deadbeat... How about a thank you?

I'd meant to buy a study-aid with the money. If I failed my exams, I was blaming her.

Anyway, after finally hashing out our terms, it took yet another thirty minutes for Shinobu to select her ten donuts from the display case (I even let her choose my five. Since we were sharing anyway, there was really no "my five" and "her five").

Shopping with girls was tough.

The former vampire also seemed to have tunnel vision and zero finesse. After spending thirty minutes "cruelly" choosing, she got a whopping three flocky choux in the end.

Chocolate flavor, apple flavor, and blueberry flavor.

Strictly speaking, they were different, but this was her chance to try out all different kinds of donuts. You'd think she'd go for a little more variation.

Maybe I should have said something, but between the way she looked and her antiquated speech, Shinobu was drawing a lot of stares. I didn't have the mental fortitude to engage in one of our slapstick dialogues right by the register.

160

Judging from the cashier's reaction, the assumption seemed to be that Shinobu was talking that way thanks to her favorite anime or something, but I wasn't adventurous enough to play along with that mistake.

Phew. So be it.

Since I was going to bring Shinobu here every month, all sorts of misunderstandings and understandings would obtain sooner or later.

It was all an anti-matter of time.

In addition to the ten donuts, I ordered two cups of free-refill coffee, after which Shinobu and I headed to a table on the second floor.

She wore a pleased expression on her face as we sat across from each other. She was on cloud nine.

"I had been keeping this privy, but in my five hundred years, the truth is that several times I have contemplated snuffing out the human race. But in surety, allow me now to make an oath! So long as Mister Donut exists, never shall I attempt to crush the humans!"

"That's some large-scale smallness. Those five hundred years must have felt very long for you."

Of course, I imagined a lot happened in that time.

Five hundred years.

While we'd formed an unseverable bond, Shinobu and I had only known each other for less than half a year—there was much about her that I still didn't know.

But I figured that was fine.

Shinobu—was an aberration.

I—was a human.

Operative word: was.

"By the way, Shinobu, there's something I wanted to ask you." Having waited for the right moment (until about five of the donuts vanished from the table, in other words), I brought up my topic. "Today, while I was on my way to Kanbaru's house, and then later on my way back? Those two people who asked me for directions—the lady who spoke in Kyoto dialect and the kid with the dashing look.

In your view—*how* were they?"

Yozuru Kagenui and Yotsugi Ononoki. I had my own grand ulterior motive for laying out this great feast of donuts. I was hoping to pick Shinobu's mind about those two.

"Hmph."

Perhaps she'd come down a bit from her donut high. Shinobu flashed me a dauntless grin—maybe a little less dauntless than intended thanks to the white powder smattered around her lips from an angel cream donut.

"My lord, what now? I misdoubt this bears mentioning… I, at least, consider it a matter of tacit accord. But since the opportunity presents itself, I will unkennel my thoughts."

"Hmm?"

"Sealed within thy shadow—and through the immutable fetters of that seal, I ever drain thy energy without unsheathing my fangs, without sucking thy blood. I am quickened by thee—and saved."

"Quickened…and saved."

"But apart from such tender circumstances, under our current arrangement I am thy vassal. Loathe and despise thee, as I surely do, much did transpire between us—so to be brief, I have taken an interest in thee."

"An interest…"

In thee, I haplessly repeated Shinobu's words back to her.

"In thee, or perhaps in thy life. Not an aberration's, but that of a mere human who has lost the vampiric power he once possessed—not an immense interest, but I am fair-curious."

And I also get to eat donuts, she added, transporting my half-eaten sugar-glazed out of my hand and into her mouth.

It was an indirect kiss. Not that I was so naive that it made me blush.

"However, my lord and master, and this is the crowning point—though I may be thy ally, do not for a moment mistake, therefore, that I am an ally to humankind."

"......"

"Of course, I am no ally to aberrations, either—at gross best they are feed and fodder. A meal, chow. Yet, though I lose my powers—though neither shadow nor form remain, it brooks not that I have therefore become human. Imagine that we come upon a human in distress. Likely ye'd lend aid to that human. I, however, would not," Shinobu declared as if she were giving an oath at the Olympics. "I will not crush humankind—but nor will I aid them. That is the rule by which I have chosen to abide."

"You mean it's not a vampire rule, but your own? A line you've drawn, for your own sake?"

"Verily. To wit, if somewhere or other this person or that person were in distress, I would not bother to inform thee—and there is no vouching that I would answer any questions with the truth. That, then, is where things stand." Through a mouthful of donut, she mumbled, *I went to great travails during the recent incident with the bee aberration, but that was to aid my master, not thy kin.*

For someone eating something sweet, her expression was quite stern—she wasn't saying any of this just to tease me or to be coy.

Well, I guess that made sense. Having been bestowed a tiny measure of vampirism, Koyomi Araragi's position was fairly complicated, but Shinobu Oshino's position after she was deprived of the greatest portion of her vampirism, and her true name in addition to her shape and form, went beyond mere complication into the realm of the inscrutably bizarre.

Shinobu Oshino.

An ironblooded, hotblooded, yet coldblooded vampire.

Whatever tremendous bargains she made with herself—were beyond my comprehension.

The legendary vampire had shut me out, giving me the complete and utter cold shoulder. It took four months for her to open those lips and speak to me again at last.

Four months. Compared to the five hundred years she'd been

alive, perhaps it was a short period of time.

For Shinobu, however, those four months—must have felt longer than five hundred years.

Turmoil, day in and day out. Uncertainty. Despair.

If my spring break had been hell—then Shinobu's hell had dragged on ever after spring break.

In which case, whatever conclusions she came to, whatever bargains she struck with herself, weren't for me to criticize.

If she wanted to vanquish the sun, or crush the human race—I wasn't going to try to talk her out of anything anymore. I could only offer up the sad little remains of my life, which should have ended long ago, and beg for her forgiveness.

If you repeat something too often, the words can begin to lose meaning, but this, I will say over and over again: if Shinobu Oshino were to die tomorrow, then Koyomi Araragi's life could end tomorrow as well—because it was only Shinobu Oshino's presence that allowed me to live on.

"Well, yeah… We do have a tacit agreement, as you say. Even I get that, there's no need to spell it out now. So, what? Are you saying—you'd rather not tell me about those two?"

"Even that question is difficult. If I tell thee I don't wish to answer, that will communicate to thee that they are, at the very least, *somebody*."

"You mean you refuse to even entertain the question? Hm, that's an austere rule."

"Well, I don't know for austere…"

Shinobu reached for her coffee as if the sweetness in her mouth had become too much. As befit her nationality, she preferred black tea, but that didn't mean she shunned coffee. Watching a little girl take a sip of coffee was a sublime sight, by the way.

"But strictly speaking," she resumed. "Perhaps I'd not mind telling thee about the little girl with the dashing look."

"What…does that mean?"

"She is not a human. She is an aberration," Shinobu replied bluntly.

Still, it must have been a gray zone in terms of her rule—her tone was flat, indifferent, and business-like. "The human shape is a counterfeit. Like myself, her appearance does not befit her true age—and her name, Yotsugi Ononoki, is likely false as well."

—*He said with a dashing look,* Shinobu appended in a business-like tone.

Joking in that way was her dry obstinacy showing through.

Or perhaps it was her unmanageable combativeness.

Maybe it was her unconquerable sense of humor.

In any case—that was her character.

"Parsing her last name, Ononoki," she continued, "gives me a general notion of her nature—but this begins to edge on the creature's privacy. More than any rule, as a matter of etiquette I would rather not speak on it. Ye'd not want me to announce thy sexual proclivities, either."

"Well, no." Well, not at all. Why would I want them announced? "But putting her last name aside—something about her first name, Yotsugi, seems weird to me. When you compare it to that Kagenui lady's first name, they almost sound like a pair."

"Ha, the name likely binds her, I'd wager." Shinobu shrugged her shoulders emphatically. Usually a shoulder shrug isn't so over-the-top, but it did accentuate Shinobu's pent-up frustration. "Just as I am bound by that shallow brat's name. In short—Yotsugi Ononoki is like a familiar to Yozuru Kagenui."

"A familiar…"

An aberration—bound like Shinobu.

The shallow brat that Shinobu spoke of was someone I, and Hanekawa, and Senjogahara, and even Hachikuji, Kanbaru, and Sengoku, considered our savior.

Mèmè Oshino.

A counter-aberration expert—an authority on sending away yokai.

In more mundane terms, the dude in the Hawaiian shirt.

For Shinobu, he was the human she bore the deepest grudge

against, apart from me—but during the time Oshino resided in this town, they lived together in that abandoned building…Eikow Cram School.

So while Shinobu spoke of him disparagingly, resentment probably wasn't all that she felt for him.

What she felt, however, was beyond my comprehension. I couldn't even begin to imagine.

To be bound—by a name.

One thing that seemed certain was that Shinobu didn't want to discuss Oshino.

"A familiar. The term," she hurried on to her next sentence, "makes her sound like a page of some sort, so perhaps it is not accurate. Hmm… To liken her to something from this country's own lore, she is akin to a *shikigami*."

"A shikigami…"

A familiar…or a shikigami. I hadn't noticed anything to make me think that. She looked human as far as I could tell.

But now that Shinobu said so, Ononoki's lack of facial expressions, her inscrutability, her elusiveness—were enough to make you think that she wasn't altogether human.

Zero or even negative in quantity.

And more than anything, placed side by side with some of the other materially, physically existing aberrations that I'd faced off against—there were similarities, to be sure.

For instance, Tsubasa Hanekawa, when she was bewitched by the cat, and Suruga Kanbaru, when she wished upon the monkey.

They clearly had something in common.

"Hrrm…"

Still, though. Were aberrations allowed to go around existing in such an unceremonious, everyday sort of way?

I couldn't tell at all. I was suspicious about her, which is precisely why I'd asked Shinobu, but I'd never have guessed that the little girl was a honest-to-goodness aberration.

That said...I shouldn't be so baffled, objectively speaking. One of those "materially, physically existing" aberrations was sitting right in front of my eyes and stuffing her cheeks full of tasty, tasty donuts in the most unceremonious, everyday manner.

Not to mention me, myself. In some ways—I was a kind of aberration, too.

"So, a shikigami..."

Maybe this association was a little too on the nose—but the first thing I thought of when I heard the word was an *onmyoji,* our native sorcerer. She'd spoken in Kyoto dialect, after all...

So if Ononoki was an aberration, Kagenui—

"That explains why they called me names. 'Fiendish young man,' 'kind monster sir.' I see. Those two—well, Kagenui at least, is some kind of expert."

An expert, an authority.

In other words, she was in the same business as Mèmè Oshino.

"Ononoki perhaps, but as for Kagenui, had she not simply espied thee mounting thy kinswoman like a post-horse and judged accordingly? Anyone who witnessed such a sight could be forgiven for thinking thee fiendish."

I couldn't tell if Shinobu was chiding me or really meant it...until she clicked her tongue and muttered, *I spoke too much*—so I guess she meant it.

How rude.

Hrmm...but I didn't get it. So Kagenui wasn't an onmyoji?

Since she'd been spot-on about Karen getting stung by a bee aberration, she couldn't be a total amateur—unless she just meant it adjectively as well, as in "fierce as a hornet." According to Karen, Kagenui posed an automotive level of danger—it wouldn't be odd if Kagenui, in turn, had picked up on my sister's fearsome combat skills.

In fact, Kagenui must have realized that no ordinary girl carried her brother around on her shoulders.

Maybe that was what "hornet" meant.

But maybe not.

"I shan't spill any information regarding proper humans. I limit myself to aberrations, or at the most, experts on them," Shinobu forestalled me before I could speak. A look of anticipation must have crossed my face. "Did thou think to avail thyself of me so readily? I am not such a cheap woman that a few donuts would loosen my lips. I am neither thy familiar nor thy shikigami. I am simply a vassal. If ye insist on answers, resort to thy authority to command me."

"I'm not insisting on anything..."

Nor did I think I could avail myself of her readily.

I didn't intend to buy favors, either.

Well, sure, it had been quite a wishful ulterior motive—she was right to nail me on that.

So long as I wasn't pinned through the heart with a wooden stake.

"I'm glad we understand each other," Shinobu said, taking another sip of her coffee.

Copying her motion absentmindedly, I took my own cup in hand.

As if she'd been waiting shrewdly, with malice aforethought, for the black liquid to enter my mouth, she said, "But if thou do insist, my lord—why not inquire with the man sitting in the corner?"

"?"

I turned to look behind me, whereupon I promptly spewed the coffee from my mouth.

Sitting there, his tray piled high with nothing but muffins and pies that he was easing down with a double espresso—was none other than a fraudulent practitioner of Mèmè Oshino's trade.

Deishu Kaiki.

008

Hitagi Senjogahara, who encountered a certain crab in between middle school and high school, was conned by five frauds during those two years before Mèmè Oshino finally resolved her physical problem—to some degree, she must have wanted to be fooled, but in any case, the first of that quintet was Deishu Kaiki.

The man who was the beginning and the end.

The first and last man.

Called the ghostbuster.

That was Deishu Kaiki.

A late middle-aged man dressed in a sable-black suit finished with a deep black tie, like he'd just come back from a funeral and was in mourning, he was visibly ominous.

A Fire Sisters act of justice had recently targeted this ominous man.

He was positioned as the villain.

I'll leave out the finer details, but he'd been circulating charms that utilized aberrations, mainly among local middle-school students. When you thought about it, it was a pretty large-scale con, developed systematically over several months—he was stopped before the damage could grow too severe, which I guess was a silver lining.

But that didn't mean we came out of it unharmed. Karen was stung by a bee—and all the follow-up was a real pain. I would in no way say that things went smoothly.

Still, it did give Hitagi Senjogahara the opportunity to face Deishu Kaiki directly and deal with her past trauma—for a closure of sorts.

She expelled all the venom from her system.

Deishu Kaiki promised never to show his face to us again and left our town for good—and yet.

And yet.

"What the hell are you doing here?"

"Don't be foolish. You thought I'd honor our promise? If so you are a dolt. The lesson for you to take home from this is that promises are made to be broken," Kaiki answered ominously while stuffing his face with a blueberry muffin.

He could seem ominous even at a Mister Donut.

You'd think his image would improve at least a bit, but it didn't make him one iota cuter.

I'd made a lot of tough-sounding claims at the time, like *I should never meet Deishu Kaiki again for the rest of my life* and *If we meet again, it will probably be to kill each other*… And now here I was bumping into him at the neighborhood donut shop.

You gotta be kidding me. All that tough talk, gone to waste.

Even after I (and Shinobu) walked over and sat down across from him without asking, he simply continued to eat, betraying not even the slightest hint of surprise—one thing Kaiki wasn't, was ordinary.

He may have been a fake and a swindler—but he was every inch the real deal.

"Or so I would usually answer."

Right when I almost opened my mouth, wondering how I might chew out the shameless man, Kaiki swiftly issued a retraction—the timing was nasty, like he was trying to annoy me.

"Relax," he said. "Exceptionally rare though this may be, for the time being, I do in fact plan to keep my promise with Senjogahara—doing so would align best with my own interests. The interests of money, that is. I never meant to revisit this town a second time."

"Yeah, fine, but you're here…"

"I never meant to a second time. Only this time."

"……"

The conman!

What a conman!

Actually, if he was going to be like that, this was his third visit at least, wasn't it?

Prior to the issue of him being the real deal or a fake, a lot of what he said and did was just so small-time.

It was like he was papering over his smallness with that baritone of his.

"Kaiki… Whether or not you intended to deceive us, you made a big show of cutting and running. Why come back here to eat donuts?"

"I remembered I had a coupon that's only good for this branch—I came back to redeem it."

"I-Is that another lie?"

"What a vexing statement. I've never woven a lie or a monk's hair," the conman insisted solemnly.

This guy really was incorrigible… I already knew that, but still.

For reals.

But you had to admit, the man had balls.

Boldfaced—or barefaced. Way too audacious.

He had to know that if Karen or Senjogahara found him, he wouldn't get off so easy this time—yet here he brazenly sat, not even trying to sneak around. He made no move to run or hide but also seemed to have no defense plan in place.

Naturally, I had never been confident in the first place that he would really, truly, in the strictest sense of the word, keep his promise.

Any promise that wasn't put in writing…

Wasn't much of a promise at all—still, for Hitagi Senjogahara, forcing Deishu Kaiki to make one had been enough.

Had been.

Right…

The issue here wasn't so much Karen but Senjogahara.

She was so nicely reborn, but a third encounter with Kaiki, at this stage, could result in a massive relapse.

If she went back to her acid-tongued ways now, I wouldn't know how to handle it.

"What I said about the coupon was the truth, and that's not all," Kaiki deadpanned using what sounded to me like the wrong conjunction. He brought his double espresso to his lips—wait, since when did Mister Donut serve double espressos?

Did he make a special order? Why was even his drink raven-black?

They speak of someone "donning an ominous air," but in Kaiki's case he seemed to exhale an ominous air. It was like he sucked in oxygen and emitted black smoke. His very existence was ominous.

"It's a boring, minor business, so don't concern yourself, Araragi. I will be out of your hair soon—"

"I'd rather you got out of it right now."

"If wishes were ponies, young man. I didn't want to see you any more than you do. I suffered some very great losses thanks to you all—the only saving grace is that your sister got busy taking care of all the follow-up and spared any expenditure on my part."

"……"

"If I am a plague to you lot, you are a plague to me as well."

As Kaiki spoke, he chomped on another muffin.

It really didn't suit him. As ominous inside as he appeared, the man still enjoyed sweet fare?

Of course, it was none other than Mèmè Oshino who'd tamed Shinobu with donuts—maybe being an expert on aberrations demanded a high sugar intake?

"The truth is, I still have more coupons remaining," Kaiki divulged. "Now that you've spotted me, though, it's best that I don't use them. I will try to scalp them to someone. I wouldn't want to tarry and have you bring Senjogahara here."

"I would never."

"I suppose not. However," Kaiki said, glancing at Shinobu, who was concentrating on eating her donuts beside me with no apparent interest in our conversation. "You're quite the wily fox, aren't you? It seems you are as wicked as I am. Look at you, out in broad daylight, in the middle of summer, sporting this little blond Lolita around town, pleased with yourself as punch."

"......"

Don't call her Lolita.

And I wasn't *pleased as punch*.

I wasn't him.

Shinobu hadn't bothered to help out during our confrontation with Kaiki (she must have been sleeping peacefully in my shadow when it went down), so in a way this was the first time the two had come face to face— hmm.

Though human, Kaiki was an expert, like Oshino. An expert other than Oshino.

I wondered how Shinobu's rule worked in this case—especially since it didn't involve an aberration.

"How about it, little girl? Would you mind if I took your picture? I'll give you 500 yen per shot—I could earn 500,000 yen with such material," the conman tried to strike a dubious bargain with the vampire at my side.

You had to watch this guy, he was a slick one.

But wait.

Did Kaiki honestly not realize what Shinobu was?

Well, I suppose he was ultimately only an expert fraud… He and Oshino were actually different types.

That's right.

Kaiki—didn't believe in aberrations.

To him, they were no more than tools that he used in his scams. The bee didn't exist—nor did vampires.

"Hmph, I suggest ye look elsewhere. I would be underselling

myself."

"You can have one of my muffins."

"A muffin?! My lord, this knave's not half bad!"

"Don't get taken in so easily."

He'd never even pay 500 yen.

In fact, he probably hadn't paid for all those muffins. In the worst-case scenario, he might have forged the coupons.

"Well, I'm not such a rube to fault other people for their predilections," he claimed. "Offer me a decent sum, and I won't tell Senjogahara about these unusual tastes of yours."

"You try to blackmail people, just like that?"

Skullduggery came second nature to Kaiki. But it was no skin off my back if Senjogahara discovered that I'd taken Shinobu out on a date (if she found out about Hachikuji, though, I might be in trouble).

"I never cease to be amazed," I said, "that someone like you actually exists. I bet you don't even have Senjogahara's contact info."

She'd destroyed his cell phone.

And she didn't move to Tamikura Apartments until after she'd been swindled by Kaiki—though maybe a conman could easily obtain a cell phone number?

Either way, I doubted Kaiki would carry through with it.

As far as he was concerned, Hitagi Senjogahara was no longer worth a single yen—in fact, when he came to this town to work his con on middle schoolers, he'd totally forgotten that there was a young woman here whose family he had defrauded.

Of course, that might have been another lie. But at the very least—Kaiki hadn't tried to approach Senjogahara.

That. And that was it.

Even taking away the issue of money, or adding it for that matter, Senjogahara was broke now and what Kaiki called "an ordinary girl"—she didn't interest him in any way.

Which…worked just fine for us.

I let out a sigh.

I'd be lying if I said taking Shinobu out on a first date hadn't put a little spring in my step, miffed though I'd been at first that she was interrupting my studies... Running into Kaiki completely ruined it.

Now I felt like I was in the pits. The guy was like a reverse leprechaun. He was just way too ominous.

What a contrast with Hachikuji, whose mere sight filled me with joy—today I was being lift up only to be cast down like in that old game show, the Up-Down Quiz.

"Stop it with those eyes," Kaiki complained. "That's no look for a kid to inflict on an adult."

"No, I was just thinking, you're really like a crow."

"A crow. I'll take that as a compliment. The crow is a tough and very clever bird."

"Well yeah, I guess..." Their jet-black color gave them a bad rep, but judging by appearances wasn't fair. Crows were even said to bring good luck in some regions. "They do toss garbage around and make a mess, though."

"They pick through garbage because humans put out garbage. On the grand planetary scale, it's humans that are tossing garbage around."

"You seem like the type who hates being environmentally friendly..."

"Speaking of making a mess, the other day I saw a crow eating a pigeon. It was a breathtaking sight, an explosion of feathers all around them."

"I'd rather not picture that..."

What a downer conversation... Small talk with Kaiki was so not worth it. Not that I wanted to have fun chatting about birds with a guy like him in the first place.

Not just crows, but birds in general, were tough and tenacious creatures—I already knew that. Forget about small talk, I should have chosen to ignore Kaiki the moment I laid eyes on him—but Shinobu had prodded me.

Because I wasn't going to insist, I needed to ask him—and came over to sit with him knowing full well that the experience would be unpleasant.

Protecting Senjogahara, though, was my strongest incentive, of course.

"Yozuru Kagenui and Yotsugi Ononoki. You know them, right?"

I'd phrased my question in such a needlessly leading manner because I didn't want to create any untoward opportunities for Kaiki. If he didn't know, he didn't know, and if he didn't feel like telling me, that was fine. The one thing I didn't want was for him to make this complicated and to demand payment for the info.

I really wasn't interested in haggling with a conman.

Unfortunately, a kid's shallow tricks were no match for the crafty wiles of an adult.

"You want to know? I will tell you. Pay up."

Kaiki thrust his chest out proudly.

What a syllogism.

Geez, the miser—though in his case it was more like plunder.

This was a man who declared that he valued money more than his own life. Just as the Fire Sisters upheld the ideals of justice, Kaiki upheld the principles of capitalism.

He'd grind justice beneath his boot—without batting an eye.

"Meeting coincidentally like this must be fate, Araragi," he said. "I could offer you a discount, considering. I won't even ask for a coupon."

"Coincidentally, huh."

Such an unhappy coincidence—but I had to make the most of it, true.

"All right…fine."

It wasn't worth arguing over. The moment he got me thinking that way, I had already fallen into the conman's trap and become an easy mark. But that didn't mean I was proceeding without a plan.

Coming off as a boob and making him underestimate me seemed like a good idea.

Why put him on his guard? A distrustful conman was no laughing matter.

"But no more lying," I cautioned. "This blond Lolita possesses the amazing ability to see through any and all lies, all right?"

"Who's lying now? I'll give you credit, you've got some nerve trying to dupe a swindler," Kaiki mocked me.

Of course he'd see through such a blatant lie—and underestimate me. I smiled inwardly, pleased with myself.

"No matter how you look at her," he continued, "the young miss is a foreigner. She seems to struggle with the language and probably can't make out half of what we're saying."

If he meant that as a joke, then maybe Deishu Kaiki had a pretty unique personality... But no, it could be another one of his ruses.

He'd already conned scores of naive middle schoolers in various ways—perhaps I wasn't the only one trying to come across as a boob. I couldn't be careful enough. This ominous man was a swindler who'd succeeded in deceiving even Hitagi Senjogahara.

Come to think of it, having been fooled by him, Senjogahara went so far as to commit the atrocity of abducting her boyfriend just to keep me from getting any closer to Kaiki—from having anything to do with him.

If she knew I was unexpectedly sitting face to face with him, she might lose it all over again.

Sigh... Now I had a secret to hide from my girlfriend.

It really was draining, though, squaring off against Kaiki like this. Not fun at all.

My health bar was shrinking by the second.

"How much do you want, then—for information on the both of them," I said, taking out my wallet as I spoke. I'd already spent about 1,500 yen to buy the ten donuts and two cups of coffee—as someone who lived off an allowance and depended on his parents, I couldn't afford to be too careless with my money.

I was hoping to take Senjogahara on another date once she got back from her grandparents' house.

I was dealing with an adult here, however, and chump change probably didn't cut it.

Would two thousand yen be enough?

I opened up my wallet and pulled out two thousand-yen notes but wasn't sure. That's when Kaiki snatched the wallet from my hand with the most natural, practiced movement, saying, "Let me see."

Oh boy, "Let me see"?

The movement was so subtle (a sleight of hand you could almost call beautiful) that I didn't even reflexively tighten my grip in order to keep my wallet from getting stolen, and he just plucked it from me—it was the kind of dexterity that better suited a pickpocket than a swindler.

From Shinobu's point of view, sitting next to me, it may have even looked as if I'd handed over the wallet without resistance. She was staring at me as if she thought her master was a moron.

"Hmph. I suppose this will do, Araragi. I will accept this miniscule amount in the way of wishing you and Senjogahara, the young couple, good luck in your future life."

You didn't need to be able to see through lies to know that his selfless words were utterly insincere. He slipped my wallet into the breast of his funereal suit.

Did the jerk just filch my entire wallet?

He was the real fiendish monster. Crows were cute compared to him.

Unless, Kaiki being who he is, I needed to thank him for leaving me with a generous two thousand yen?

But this wasn't some heartwarming story where the wallet actually only contained coins now. My precious 10,000-yen bill was in there, okay?

"Ah, if I had acted likewise, I might have feasted on many more donuts…"

Shinobu nodded her head up and down several times with deep interest as she said that.

As an aberration, she was susceptible to surrounding stimuli, and she was receiving some bad influences from the human world in the present progressive tense.

Some people couldn't help but be a negative influence, but I wished that Kaiki would show a little forbearance.

Or true forbearance.

"Of course, there is no such thing as a miniscule amount of money to me," Kaiki noted. "I'm actually the one who came up with the phrase, 'Look after the pennies, and the pounds will look after themselves.'"

Kaiki was going from lies to deluded boasts now. He was ominous, and the stuff he said made no sense. Just what kind of everyday life did this guy lead? I couldn't imagine what he did in private when he wasn't running scams.

Or maybe he was on call 24 hours a day, 365 days a year as a constant, tireless conman.

As the real deal, and as a fake.

But since things had already gone south, it was probably better if I hurried and asked my questions—otherwise, he might charge me extra like one of those greedy binoculars at an observatory deck.

"Now tell me. About Yozuru Kagenui and Yotsugi Ononoki."

"Hmph. Of course I will—I've received currency so this is now a valid transaction. But Araragi, the fact that you're asking me must mean that you already have some notion of your answer," Kaiki pointed out calmly.

His face was hardly expressionless, but I couldn't read anything from it—and even if I could, I would no doubt be mistaken. His was the real poker face.

This, too, was something that Hanekawa told me.

The term has come to mean a completely expressionless face, as in one that betrays no emotion, but apparently its original sense was different. The ability to evoke a completely unrelated emotion on your face than the one that you were actually feeling—that was the true poker face.

It only made sense since a game had given rise to the word. Just wearing a blank look wasn't enough to deceive your opponents.

You couldn't deceive them, or fake yourself.

Not hiding expressions, but making them. Or to take it a step further...

Not hiding emotions, but making them.

That was how you did it.

In that light, Hitagi Senjogahara, whose face had been like cast iron until recently, would have made a second-rate con artist.

Maybe she could hide expressions.

But she couldn't fake emotions.

If she could, I'd never have seen through her act...

She was pretty clumsy that way.

"Those two are experts. Ghostbusters, like me," Kaiki stated as if he were telling me nothing more special than an acquaintance's culinary preferences. "However," he added, "whereas I am a fake—they're the real deal. If I am a conman, they're onmyoji."

"......"

Onmyoji.

At that word, I turned toward Shinobu, but she was completely absorbed in her donuts like nothing he had to say could possibly interest her. Talk about antisocial.

"I said 'they' out of habit," Kaiki proceeded to correct myself, "but strictly speaking Kagenui would be the onmyoji, whereas Ononoki seems to be a shikigami—seriously. Yokai, ghosts, those two are a pain in the neck with their passion for the occult."

Why don't they just tell fortunes by blood type instead, he griped.

The pair hadn't struck me as all that unpleasant—but maybe it went beyond appearances.

I asked Kaiki, "So you know them?"

"What makes you think so?"

"Well, the way you were talking... I don't know. Something about your choice of words."

"I only know their names. Kagenui is fairly well-known in the business... The aberration roller, they call her. You'd have to be a quack not to know of her, but I haven't actually met her. A real deal like her pays no attention to fakes like me... In any case, I am in fact a quack of sorts."

He had answered me in the negative.

Hmph.

It seemed somehow significant to me that he'd referred to Kagenui and Ononoki as "those two," which sounded personal...but it was no more than a matter of word choice.

Word choice could be like wordplay, but they weren't the same thing. There were plain slips of the tongue, too. Just like brothers and sisters had their sibling-speak, maybe experts formed a community via language.

"While we're at it, Araragi, there is something that I would like to ask as well—though obviously I will not be paying for the honor."

"......"

Sure.

Ask away.

"How do you know of that pair? As long as you're on the straight and narrow, you're even less likely to get involved with them than with me."

"I don't know about involved... They asked me for directions, that's all."

"So you didn't just come across their names but met them face to face? That is even less believable—are you trying to pull a fast one on me?"

"You're the last person who ought to be doubting someone's sincerity."

"Are you sure you're not mistaken? Perhaps they gave false names..."

"Does standing on top of a mailbox or saying 'with a dashing look' with a blank look ring a bell?"

"Hmph. That's them."

Kaiki nodded.

So that was enough to verify their identities…

"Come to think of it, today's been weird," I observed. "I can't believe I've run into three 'authorities' in one day—ugh, coincidence is a scary thing."

Maybe because it was *Obon*?

Though that would be occult thinking.

The scariest part was that the day was barely half over—at this rate, I might run into yet another expert in the afternoon.

Was Mèmè Oshino's return being foreshadowed here?

Was it a lead-up to Mr. Aloha's reentry?

In which case…uh, well, I don't know, man!

"Coincidence, huh," Kaiki picked up on my word. "Araragi, I used the word myself just a moment ago to say that meeting like this must be fate, but 'coincidences' as they're generally understood are a tricky affair—and, by and large, a product of malice."

"Malice?"

"Yes, malice. Nothing like fate."

Malice—as opposed to justice.

Although Shinobu was supposed to be just some blond Lolita, not a vampire or anything as far as he knew, Kaiki glanced at her meaningfully as he repeated the word.

"Yozuru Kagenui and Yotsugi Ononoki," he went on. "Implacable latter-day onmyoji—but Araragi. Even as experts go, they have a very narrow area of expertise. That two-man cell specializes in aberrations of the immortal kind."

009

Not that that means anything since there are no immortal creatures in this world, the tardigrade perhaps, he ended on a deflating note, and that was the full extent of the info I gained from Deishu Kaiki, the con artist.

It was hard to say if it was of any use—at least, I had my doubts that I'd gotten my money's worth.

Specializing in immortal aberrations.

Guillotine Cutter from spring break was an authority specializing in vampires—was it like that? Was it also like Deishu Kaiki being an expert on fake aberrations?

I couldn't say.

Hmm. In that sense, despite his clowning, the expert we knew best, Mèmè Oshino, actually had an almost ridiculously broad scope.

Just who had we been dealing with?

In any case, now that we were done, I had no reason to remain sitting with Kaiki. It's not like we were best buds ready to chat away, and even if we were, trading gossip, let alone barbs, with a guy who played dirty and was so settled in his ways wouldn't be very fun.

A comic-relief segment with him was out of the question.

Getting up, tray and all, and returning to my original table, I noticed just in time, precariously enough.

"Oh, right," I called out to Kaiki, "you can keep my wallet and money, but there's one thing that I want back."

"...? That you want back? Would it be a credit card?"

"Why would I have one? I'm just a high school student. A photo... There's a photo in there."

"Ah."

Kaiki reached into his breast pocket and pulled out my (scratch that, no longer my) wallet, opened it, and removed a photo—when he saw who it was of, he furrowed his brow a little.

Whether or not that was his poker face, I couldn't tell you.

"Senjogahara... So she cut her hair."

"Mm... Yeah, well."

The picture in my wallet was of Hitagi Senjogahara.

The photograph had been taken recently—with the digital camera I'd unearthed in Kanbaru's room at the end of last month.

This was a printout.

Maybe I had talent, and it was such a great pic that I'd stuck it in my wallet like a lucky charm for exam-takers—doing so might have been somewhat old-fashioned for a high-school boy in this day and age, but I still sure as hell didn't want to let Kaiki have it.

I simply didn't want to part with it in the first place. No amount of information could make up for it.

"Hah...what a broad, insipid grin," lamented Kaiki. "When people lose their spark, they truly do lose it—I knew her back when she shone, and to me this looks like a completely different person. There is no shadow nor a trace of who she once was."

I thought he might demand my last two thousand yen in exchange—but unexpectedly, he handed back the photo without ado.

Without trying to bargain, seeming genuinely uninterested, like he couldn't begin to find any value in it—he returned it to my hands.

"As far as I'm concerned, this is a very regrettable development," he opined. "I don't know what to say other than I am disappointed.

A cheerful Hitagi Senjogahara is worthless. To be cursed not to know your own worth, or to be cursed not to know your own worthlessness. Which to choose, if we must, is a question we bear all-life long—but children ought to grow and mature, so a man as old and finished as I am might keep such comments to himself."

Old and finished—that was Deishu Kaiki's own appraisal of himself.

True, to someone his age, Senjogahara and I probably seemed like kids who'd just started out.

And further—I gathered that Deishu Kaiki and Hitagi Senjogahara's relationship was a little more complicated than that of conman and victim. If not, there was no way that her reunion and confrontation with him could offer such definite closure.

It wouldn't have served as such a detox.

But regardless of what I did or did not gather, I shouldn't pry into my girlfriend's past—I didn't need to be told by the likes of Kaiki that kids should have their faces turned toward tomorrow rather than yesterday.

Not finished, but starting out.

Now then.

As for the immediate future—I obviously needed to be thinking about Kagenui and Ononoki.

Yozuru Kagenui and Yotsugi Ononoki.

I'd learned that the two indeed formed a pair...a two-man cell.

And I'd also learned—that they were indeed experts.

So they hadn't called me a fiendish monster for my awful behavior toward Karen and Hachikuji, after all. They were referring to the modicum of vampirism remaining in me.

In a sense, I was being permitted to keep treating Karen and Hachikuji in the same way.

That was encouraging.

Obtaining the info I'd been seeking, however, didn't mean that anything was actually settled—in fact, it seemed to have enlarged the problem.

The plot thickened.

Ghostbusters specializing in immortal aberrations.

Immortal, immortal...

Vampire.

Kaiki insisted that such things didn't exist. Broadly speaking, his denial made perfect sense, but strictly speaking, there were creatures in this town right now to whom the term did apply—two of them.

Shinobu Oshino and Koyomi Araragi, needless to say.

"Wherever there be immortals, so too one finds their quellers—in myth and legend, immortal beasts, even gods, appear in legion. Immortal though they may be, these aberrations are frequently slayed. If immortals exist, then so do—their killers. That is what those two are," Shinobu said as we returned home from Mister Donut.

We were riding two to a bike, which I'd avoided doing with Karen.

I would rather Shinobu hide in my shadow while we traveled, but now that her stomach was full, *I might as well feast my eyes on the daytime world,* she decided all on her own, and I lacked the means to check her wayward desire.

Well, I had the means but wasn't going to.

Shinobu looked to be about eight. If we claimed she was only six, people would believe us—even though she was actually five hundred years old.

So riding two to a bike with her wasn't (at least appearance-wise) illegal, but that was only if she sat nicely on the rear rack. Instead...

"Mm. It would be much easier to converse from here."

Shinobu had fit herself snugly into the front basket.

She was facing me as I pedaled, her butt wedged into the basket and her legs propped on either handlebar. It seemed she didn't quite understand bicycles.

Ignorance was a powerful thing—mere novices like the rest of us would never dream of such an outlandish riding style.

I name it the reverse ET.

That said… She'd simply been alive, not sealed up, for five hundred years, so even if her grasp of Japanese culture was weak, you'd think she'd have learned about bicycles somewhere along the line.

Maybe it had nothing to do with being a vampire, and she was just generally aloof.

It was a little difficult to steer (I had to lean forward to make sure my shadow stayed over the basket), but I could still pedal so that's how we rode.

It wasn't beyond the pale.

"An onmyoji who specializes in immortal aberrations, huh?" I said. "Yikes, their target must be you and me in that case."

Not that Shinobu and I could currently be called immortal—but our bodies certainly encompassed an immortal factor, or fragments of immortality. Even if the vestiges only meant healing quickly or taking longer to get hungry, if they persisted, that probably was an immortal quality.

Come to think of it, according to the conman Deishu Kaiki, he'd chosen this town as the backdrop for his large-scale scam because a legendary vampire (Shinobu, in her previous form) had descended upon the area, making it conducive to occult-oriented work (Kaiki's fraudulent activities).

Even if we weren't his targets, you could say in a broad sense that our existence had lured him here. At the very least, it wasn't for a wistful or sentimental reason like revisiting the town where his former mark Senjogahara lived.

"Hah, thee and me, their targets? There may be other possibilities, my master…"

Shinobu leaned back arrogantly in my front basket and folded her arms behind her head.

It was the wrong place to be acting like a big shot if her goal was career advancement.

She really was petite, though.

I bet she could slip right into my pocket.

"I've devoured nearly enough immortal aberrations in my time to make myself sick. I am a proper slayer of them, myself... Yet if we are to speak of it thus, aberrations do not live," Shinobu blew up the whole premise.

"Ah. Right, if it's not even alive, then how is it immortal? Or maybe, all aberrations are immortal in a way... Oshino said something to that effect, too. But semantics aside, Shinobu, when you say there are other possibilities, are you saying there might be another vampire in this town besides us?"

"Not necessarily a vampire—it would not be so odd, either. Or rather, it would be odd."

Hmm. If we put aside the immortal part of it, then even in my immediate circle, there were actually a few people who were host to these aberrations.

For instance Suruga Kanbaru, who had a monkey residing in her left arm.

For instance Tsubasa Hanekawa, who had a cat residing in her psyche.

"I see. If someone I didn't know were living with an aberration, that wouldn't be so unnatural—well no, actually, it would be. Just how many aberrations could there be in one town?"

"Are there not eight million gods in this country? Around 170,000 per prefecture. Ten in one town would seem toward enough."

"You can't mix up gods and aberrations—"

...Or maybe you can.

An aberration pretty much equaled divinity in Japan, according to Oshino. Incomprehensible happenings were the gods' doing, incomprehensible things were their form.

Right, he'd said so.

"Kaiki doesn't even believe in vampires, but apparently it was a visit from a gold-class aberration like yourself that stirred up other ones in the area. I even hiked up to a shrine that was becoming their hangout—that's how I met Sengoku again."

Still.

Realistically speaking, it was probably best if we assumed that we were Kagenui and Ononoki's target.

Coming after another hypothetical immortal and just happening to ask me for directions, by coincidence, seemed untenable.

It sounded like wishful thinking.

A hopeful outlook is a necessary and wise stance for humanity's survival, but in this case, it didn't seem like optimism would be in our best interests.

Being asked for directions was already far too convenient to be a coincidence.

Coincidence. By and large, a product of malice—for such a nasty guy, Deishu Kaiki did say nifty things.

I suppose that came from a life lived on the front line. He'd been under fire, but instead of turning into a fighter, he'd remained a fraud—and an expert.

An expert and an authority—and Kagenui, too, was an expert and an authority.

An onmyoji.

The aberration roller.

Hm? I seemed to recall Shinobu having some hang-up about the word *onmyoji*—unless she was just hiding her tracks due to her so-called rule?

"What is wrong, my lord? Are ye thinking?"

"Thinking… Yeah, you bet. Or worrying." Well, it was no use asking her. Pressing her wouldn't get me anywhere. Right now, it was better if I focused on what to do next. "Kagenui and Ononoki… Picking those ruins as their base does seem like something a colleague of Oshino's would do. I probably need to attend to this sooner rather than later. In fact, I ought to go ahead and take action today—"

"Ho-ho. Time for another battle? I can feel my spleen tingling already."

Shinobu was grinning, visibly amused.

I considered getting into an accident on purpose, maybe ramming us into a telephone pole, but if I did, neither Shinobu nor I would emerge unscathed.

Some immortal pair we were. We couldn't even crash a bicycle safely.

"No battles. We're going to talk, just talk," I said.

According to Karen, her master would be an even match for Kagenui—and we had a bona-fide aberration in Ononoki.

These weren't opponents I was eager to take on.

I didn't belong to some warrior race. When I came back from the edge of death, there was no exponential burst of power.

"It's what Oshino would call a negotiation—if they can be made to understood that you and I are harmless, we won't get hunted," I explained.

"Hunted, eh? Perhaps that is not what they are here to do."

"Why are they here, then?"

"Who can say? I am simply diverting myself by toying with thy words. My job is to be the voice that asks, 'Is it?' Heh. But calm thyself. We are one in body and spirit and share a single fate. In the push, my strength is thine."

"Good to know."

Not that I planned to rely on her.

Even if I didn't use Shinobu as backup, she'd be in the background—the mere fact that we were one and our fates were linked would give me strength in a pinch.

It was at the end of the previous month that I reconciled with Shinobu—but come to think of it, she'd joined with me in body and spirit, joined in my fate, from the moment we first met. I'd failed to notice such a huge thing until just recently—had never thought to notice.

"'Tis hot… I must avouch that I hate the sun. Perhaps I should have hidden in thy shadow as ye urged. My body is turning to ash. This cap is worthless. Yet would I melt were I not a vampire."

"Ha, I bet. Even the asphalt melts in this sort of heat."

"Is this the global warming they speak of? Hmph—the Earth has been warming and cooling erst long ago."

"Right?"

"Why the clamor over a change of a mere hundred or two hundred degrees?"

"If it went up and down by two hundred degrees, we'd be past clamoring."

Okay… I should probably head straight for the ruins after I got home.

It wasn't just a matter of wanting to handle this as quickly as possible. As a basic negotiation tactic, I wanted to take the initiative.

Lately, in *shogi*, the consensus seemed to be that the player who makes the first move is actually at a disadvantage, but it wasn't like I was going there to confront them. This wasn't a match.

We were going to talk.

Even if the two-man cell of Kagenui and Ononoki hadn't come to our town for Shinobu and me, they were experts, so I highly doubted they were just here on vacation.

It probably had to do with aberrations.

In which case, I ought to clue them in on the town's peculiar circumstances even if that made me a busybody—or else, this might come to affect Kanbaru or Hanekawa.

As it occurred to me earlier, the aberrations that resided in those two weren't particularly immortal, but there was no guarantee they might not get tangled up in some mess and collaterally slayed.

It almost sounded laughable when I put it into words, but it would be just like those two. Suruga Kanbaru had the worst luck, and Tsubasa Hanekawa easily got mixed up in things.

I wouldn't be doing any studying today.

I'd rest my liver for a day, so to speak.

It was fine—I was prepared for this.

Over spring break, when I decided to spend the rest of my days with an ironblooded, hotblooded, yet coldblooded vampire, and to live until we died—to die until we lived, I knew I'd be dealing with this sort of stuff. It was my natural duty, even a right.

This barely qualified as trouble. I wasn't even on the front line, and this was no match. To me—to *us*, it wasn't even a minor event.

There was no flag to trigger and no choice to make. Imagine what Oshino would say if I panicked over this much.

"Well, if that's the deal, I could even drop by the ruins on my way home…"

Glancing at Shinobu, who was beginning to nod off in the basket—it was the middle of the day, so I guess she was sleepy after all—I considered going to the abandoned building right away.

But before we left Mister Donut, I'd spent one of the two thousand-yen bills that Kaiki had mercifully spared on a box of donuts to bring home as a present to my little sisters (Shinobu kept nagging from the side, "What about me? Where is my present?!" like that was going to happen), so instead I decided to drop it off first.

I could also give it to Kagenui and Ononoki, but I had to admit that it seemed a little insincere to repurpose something as a peace offering. Moreover, Ononoki might not love Mister Donut as much as Shinobu did just because they were both aberrations. Despite her calm expression, maybe Ononoki preferred super-spicy food.

It would be a shame if it backfired. I also didn't want to seem too obsequious.

I just wanted to make the first move.

As I pondered how best to proceed, I was under the impression that I was approaching the issue with a fair sense of urgency—but I was in fact operating as slow as molasses, at a turtle's pace, and soon I was in for a rude awakening.

Really soon.

Pedaling my bike and arriving home, I spotted, believe it or not, the very two people in question—Kagenui and Ononoki—at our front gate, ringing our doorbell.

Kagenui noticed me and said, "You again." Ononoki also turned in my direction, as if in imitation, her face expressionless.

Incidentally, as the one being stared at, what with a blond Lolita crammed into the front basket of my bicycle like a sack of groceries, I made for a pretty indecorous sight.

Downright indecorous.

"Hello…" I bobbed my head.

Seeing them side by side like this, they really did come across as a two-man cell—if I were to say every cracked pot has its broken lid, it might not sound very generous, but Kagenui and Ononoki seemed to fit together perfectly like two pieces of a puzzle.

Human and aberration. Onmyoji and shikigami.

"First your sister and now this waif, eh, fiendish young man. Quite the basket of eggs you've got there. Or should I say an orgy of them? Ha, I wouldn't mind luck like yours."

Like before, Kagenui's feet weren't touching the ground as she spoke.

This time she was squatting agilely atop our gate—like a thief about to jump over it to sneak into our house.

I take that back, she didn't look like anything. She in fact was a suspicious person.

"Sister, that is not a waif, but a vampire. If you must, she is closer to a hag—he said with a dashing look."

Her face actually blank, this was Ononoki, her finger still on the doorbell.

Shinobu twitched at the word "hag" and woke up moodily.

Maybe she felt more offended than moody.

Hmm, I knew that Shinobu was dissatisfied with her current Lolita appearance (More than once, in the middle of the night, I'd witnessed her patting at her own flat chest and heaving a poignant sigh. It was sad), but she didn't seem to appreciate being called a hag, either.

For someone who'd been alive for five centuries, she could be surprisingly touchy.

"Hmph. How the little rookie ba—"

Barks, kakak. I think Shinobu wanted to say so with aplomb and elegantly leap to the ground, but alas, the basket wasn't designed to be exited with any ease by a person crammed in there (to be ridden in, actually), and her struggles began. She should have accepted my help, but stubbornly refusing it, she finally freed herself from her reverse ET by twisting and tipping the bike over sideways.

She didn't have a shred of dignity left. It was decidedly unimpressive.

"Ah. Literally from the cradle to the grave, eh, fiendish young man," teased Kagenui. "I reckon you'd even fancy a zombie caller from the dirt. They say necrophilia is an aristocratic predilection. Kakak, a fair playboy."

"……"

The Araragi residence's gate, nowhere as grand as the one for Kanbaru's mansion, was just a narrow steel fence—but Kagenui's balance did not so much as falter as she perched atop it on the tips of her toes.

Agile didn't begin to describe it.

I've never seen a circus, but from what I've heard and imagine—in balance tricks like the tightrope, performers maintain equilibrium by actively swaying their bodies. That might seem risky at first glance, but apparently it's more dangerous to stop and hold still—I guess it's like how bamboos are less likely to snap than cedars in a typhoon?

Kagenui, however, directly contradicted that theory. It was like time had frozen in a bubble around her or as if some invisible pane of glass spread underneath her feet—she didn't even budge. The spot was high, and her footing wasn't exactly stable, but as far as I could tell, she wasn't even trying to balance herself.

She was beyond advanced. With equipoise like hers, she could probably do a handstand on a balance ball and make it look like child's play. In fact—she almost looked like she could walk on water.

Karen might have sensed more, but an amateur like me wasn't able to comprehend even the basic wonders of Yozuru Kagenui.

I just found it mysterious.

Mysterious—and inexplicable.

"Man, I don't know," I blurted out without meaning to.

If it was as Shinobu said (her testimony was much more reliable than Kaiki's), Ononoki was the nonhuman and, whatever her true nature, an aberration—but she seemed the more normal of the two.

Maybe that was part of the onmyoji-shikigami deal: a proper, hierarchical master-servant relationship with a clear and precise chain of command, unlike the strange and complicated bond between Shinobu and me.

Ononoki did just refer to Kagenui as "sister"—but that didn't necessarily mean they were sisters, did it? Wasn't it only a mode of address like "big brother"?

"Ah, right, right, I ought to thank you first. What a great help you were. I found Eikow Cram School just where you said it would be. It's so difficult getting there, I reckon I might not ever have without your instructions—and you actually helped Yotsugi, too." Kagenui said all this in such a laidback, easygoing manner. There was no hint of hostility or menace. "Maybe you've heard this before, but they say that folk what are easy to ask directions from have a mentor's soul. Their aura beckons people. Not that I put much stock in jaw like 'auras.'"

Her face broke into a smile.

It was a pleasant smile. A very—pleasant smile.

If I hadn't heard that she was an expert on immortal aberrations, I would've seen her as an ordinary, friendly lady. The source of that info happened to be the world's most unreliable and ominous man, so it was all the harder for me to settle on a stance.

"I don't know if a body has asked me for directions once in my life—do you reckon that means I don't have an aura?"

"That is why you walk no road, sister... None stretches before your feet, and none behind—he said with a dashing look."

I couldn't even tell if Ononoki's words were meant as consolation. Maybe it was sibling-speak? An inside joke?

I didn't know how to react—and had never met anyone so hard to converse with as these two. It wasn't like they put up barriers, they were frank—but Kagenui and Ononoki seemed to have their own little world. They didn't seem to need anyone else.

Honestly, it was as awkward as being invited to another family's family gathering—and we were standing in front of my house.

I couldn't just stay silent, though. If I let them lead, this negotiation would never get off the ground.

"Actually...there's something I wanted to get straight."

Negotiate—I had to negotiate with them.

My inept strategy was already derailed, unfortunately, and they had made the first move—but if I didn't get overwhelmed any further, I had a chance to turn things around.

The consensus—was that going second gave you an edge.

Waiting for Shinobu to struggle free at last from under the overturned bicycle, I screwed up my courage and said, "You two came to this town because you're hunting us—an unholy immortal and its thrall." As for who was whose thrall, I skipped all that because it was too convoluted. "You came here to kill us, didn't you? It wasn't just coincidence that you both asked me for directions—you were scouting us out."

"......"

"......"

I cut straight to the chase, with no plan, letting the chips fall where they may. We weren't going to get anywhere unless we spoke the same language, so I decided to just go for it and see how things turned out. You could say I was swinging blindly.

In response, however, Kagenui and Ononoki—cocked their heads at me simultaneously, in apparent puzzlement.

As for Kagenui, she even wore a wry smile. "Oi, I don't know what you're on about, fiendish young man, but I reckon you've got the wrong idea," she said.

The wrong idea?

Huh? Had Kaiki duped me, in fact? Had I let him shake me down for some pocket money?

Possible!

If so, then I probably looked like a total head-case to them—accusing someone of wanting to kill you just for asking directions? Talk about having illusions of grandeur.

Yikes. Now I was in a whole different kind of hot water. How was I going to worm my way out of this? At this rate, I was going to be negotiating with a psychiatrist.

Just as I was starting to panic: "W-Well, it's not like you're coming out of left field—but you've sure got some britches on you," said Kagenui, seeming honestly put out. "The matter regarding the ironblooded, hotblooded, yet coldblooded vampire, the king and slayer of aberrations, Kissshot Acerolaorion Heartunderblade, is considered resolved. As an aberration, she has already been thoroughly slain—as an aberration, her thrall is only present as an absence. You're each other's alibi and proof of nonexistence, and regardless of the type of specialist, you're untouchable now. Besides, in our business we've got better things to do than squander resources on an ordinary human experiencing a few aftereffects."

"......nkk."

Just as I was starting to relax, I felt myself tense up again. Kagenui knew Shinobu's former name—only Hanekawa and I were supposed to at this point, and no one still called her that.

An expert.

A ghostbuster—a professional.

The immortal slayer and aberration roller—

"I suppose Oshino's meddling is to thank for it. Sticking that beak where it doesn't belong is his specialty," Kagenui muttered almost as if she was talking to herself—wait.

Just now—did she mention Oshino?

Judging from the context, she couldn't have meant Shinobu—so who was she talking about?

It wasn't very hard to figure out.

Our savior—the slacker in the Hawaiian shirt.

This woman, Yozuru Kagenui—knew Mèmè Oshino?

"My lord," Shinobu interrupted us—while she had extricated herself from beneath the bicycle, she was still sitting with her butt planted on the ground. I don't think she was somehow trying to vie with Kagenui that way, but she spoke without getting up. "This is no time to be losing thy wits—do not let idle matters distract thee. Is there not something else that thou should be thinking about?"

"Huh?" My physical and emotional sensations transmitted directly to Shinobu—so when I was upset, she could tell in a tactile and not just intuitive manner.

True, I was upset. But I didn't see why she should be admonishing me—except...

No. Think, Koyomi—just think.

About the non-idle matter.

Kagenui may not have been a con artist, or even really an onmyoji, but that didn't mean I should let her string me along and swallow everything she said hook, line, and sinker.

Even if everything Kaiki said had been lies, and even discounting the stuff that Shinobu had told me—originally, it had been my own hunch, hadn't it, that there was something suspicious about these two.

Suspicious.

Right off the bat—I'd thought they were different.

I still hadn't heard anything, from anyone or from anywhere, to contradict that feeling.

I knew damn well that evading questions and spinning half-truths were these experts' stock in trade.

Of course.

Of course!

If they weren't targeting Koyomi Araragi and Shinobu Oshino—then why were they *here*?

Why were they at the Araragi residence?

Why was Kagenui squatting on our gate?

Why was Ononoki pressing our doorbell?

Just as I put up my guard again and was about to take an obvious defensive stance—

"Argh, shut up! Shut up shut up shut up! How long are you going to keep ringing that bell?! Can't you see I'm pretending no one's home?!"

Our front door burst open—to the sound of shrill, hysterical screaming from the other side.

I didn't even need to turn my head. Didn't need to look.

Naturally, it was my sister, Tsukihi Araragi, the strategist of Tsuganoki Second Middle School's Fire Sisters, who came bolting through the door—still half-naked in her yukata, the idiot hadn't even bothered to put on sandals before rushing outside.

I guess you had to give her some credit, though.

She must have at least had the common sense to think, *I probably shouldn't step outside in my nightwear.* And: *I shouldn't carelessly answer the door when the rest of my family isn't here.* That was why she'd been ignoring Ononoki's ringing for so long.

She was pretending no one was home.

But Ononoki wasn't just ringing the doorbell. She was hammering it fast. Tsukihi was hysterical and all, but even I would have come running out in a rage. That was more heinous than a ding-dong-ditch.

For someone with such a calm face, Ononoki was a bad girl and a prankster.

Of course, even assuming I did come running out, only Tsukihi would bother to do so with an awl gripped in her good hand.

She was ruining the reputation of awls.

An awl was actually a useful tool. What a shame.

"Committing a terrorist act against the Fire Sisters' home, this little house on the prairie where justice dwells—you've got some guts. Hmm?"

Tsukihi was just starting to get worked up, spewing nonsense as her claws came out—when just as suddenly her rage deflated, the claws retracting immediately. The sight that greeted her eyes must have been too much to process.

There was her brother, Koyomi Araragi. That part was fine. Nothing unusual there.

But what about the blond Lolita sitting on the ground beside him? The strange woman squatting with perfect balance atop the thin railing of our front gate? The bizarre girl hammering the doorbell with her finger even now?

It made no sense—no sense whatsoever for any of the three to be there. Indeed, the fact that there was one person, namely myself, whom she could expect to find there mixed in with the other three bizarre figures probably made it even harder for Tsukihi to make sense of the picture.

She possessed the unusual skill, Regulate Emotion, flying into hysterics at the drop of a dime and putting that hysteria back on the shelf at a moment's notice. First things first, she took a step back to get a better view.

"Um," she said, as if thinking out loud, "I'm pretty sure that blond girl there is the one I saw in the bathtub with my brother before..."

Why was she bringing that up?

Just process that as a hallucination.

In any case—this was looking pretty bad. I had managed to keep all this occult and aberration business totally secret from both Karen and Tsukihi. Even after Karen got stung by the bee, I'd concealed that aspect of the incident from them.

I probably needed to tell them about my condition and about Shinobu, the aberration that lived in my shadow, at some point—but I didn't think it was the right time for that yet. I didn't have my own thoughts in order enough to talk about it—but more than anything, Karen and Tsukihi were still too young, in my opinion.

Which is why, at the very least, I wanted to avoid dumping that stuff on them in the form of a traffic accident of a run-in. Especially if it meant starting with Tsukihi rather than Karen...

Tsukihi's appearance threw me back into a panic after all the trouble Shinobu had gone through to get my head back in the game. The caution and composure I'd regained was in tatters.

Yotsugi Ononoki, one half of the two-man cell—seized the opportunity.

"*Unlimited Rulebook*, rules consisting mostly of exceptions—he said with a dashing look."

Did I really say that compared to Kagenui, Ononoki seemed like the normal one? Because I must have had no idea what I was talking about if I did. Talk about underestimating a person.

Her index finger, which was pressing the doorbell even after Tsukihi had come rushing out, exploded.

No, not exploded.

Rather—it expanded in volume, in explosive fashion.

I was already familiar with Dramaturgy—an expert vampire hunter that I had encountered over spring break, he hunted vampires despite being a vampire himself. A kinslayer aberration.

Dramaturgy stretched the limits of his unique vampiric transformation abilities to hideously contort and disfigure his arms, wielding them as exquisite twin flamberges—I can still recall, with perfect clarity, the pain those blades inscribed into my flesh.

And as much as I disliked it, I was flashing back on that memory.

But whereas Dramaturgy transformed his arms into blades, Ononoki transformed her finger into a blunt instrument.

The first thing I thought of—was a humongous hammer.

A giant hammer—like the thunderbolt of the gods.

Ononoki's enlarged, swollen, ginormous index finger completely obliterated the columns on our front gate as if they were no more than Styrofoam.

I hadn't just been upset. I'd also been careless.

It was the middle of the day, the sun still high in the sky—I can't deny having assumed that there was no way a battle could unfold in a residential neighborhood.

But I was wrong.

My assumption could not have been more misguided.

Although night was the time for aberrations, even when the sun was up, even in the middle of the day, whenever, wherever, they were always near.

There, and also not there.

Oshino had drilled that into my head!

"Nrk…"

My most flagrant assumption, however, was yet to be exposed—not just my physical, but also my mental stance had been all wrong.

I was sure that Ononoki's sudden hammer strike must be aimed at me, or if not me, then Shinobu—but I was wrong.

Very, very wrong.

Her hammer, Unlimited Rulebook, obliterated the columns of our front gate like Styrofoam…and then kept going.

And going.

And going.

Until it obliterated Tsukihi Araragi's top half.

"………nkk?!"

Enlarged, swollen, and ginormous—it devastated her from the waist up, along with the door behind her—like mere Styrofoam.

"Tsu-Tsukihi-chaaaan!"

I couldn't even grasp what had happened, what I was seeing.

But I didn't need to understand—my body began moving on instinct.

Sending me flying toward Ononoki, who wasn't paying any attention to me. Shinobu, attached to my shadow, dragged along by the momentum, helplessly tumbled across the asphalt.

But I was incapable of worrying about even Shinobu, now.

All I could see was red. The whole world was red.

Searing, crimson rage.

What had she done?

To Tsukihi Araragi. To Tsukihi-chan.

To my little sister who was more precious than anything else in the world!

"Cool your head, fiendish young man. Don't get so hotheaded. Don't young people these days know? Anger is a hellfire that burns the wielder—it's fire, pure fire."

I remember up until the point I was about to grab Ononoki by the neck—but after that, my memory cut off like a sandstorm. The next thing I knew, I was lying folded up on the ground.

Folded up.

That may sound vague, but it was the most accurate expression for my predicament.

My legs, my knees, my waist, my arms, my elbows, my shoulders, my neck, were all folded over and under, in and out, like the gussets of a bellow—neatly, like in some celebrity homemaker's storage tips.

And the very person who had reduced me to this state, Yozuru Kagenui—was balanced atop my folded-up back, in a squatting position exactly like before.

Smiling. In an amused—even a good-natured way.

"You reckon what Oshino would say at a time like this? You're so spirited, did something good happen to you?"

"Ngh…"

Why—just why?

Why did she know so much about Oshino? Why was she able to quote him? And at a time like this!

"Damn you! You…you pieces of shit! My sister! You killed my sister…Tsukihi! You won't get away with this!"

"Huh? No kidding—that child is your sister?" asked Kagenui, surprised. She nodded, as if something suddenly made sense. "Of course. I just reckoned you happened to have the same surname."

What?

The two of them…didn't even know that this was my house?

Then what in hell were they doing here?

"I see. There was some noise in my information. This must have been a very shocking sight for you, then. So sorry about that," Kagenui apologized offhandedly like she'd spilled some water on the table.

An apology.

An apology?

"Ngh… You think an apology is going to cut it?!"

"Watch for yourself."

I couldn't turn my neck. It was pressed against the ground as stiff as if it had been set in plaster. But Kagenui jerked my neck forcefully in the direction of our front door—as easily as you might twist a baby's arm.

Forcing my eyes to behold the scene once more.

The destroyed pillars, the demolished gate.

No trace of the front door remained, and just inside that opening, gruesomely annihilated, lay Tsukihi Araragi's lower half—

"Wha…"

When I saw what Kagenui meant—I could barely believe my own eyes.

"H-Huh?" I sputtered.

Tsukihi—didn't have a scratch on her. As if in inverse proportion to the demolition around her, her upper half, which ought to have been blown clean from her body, was attached firmly to her lower half, right where you would expect to find it.

She was propped unconscious against the wall in the hallway—but was perfectly alive.

Completely fine, as if the dramatic scene I had just witnessed had all been an optical illusion.

She was healthy and whole.

But considering how all of the non-corporeal parts of her upper body—her scanty yukata, the accessories in her hair, and so forth—had, indeed, been obliterated, blown to kingdom come just as had been seared into my memory… Considering that the only thing that remained whole was Tsukihi's now exposed, naked upper body…

Perhaps the real optical illusion was what I was seeing now.

"Nope," I muttered without thinking.

Nope.

I knew this—knew it like the twists and turns of hell. I had seen it, had been shown it, time and time again.

I recognized this hellish truth. It wasn't an optical illusion—but regeneration.

Healing, recovery—and immortality.

To be injured and injured and not to die, to be obliterated and obliterated and not to die, to be killed and killed and not to die, to die and die and not to die—this was immortality, perennial and everlasting.

Shinobu Oshino had been living and dying for five hundred years like this—I, too, had lived and died this way, if only for two weeks.

I had died again and again.

Which is why—I was accustomed to this sight, the upper body blown wretchedly from the rest regenerating exuberantly in the span of a few blinks.

A sight I was accustomed to and tired of. A death I was accustomed to and tired of.

Immortality. This was immortality—but.

Why did my little sister, of all people, possess the skill of an aberration?!

"Mister Koyomi Araragi—kind monster sir. It seems your fate is closely entwined with such immortal aberrations. You're a daredevil who'd leap over hell. I'm the one who's surprised here."

Her index finger having returned to normal size at some point, Ononoki stated the facts with a blank expression.

"Your sister is afflicted with an immortal bird of omen. From the outset she was your sister but not your sister, Tsukihi Araragi but not Tsukihi Araragi, human but not human. What you see there is a rare bird of fire, the evil phoenix—he said with a dashing look."

0 1 0

"*Shide no tori.*"

Afterwards, that was how Shinobu Oshino began her explanation as usual. "To wit—a lesser-cuckoo aberration."

The lesser cuckoo.

Family Cuculiformes, Order Cuculidae.

A summer bird, eleven inches in overall length, with a wingspan of six inches and five-inch tail feathers—its back is fawn-colored while its stomach is grayish with white mottling.

"*Young leaves in my eyes, lesser cuckoos in the mountain, first bonito of the season*—that lesser cuckoo. Those two spoke of it as a phoenix, but this bird of death is ill so grand as that word would suggest. In Japan, most people think of peacocks when they picture a phoenix, according to that shallow brat."

Known primarily as the *hototogisu*, there were many ways to write the lesser cuckoo's name in Japanese characters—and nowadays few remembered its association with phoenixes. Once upon a time, however, it was believed to be a migratory bird that could pass to and from the afterlife.

A fitting bird for the *Obon* season.

It went without saying, but the lesser cuckoo was one of the most familiar birds in Japanese culture. For instance, in the oldest surviving collection of Japanese poetry, the *Man'yoshu*, which was compiled during the Nara Period, there are over 150 poems dedicated to the cuckoo—as one of the season words utilized in classical poetry, it symbolized summer.

Unlike even the katydid and cricket, which had switched names over that time, one of the most surprising things was that the bird had already been known as the *hototogisu* over a thousand years ago, like some universal constant.

One of the bird's most distinctive features is its cry—extremely distinct and immediately recognizable upon hearing, it is often written as *teppen kaketaka*.

O lesser cuckoo—do you feed on lizards too with that cry of yours?

"And 'tis not only the diversity of characters used to inscribe the bird's name. It also sports an unparalleled number of aliases—outfacing any other species of bird. The brat jabbered a few. These are only the ones I remember, but there was the evening bird, the nightwatch bird, the bird of murk…the shoeclaw bird, the five-dew bird, the kokila, and of course—the *shide no taosa*."

Shide no taosa. Like *shide no tori*—a bird that could travel to the land of death.

"I suppose that name might be the source of the legend—*shide* as in death, to depart to the afterworld. *Shide no taosa* becomes *shide no tori*, the lesser cuckoo. 'Tis aught but secondhand knowledge, of course," Shinobu said.

Indeed, as a former vampire, aberrations were no more than feed and fodder, a meal or chow to her—and she was hardly enough of a gourmand to the finer points of her meals.

She was a glutton, not an epicurean.

Therefore—all of this knowledge must have come courtesy of the shallow brat, Mèmè Oshino.

It was just one portion of the great wealth of knowledge that Oshino had crammed into Shinobu's head—during the three months they lived together in that abandoned building. Why Oshino would plant such knowledge into Shinobu's mind (utterly useless from her point of view) was anyone's guess.

"This aberration has no distinctive features that particularly stand out—it is twice-sod simplicity. With so little to spark interest, it is an aberration that few labor to study. Of course, since it falls under their *field of specialty*, I think it only natural that those two would be aware of the creature."

From the ashes. A sacred bird, a bird of omen. The phoenix.

"Verily, the *shide no tori*'s identity can be compassed in one single point—*it does not die*. That is the import of its existence. It galls me to say this, but supposedly its immortality surpasses even that of vampires."

Immortality—that surpasses even that of a vampire's. Imperishability. Like the incarnated spirit of life.

"*For every three generations of deer one generation of pine, and for every three generations of pine, one generation of bird.* That is how long-lived birds were once imagined to be. Cranes were previously fabled to live a thousand years, and tortoises ten thousand, but anything that could live a thousand years must surely be considered a monster. Even I have lived but a half that span."

Indeed.

Not only the lesser cuckoo, but birds of the air throughout the world were often compared to life itself—the idea that storks came delivering babies was a perfect example.

Perhaps the reason for this was that the manner in which birds built nests, warmed their eggs, and cared for their offspring with devotion caused humans to see birds as a metaphor for ourselves—as an extremely straightforward instance onto which we could project our own notions of childrearing.

Indeed, birds may have felt even closer to humans in this regard than other mammals.

However—if that hypothesis was correct, then the lesser cuckoo was an exception.

One of the most commonly mentioned characteristics of the lesser cuckoo was that it planted its eggs in other birds' nests.

It was a brood parasite.

In addition to the lesser cuckoo, this was a well-known practice shared by the common cuckoo and the Hodgson's hawk-cuckoo. They waited until a bird from another species left its nest and then knocked some of the eggs to the ground to lay their own—tricking the other species into warming and hatching them.

Nor do hatched cuckoo wait haplessly to be reared, instead using their backs to shove out eggs that were already in the nest, as well as chicks that hatch before them—that way it claims for itself all the nourishment that the parent bird brings.

"Among the eggs / Of nightingale / A lonely cuckoo / Is born / You cry not like / Your father / You cry not like / Your mother / From the fields where / The hare blossoms bloom / Come vaulting / Your echoing cry / Where you sit / In the flowering tachibana / It would cheer me / To listen still / Do not go far / I will give you a present / Stay here in the / Tachibana flowers / Of my home, sweet bird.

"That is a long poem from that *Man'yoshu* or whatever I mentioned earlier. I find it a wonder that in the days of antiquity, long before I or indeed any vampires were birthed into this world, a creature with such traits would exist. Of course, a concept such as childrearing is beyond my ken."

Vampires multiplied not through procreation but rather through the drinking of blood. Obviously, as a vampire, Shinobu would have no reason to project onto the childrearing of birds. But, I ought to add, why the lesser and common cuckoos lay their eggs in another bird's nest is still something of a mystery. That aspect of ecology exceeds not just vampiric but human understanding. Or perhaps, it isn't that it's poorly understood—it just seems incomprehensible.

If it was just a matter of outsourcing childrearing to other species of birds, then that made a world of sense since they could propagate with minimal effort. It sounded very efficient—but it was easy enough for them to be found out (naturally, if the parent bird found out, the cuckoo chick would not be reared), and even if the whole affair went perfectly, the end result was still that the original family in that nest would be uprooted and exterminated, reducing the number of families that could be targeted for outsourcing in the future—and since cuckoos were dependent on other species for their rearing, their own numbers would be forced to dwindle as well.

In that light, it was just like Shinobu said. It was amazing they had survived into modern times while relying on such an inefficient method.

"The aberration, as well—the behavior of the *shide no tori* takes after the real lesser cuckoo. To wit, it is a brood parasite—it lays its eggs in human nests."

A brood parasite—that targets humans. That targets mothers.

"As a phoenix, a bird of the ashes, it transmigrates into the womb of a mother who has conceived—of course, the widely known phoenix of legend throws its body into a blazing fire once it grows old, only to be reborn from the flames as a tender hatchling once more."

A blaze. A flame. Fire—a bird of fire.

Come to think of it, the lesser cuckoo was also said to traffic with the moon...

Turn your eyes / In the direction / Of the lesser cuckoo's cries / And all you will see / Is the new dawn moon.

That was a famous poem even included in the *Ogura Hyakunin Isshu*.

In other words, Tsukihi—her name was written with the characters for "moon" and "fire."

A cheap pun. It wasn't very funny.

"In this case, the *shide no tori's* case, the fire is, to wit, the mother's womb. And so, strictly speaking, it is not thy sister that the bird possessed, but rather thy dam. Thy mother. Fifteen years prior, an aberration took up lodgings within her..."

And then one year later it was born.

Reborn—as Tsukihi Araragi.

The *shide no tori*.

"Like the bee aberration, this one has no even form of its own—but a major difference is that the *shide no tori* can mimic humans. Nay, perhaps we should say—*it can only do so*."

Mimicry and camouflage—faking.

An aberration—that faked humanity.

Not the real thing, only an aberration.

"Broadly speaking, it is a harmless variety of aberration. It carries out no mischief on human beings—it is simply a fake. Verily—it is only immortal. It lives its allotted span, omitting any injury and healing any sickness. And when it expires—it reincarnates once more. Thus has it survived into the modern day—much like the lesser cuckoo."

A Rolls Royce doesn't break down.

I remembered the urban legend that Hachikuji told me. At the time I thought it was just small talk and safe to ignore.

A Rolls Royce doesn't break down, and the *shide no tori* doesn't die out.

It doesn't die out, it doesn't get injured, and it doesn't fall sick. It was an aberration of the sacred realm, a phoenix. It simply continued to be reborn.

After a hundred years—two hundred years. Even a thousand years.

It survived—to arrive here? In my mother's womb?

Karen was born in June and Tsukihi in April, making the math between their birthdays haphazardly close—but once you presupposed the existence of that aberration, even that unnaturalness seemed natural.

There's a common riddle: "There are two girls. They are the same age and in the same class at the same school. They live in the same house and have the same mother and father. But if you ask them if they're twins, they answer no. If the two girls aren't lying, then what is their relationship?"

Saying that they are "triplets" wasn't the only possible answer. If the older girl was born in April and the younger girl was born in March, they could be sisters. Logically speaking, there are in fact sisters born in consecutive years who're the same age for a period of time, like Karen and Tsukihi.

They were often mistaken for twins—and cases like theirs were indeed rare.

Like nonexistent aberrations.

A rare case—unnatural, yet natural.

"To wit, the aberration is deathless, but it is nary ageless—though now that ye know all of this, are there not many points that make better sense? Has it not occurred to thee that there has always been something off about thy kinswoman?"

When she put it that way—yes. I didn't know about always, but—hadn't I noticed something just today?

The scars on her body—had vanished.

Her injuries—had mended.

From the scar on her body that the doctor said would last her lifetime, to the more recent nicks and bruises—they had all disappeared, without a trace.

Even if wounds did heal—they shouldn't have been cured.

It wasn't possible. Or if it was—something wasn't normal.

"The immortality does not seem to be hard-fast and continuous, as thou and I once were—that would not pass as human. The brat did not delve so far, but I have my own travails in immortality so I would know. From what I could note, the *shide no tori*'s immortal properties increase exponentially in response to stimuli. As thou saw even now, in response to a life-threatening injury such as having her trunk razed and blasted from her body, she regenerated in mere moments much like a vampire—for a minor gall that does not threaten her life, the immortality seems to execute by degrees. A prudence that allows it to live in the human world—an example, if ye will, of an aberration adapting to its environment."

Aberrations were easily influenced by their surroundings. I guess this was just another case in point.

In order to avoid detection, as a fake rather than a human, it concealed excessive immortal traits that would impede its ability to live as a human being—barring emergencies.

I had to admit—it made sense. Whether I liked it or not.

Truck canopy or not, jumping off the roof of a school would usually kill a person—rightfully speaking, it should have been unthinkable to carry out an acrobatic stunt like that and not pay the price for it. Getting off with just "battles scars" seemed a little ridiculous.

It wasn't some kung-fu movie—yet, on top of that, she'd been cured of her wounds.

Plus, the Fire Sisters business.

Playing at defenders of justice—it was one thing for Karen with her crazy martial arts skills, but it was pretty bizarre that Tsukihi managed to stay able-bodied while engaging in such perilous behavior.

Kidnappings, ambushes…

I doubt she could have been so lucky. While she may have been the strategist, it was actually Tsukihi, and not Karen, who had the more aggressive personality.

And—once I started, there was no end to all the strangeness, but there was also something more commonplace to consider.

Her hair.

Her hair grew much too fast.

Even though she didn't wear wigs, she was able to change her hairstyle constantly, every few months. Now that I thought about it, that explained it—just recently, her hair had been in a bob, but now it was already longer than mine, in a single-length cut with the tips reaching all the way to her shoulders. There was no way her bangs could grow all the way down to her shoulders in just a month or so, was there?

Kanbaru once said that her hair grew so fast because of all her sexy hormones—but this was on a different level and no joke when I

214

thought back to it.

Ha… No laughing matter.

The abnormal speed at which it grew qualified as regeneration.

Of course there was no danger of dying from cutting your hair, which is why the regen from cutting her hair wasn't very dramatic—but with such an increased metabolic rate, Tsukihi's nails probably grew pretty fast, too.

Her metabolism—was *too* good.

Right, just today she was taking a shower in the middle of the day, and it did seem like she cut her nails frequently—of course, this was a "now that you mention it" kind of deal. It was too trivial to bring up in its own right.

Now, a torrent of things came to mind—almost too many realizations.

In the end, however—perhaps I had simply turned a blind eye because we were family.

After all, things were only strange when you took the time to notice.

A fake can't be told apart from the real thing—that's how it qualifies as a fake.

Being like the real thing was the fake's only proof of existence.

This example isn't as modern as the urban legend of the Rolls Royce, so I guess you could call it half-knowledge—but tales of children being abducted by spirits have been passed down for ages.

One day, a child suddenly vanishes—only to return several days later as if nothing happened. And though there is nothing different, to put your finger on, between the child that comes back and the child before it disappeared—despite nothing seeming off…

It's a different child without anything seeming off.

Unlike Senjogahara's rehabilitation making me wonder if she'd been replaced while I wasn't looking, this wasn't a matter of change or growth—but a simple substitution.

In other countries, apparently, it was sometimes said that "Pretty children are replaced by fairies." Those stories probably have similar origins, and the *shide no tori* was a similar tale.

Only, the child was replaced before it was even born.

The Game of Life.

I used to play that board game back in the day with Sengoku and Tsukihi, but the bird aberration that currently went by the name Tsukihi Araragi was playing an eternal game of life, constantly proceeding to the goal and then returning to the start of the board—with neither beginning nor end, spinning forever.

An infinite loop, a transparent, colorless life.

The final nail in the coffin was how susceptible Tsukihi was to external stimuli.

Her sense of justice owed to Karen's overbearing influence—all birds learn to cry by mimicking their mother, but the way that Tsukihi followed after Karen was almost desperate. Her own self didn't seem to figure.

She wasn't there—no one was there.

No human…

Not human…

"I'm repeating myself," Shinobu said, "but the *shide no tori* is a harmless aberration—its only reason for existence is its immortality. It aims only to survive and to exist—living as humans, breathing as humans, eating as humans, speaking as humans and—dying as humans."

And yet.

Despite all that—it was still an aberration, wasn't it?

Wasn't it fully and thoroughly an aberration?

However minutely it modeled itself after humanity, however closely it imitated us, wasn't it unmistakably—an aberration?

Shinobu must have heard my rebuttal, but she ignored me. "'Tis no surprise that thou did not notice."

Even I failed to see it, she added. Coming from a vampire as haughty and imperious as herself, it almost sounded like an excuse.

216

On second thought, however, she may have meant it as an apology.

She had no reason to apologize to me, though.

In fact, if anything, I felt guilty—for making her attempt such an apology.

As the king of aberrations, it wasn't just fellow aberrations that Shinobu didn't care to sort out. Humans were the same for her—no, let alone one human from another, perhaps she didn't even distinguish between humans and aberrations.

That was what it meant to be royalty.

The title of king—it meant standing at the pinnacle.

In the end, perhaps the only human that Shinobu Oshino really recognized was me—truth be told, she lumped even Karen Araragi and Tsukihi Araragi together in her mind.

If they were standing in front of her, she might discern some differences, but once they went away and a few minutes passed, she almost entirely forgot about them.

It was impossible to be cognizant of something that didn't interest you.

Or rather, even if she was interested—it was like a Japanese person who didn't understand English browsing an English newspaper. Once you folded it shut again, you wouldn't even remember how to spell words you'd just seen.

So even if she hadn't tried to explain herself, I wouldn't have thought that Shinobu had registered Tsukihi, realized what was up, and kept it a secret from me.

Just as Shinobu was no ally to humans, she was no ally to aberrations.

And despite all the abuse she hurtled at me, I knew that Shinobu was indeed my ally.

In fact…

If Shinobu hadn't been with me back there, the whole situation would have gone belly up. Suddenly thrust into the deep end like that, without knowing my left from my right, I fell completely to pieces—

and even if I hadn't, folded up by Kagenui as I was, there was nothing I could have done.

By the time I lost my cool and went flying at Ononoki, I had already made a serious mistake—not that I wanted to become the kind of person who could remain calm after his little sister's torso was blown clean from her body.

Still.

I'd meant to negotiate and talk things out…

I bet Mèmè Oshino would have snorted if he'd seen me.

Actually, he would have laughed in my face.

The one who actually carried out the negotiations afterwards—was the vampire who inherited Oshino's wealth of aberration-related knowledge. Yes, Shinobu Oshino.

"Hold—traveler. I will brook no more violence. I imagine ye wish, also, to avoid causing further trouble here."

Shinobu must have judged that the one more likely to come to the table was not her fellow aberration Ononoki, whom she ignored, but Kagenui, who was still standing on my back. It was to the onmyoji that the words were addressed.

"Hmm? But I don't wish to avoid trouble. I'm not so well-behaved that I'd choose a time and a place," Kagenui shooed. "You won't brook it? What can you do to stop me now, vampire—former vampire? You've lost your powers. You're no threat to me."

"Perhaps."

Perhaps? Shinobu was almost completely powerless these days. Thanks to being sealed in my shadow, she could invoke a few skills while she was there—but even that didn't go beyond creating a DS. She could hardly take on an expert.

And to make matters worse, Kagenui was an onmyoji who specialized in immortal aberrations—Shinobu at the height of her powers might be a different story, but she was no match at the moment.

But that was the art of negotiation—what they called chutzpah.

"That may be fine for thee, but what about the little maiden?"

continued Shinobu, not letting on to the truth. "As aberrations go, she does not look strong enough to withstand my energy drain. And once I drained her perfect, I would be more than hale enough to go toe to toe with thee."

It was a bluff.

Ononoki had just obliterated the entire front door along with Tsukihi's torso. There was no way Shinobu could cope with such monstrous power—she'd only get herself blasted to smithereens like Tsukihi. Actually, Tsukihi only had her top half blown off, but Shinobu would get every inch of her pulverized.

It would be a miracle if a single blond hair remained.

However, Shinobu's brazen attitude, arms crossed and chin thrust out, betrayed no hint of uneasiness. She just stood there quietly, acting the part—a vampire of inscrutable measures.

She might get angry with me for putting it this way…but she hadn't lived for five hundred years for nothing. Considering how oblivious Shinobu was to the ways of the world, though, maybe it was less those five centuries than the three months spent with Oshino that were proving useful.

Three months with a man who could negotiate aberrations and humans alike under the table on the strength of nothing but a bluff—three months with Mèmè Oshino, who never resorted to violence even under the most extreme circumstances.

"I shan't interfere with thy business—I bespeak only a temporary withdrawal. Thou can surely agree to something so trifling. I doubt that time is such a pressing commodity for thee."

But still, that bluff… Maybe it would fool me, and maybe it fooled Ononoki… But would it actually fool Yozuru Kagenui, an expert operating in the same field as Oshino?

I was a little worried on that score. Actually, massively worried. But in the end…

"Hmph." Kagenui withdrew her hand from my head without protest. "Fine, then—I will withdraw a spell, as you say. While I might give two hoots for time and place, even I am not keen on eliminating the child in front of her own brother—although, haw-haw, it's not his sister, now, is it?"

"......"

She wasn't really my sister.

A fake—sister.

"This fiendish young man might want to put his affairs in order as well—as a show of respect to a legendary vampire, I will give you that time. I'll let myself be taken in by that admirable bluff, so go, get your thoughts in order, rest your body, and whatnot. Hm, I reckon this was our mistake. The truth is I had planned to settle this affair before the foster parents and family found out—ah, noise."

With that, Kagenui—jumped from my back onto Ononoki's shoulders.

After all this, she still hadn't stepped on the ground.

It seemed less like a childish game and more like a religious vow of some sort at this point.

But the bigger surprise was Ononoki, who didn't so much as bat an eye even when Kagenui, who looked about twice as large, landed.

This wasn't simply carrying someone on her shoulders.

I was reminded, once more, that this girl was indeed an aberration, the *Unlimited Rulebook*.

"I will come again tomorrow. Finish your preparations by then—and it's no use running. I'm no pushover like Oshino, I'll tell you that now—I never let my prey escape. And if you fix to get in my way, your certification as harmless be damned, I will eliminate you as well."

Until then, promised Kagenui.

Ononoki pivoted with the onmyoji still on her shoulders and began plodding away at a brisk pace—it was as if all the destruction and regeneration had never even taken place.

"Why," I entreated their backs, just barely croaked—I was in a turmoil of shock and pain. "Why go after...Tsukihi?"

Prey, she'd said.

But surely—there was no reason to go after my little sister.

This wasn't like Shinobu getting marked for death by expert vampire hunters.

"You've got no reason…to come after Tsukihi."

"There is. She's an aberration, a monster," Kagenui charged without turning around, from her perch above the ground, as if it were the most obvious thing in the world. "However dotingly raised, she is still a lesser cuckoo—a monstrous fake what lives by deceiving folk, mingling with a family and pretending to be human—we two fix to call that evil."

"……"

"We *defenders of justice*—don't bide by such. We don't pardon fraud."

With those words, Yozuru Kagenui and Yotsugi Ononoki, the aberration and the human, the two-man onmyoji cell, left our house in their wake.

011

"I'm home! Let me tell you, today was some fun! Even among the many trials and tribulations of my breathtaking existence, today was a day to truly commemorate. I doubt a treat like this will ever come again in my lifetime. Nothing will ever surprise me again after... Huh? Holy smokes?! What the heck is this?! The entrance to our house is completely gone! I've never been so surprised in my life!"

The time was approximately 5:00 p.m. Karen came home sooner than I thought, and her reaction to the state of our house was even better than I had anticipated.

"Koyomi, I already took my key out. Where am I supposed to put it?! Cutting through packing tape is all it's good for now!"

"Well..."

Karen's stupidity could be a real breath of fresh air, sometimes. She had a brain like a beehive. She'd make a great test subject for anyone who wanted to study how humans could get so scatterbrained.

"I figured it would be a little while until you got home," I said. "Since mom and dad will be back late today too, you could have fudged your curfew a little."

"Ahh, I couldn't, I couldn't. In the end, I was too nervous around Kanbaru-sensei. If I stayed there any longer, my head might explode, so I decided to say goodbye early. I kept tripping over every word. Can you believe it? I was a total wreck."

"I wish I could have seen that."

"But she's really great, isn't she? Is 'great' the right word? She's really got it together? Like a woman of character? In any case, she's really gallant."

"Yeah, I'll be the first to admit that Kanbaru is as gallant as they come—and her personality is genuine. I could learn a thing or two from her."

"The funny thing is, though, she kept slapping her own cheek. I guess to keep her spirits up? She did it whenever my face came close to hers or our bodies touched."

"……"

That was probably to control herself. A valiant fight against her own wicked impulses—maybe it had approached wiccan levels.

"We played a game of street ball at the park. One thing, though. She was a real hellcat on the court, but when it came to rock-paper-scissors, she was abysmal. Seriously. I didn't even have to use my surefire method. I won almost every round."

"You're telling me. She's absolutely terrible at any game that relies on luck."

She didn't have bad luck so much as no luck. For some reason, hard work and effort didn't seem to earn her happiness—which, of course, is how she ended up wishing upon a monkey.

In any case, it seemed like hiding Kanbaru's sexual predilections from Karen had been the right choice—my sister was so simple that if I'd told her, she might have offered her virginity up to her revered Kanbaru-sensei.

Either way, it sounded like Kanbaru had done right by Karen—I could rest easy now. Breathe a sigh of relief, or whatever.

I would have to thank Kanbaru later. I'd work extra hard to clean up her room tomorrow, as repayment.

"But more importantly, Koyomi, what is this?! What happened?!

Was it cannon fire?! Did a posse from the organization track us down and bombard the house?!"

"……"

A posse from the organization? Karen certainly had a goofy imagination. What was she watching that put those kinds of thoughts in her head? Animes and movies weren't enough to explain it.

"Whoa there, Karen, don't say 'more importantly' when you were telling me about Kanbaru. Just think of how disappointed she'd be if she heard you say that."

"Ah, good point. That's true, telling you about her is clearly much more important than our measly front door. Okay, listen then. After basketball, we played a game of tag on the monkey bars and—wait a second! Obviously the fact that our house is in shambles is more important right now!"

Karen was playing the straight man with great gusto.

That was all well and good, but she and Kanbaru playing tag on the monkey bars surpassed anything I could imagine… I needed to hear the details.

"Yeah, I guess," I nodded.

After Kagenui and Ononoki had left, I'd remained right where I was, in our front doorway, since the destruction wasn't about to go anywhere. Several of the neighbors came by to voice their concern, but I managed to play it off well enough—it was a lucky break that there had been no witnesses.

A lucky break.

The phrase was a little too convenient, considering the situation— just like the three vampire hunters, Kagenui had probably just done her groundwork and ensured that there would be no witnesses before carrying out her violence.

Even if she didn't care about the time or place, I'm sure she had her own logic.

They probably didn't consider their use of force criminal. Having laid waste to a private residence, they proudly spoke of justice.

In any case, no matter how burglary-free our country town, I could hardly leave with our front door gaping open to the world. I'd waited like the faithful dog Hachiko for Karen Araragi's return.

Besides—I had some stuff to think about.

I'd grown tired of waiting—but it's not as if I'd had nothing to do with my time.

"What happened here?" asked Karen.

"Actually, a posse from the organization showed up."

"I knew it! It was them, those sons of bitches! Targeting my family, those cowards!"

"So you think you know who did this…"

"My temper's running high! In fact, I'll run myself! Straight for the sun on the horizon!"

Apparently my little sister's imagination wasn't the only thing that was goofy. She also led a goofy life.

I wish she'd mellow out eventually.

Either that, or she could die.

She could join Shinobu and go vanquish the sun.

"Hrrm?!" my sister exclaimed. "You know, saying 'cowards' just reminded me of beef! Is anyone else hungry?!"

"Are you thinking about something else already?"

"That settles it, tonight let's have *oden* for dinner!"

"That conclusion doesn't make sense…"

When it came to remembering things, Karen was the real birdbrain.

"Anyway!" she yelled. "I'm pretty sure I don't know anything about any organization!"

"That's what I thought."

"Koyomi, would you just give me a serious answer?!"

Karen looked angry, her hair standing on end. But if she wanted a serious answer, maybe she could ask a little more seriously.

She was so high that it was almost impossible for us to have a serious discussion.

"Uhm…actually I'm not sure," I said. "I took a break to run to

Mister Donut, and when I came back, it was already like this." Yeah, I never intended to answer her seriously. "I figure a dump truck or something probably ran into the house…"

"Oh, you mean a hit and run. This one sure is a doozy, though. Who knew stuff like this really happened."

Karen seemed to buy my story without suspicion. She was far too trusting.

Sure, with the house in that state, there didn't seem to be any other reasonable explanation, but seeing how easily she was convinced was a bit of a letdown. While I didn't see anything wrong, per se, with lying to my sisters, when it was this easy I couldn't help but feel a little guilty.

"Karen. You're amazingly smart and very cute."

"What? Me? Oh, stop!"

Karen twisted back and forth in embarrassment. There. Guilty feelings gone. Though I suppose I had just lied again.

"Huh, I see. So that's why you're sitting here keeping watch, Koyomi. Good work. But I bet you didn't get any studying done today."

"You're right."

I could hardly study under the circumstances.

But in the greater picture of life—I guess today had been a pretty huge lesson.

"It's settled then, Koyomi. Let me take watch. It's my turn now. Until mom and dad get home, I shall serve as Cerberus at the gates of hell. Or Dekamaster even, hell's own guard dog!"

"You really like the Deka Rangers, don't you?"

"Nonsense."

"Nonsense, yourself."

"Seriously, though, I'm really hoping to join the Fire Squad. Based on how often he does handstands, I guess I'd be the green ranger."

"Then how come you don't have any bright ideas?"

That was supposed to be his thinking pose.

Geez, what age range were they trying to reach with that show?

I don't think their message was getting anywhere.

"You go ahead, Koyomi, and study at least a little in your room—they say if you take one day off, it takes three to make up for it. Of course, that's for muscle training."

"Don't talk to me about muscles."

"Actually, it's important to rest properly after training. It's called supercompensation."

"Why are you still talking to me about muscles?"

Karen better wise up soon. How was a meathead like her going to make it in this world? Sometimes I wondered if she thought her noggin was just a tool to be used for headbutts.

"Hrm? Wait, what about Tsukihi? Did she go with you to Mister Donut?"

"No." Handing Karen the box of donuts I had brought home as a gift, I shook my head—adding yet another layer to the lie.

It was a mille-feuille of lies.

"Apparently, Tsukihi was on the second floor when it happened," I said. "She kept watch until I got back. But I think the shock really got to her, being so close when it happened—she's in bed upstairs."

"Ah." Karen glanced up with a worried expression on her face—not that she could see through the ceiling or anything. "Tsukihi can be kind of sensitive and delicate."

"I'm sure you want to talk to her, but she was sleeping pretty soundly, so don't wake her for a while."

"Aye, aye!"

"Okay then."

I finally stood up.

Karen had come back sooner than I'd expected, but that was only good news as far as I was concerned. The quicker we could get this over with, the better.

I started to climb the stairs but turned around once more.

"Karen."

She'd already plopped herself down where I'd been sitting.

She faced me. "Hmm? What is it?"

"Would you be willing to die for my sake?"

"Of course. But why ask?"

......

It was the reply I'd expected her to give, but the way she answered so readily was pretty gallant...

She really was like Kanbaru.

If she weren't my sister, I'd be crushing on her.

A big if.

"Then, could you die for Tsukihi's sake?"

"Of course," she replied. "I would do it smiling."

And she actually smiled.

It was such a brilliant smile—it made me think that even if her head were to be lopped off right now, she'd have no regrets.

"Tsukihi is my sister—of course I would."

"Yeah, of course..." I nodded deeply. "I'd die for your sakes as well. Over and over if necessary—I'd be Dracula for you guys and die as many times as it took to be dead."

Speaking those words over my shoulder, I walked away and went up the stairs once again, to the second floor—but not toward my desk. I went directly to my sisters' room—straight to Tsukihi.

I didn't bother to knock and just opened the door.

Tsukihi was on the top bunk—sleeping peacefully with not even a light snore.

She was a pretty still sleeper. As quietly as I could, I climbed up the ladder and gazed at her face.

A restful sleep. As deep as death.

But—she wasn't dead.

Tsukihi Araragi was alive.

"......"

After getting her torso blown off by Ononoki, Tsukihi's body recovered as if none of it had happened—but since then, she'd remained unconscious. Like a bird scared from the bush, she wasn't coming back.

It had been a mighty struggle, but I'd hoisted her unconscious body onto my back and carried her piggyback up to her room. I could hardly leave her there with her naked upper body exposed.

The difficult part hadn't been carrying her so much as changing her out of her tattered clothes. I had never put clothes on an unconscious person before, but it was a lot harder than I expected—of course, it was just a yukata, which made it a lot easier than dressing her in Western clothes.

In the end, I wound up wrapping the yukata left over right (seen from my side), like they do for a funeral. Under the circumstances, that seemed more than a little ironic.

Oh boy, she was certainly a handful.

My sister was—such a handful.

"Immortal, huh? Not a vampire—but a phoenix."

I leaned my weight against the bunk railing and peered into Tsukihi's sleeping face.

Right now, she looked completely human to me. It was hard to believe she was a fake.

"It's not even funny—it's such a hilarious punch line, but I don't find it funny at all. And that's coming from me, who's been calling you and Karen fakes for years."

But it was the truth. I had seen Tsukihi's uncanny powers of healing with my own eyes—witnessed real "supercompensation."

To be killed and not to die—immortality.

Of course, when it came to immortality, I had experience in that myself—it was only for two weeks, but I'd been turned into a creature that could be killed and still not die. Looking at it another way, if it wasn't for that experience, I probably wouldn't be buying, even now, that Tsukihi was an aberration. It would be as ludicrous to me as the idea of drawing fire from a well.

I'd have decided that my eyes had deceived me.

Vampire.

Phoenix.

However—there was one big difference between my immortality

and Tsukihi's. Mine had been *acquired*, whereas Tsukihi's was *congenital*. She was born immortal.

While Shinobu clearly didn't consider vampires inferior in rank as aberrations—according to her, in terms of immortality at least, the phoenix was far superior. The top of its class when it came to not dying.

She had a point. When you thought about it, there were plenty of ways to kill a vampire—sunlight, wooden stakes, garlic, crosses, and so on. Whereas, with the phoenix, no weak points immediately came to mind—everything Shinobu said while riding in the front basket of my bicycle made sense, but I still couldn't recall any legends about anyone putting an end to a phoenix.

Of course, that may have just been ignorance on my part. In fact, it probably was—considering the fact that Kagenui and Ononoki had attacked. That onmyoji two-man cell must possess a strategy of some sort to exterminate Tsukihi Araragi, the Shidenotori.

Kindly adding new ventilation to the entrance to our house with Ononoki's *Unlimited Rulebook* must have been the outcome of a trial run—a test of Tsukihi's immortality and a sort of calling card.

Scarily enough, *that* had only been the beginning. They were experts on immortal aberrations, after all— they surely knew how to kill a phoenix.

"This is all happening so fast I don't know which way to turn... Just this morning I was having fun, letting Karen carry me on her shoulders. And now... Tsk, I'm not even sure what I should be worrying about most," I muttered, brushing Tsukihi's chin lightly with my fingers.

I must have sounded pathetic.

It indeed was pathetic.

Not even sure what I should be worrying about? How dumb could I get?

What was there to worry about? There was no need for angst.

The Shidenotori. The lesser cuckoo.

A bird of omen—an aberration.

The flip side was that this Shidenotori was just an aberration—

an aberration, with no clear will of its own. At the end of the day, aberrations were no more than phenomena.

Even when manifested, even when made real—they were phenomena.

Transitory.

The will and consciousness of Tsukihi Araragi belonged solely to Tsukihi Araragi—and every kernel of Tsukihi Araragi saw herself as human. Naturally, if she didn't, she would be incomplete as a fake.

In other words.

Tsukihi Araragi had no idea she was an aberration.

She was born as the true Tsukihi Araragi.

Raised as the true Tsukihi Araragi.

She lived as the true Tsukihi Araragi.

She would die as the true Tsukihi Araragi.

A fake Tsukihi Araragi—who was every bit the same as the true Tsukihi Araragi.

"Hmph…"

So then, how was she different from the real thing?

Exactly the same in every single way but still a fake—did that mean like a synthetic diamond? Something with the exact atomic structure as the real thing but with a value as different as heaven and earth, night and day…

It was Hanekawa, of course, who taught me about the uncanny valley.

I think it was during art class—the idea is that when a depiction of a person too closely resembles the original, it can inspire extreme discomfort rather than appreciation.

For instance, the fear felt at the sight of a mannequin. Or at a robot that too closely resembles a human being.

When something not human takes the shape of something human, the closer it resembles the original, and the more exquisite the fake, the deeper the sense of primordial rejection in the viewer—those coordinates are what is known as the uncanny valley.

Man, there sure were a lot of these terms.

If Hanekawa only knew the things she knew—then as for me, I didn't even know what I do know.

I didn't even know—about my own sister.

After being attacked by Shinobu, thrust head first into hell, and transformed into a vampire—all I wanted was to become human again.

I risked my life for that. Offered my life up to that end.

But when push came to shove, I remained irresolute, returning instead to an imperfect half-vampire, half-human sham. In Tsukihi's case, however, she didn't even have an original human state she could revert to.

Tsukihi Araragi had always been in the aberration column. As a human, she was a sham from the outset.

"I thought *I* was supposed to be like a phoenix to the flame—but really it was you, Tsukihi."

A fake family—an imitation sister. Without even being conscious of it, simply by existing, Tsukihi had been deceiving us all this time...

"Uhn..."

I kissed Tsukihi on her sleeping lips.

"What the heck are you doing?!"

Her eyes flew open.

Just like Sleeping Beauty in the fairy tale—immediately shoving the prince (i.e. me) off her as hard as she could and sending him flying from the top bunk was where the stories diverged.

Tsukihi bolted up with a start and began scrubbing at her lips frantically, nearly in tears.

"I-I can't believe it! I-It's a lie! My first kiss! The kiss I was saving for Rosokuzawa!"

"Heh...the same reaction as Karen."

"The same... Wait! You mean..."

You did the same thing to Karen?!

With that anguished cry, Tsukihi glared down at me on the floor where she had tossed me. Her eyes were brimming with tears.

Drooping, tearful eyes were some crazy peepers.

"I knew things were funny lately between Karen and Mizudori, but I would have never imagined the reason why!"

"Who cares about that? The real surprise is that you and Karen reacted in the same way."

"That's what you care about?! What kind of big brother ruins his sisters' love lives with stunts like this! Who cares if our reactions are the same—we're sisters, of course we'd react the same!"

"Yeah..." Of course. Because—they were sisters. "Haha... Ahahaha!"

I couldn't hold it in. I burst into full-throated laughter without meaning to...

Without missing a beat, Tsukihi snarled, "What's so funny?! What kind of person steals his little sisters' first kisses and then laughs about it?! A hamster is more principled than you! It wasn't an accident either, was it?! You were clearly aiming straight for my lips! I bet you attacked Karen in her sleep, too!!"

"No, you've got it all wrong. I kissed you in your sleep, but I kissed Karen while she was too sick to fight back."

"That's terrible! Listen up, neighbors, we've got a real degenerate here! The kind of low-life miscreant who sexually abuses his own family!"

"Come on, don't be like that. I'll explain everything to Rosokuzawa and Mizudori."

"Oh, thank goodness. Now I can rest easy. Once my brother explains things—I'll never see my boyfriend again!"

"Hahahaha."

"I thought I asked you what was so funny! Is our heartbreak so hilarious to you?! Does it just fill you with delight?!"

"No, I was actually just thinking about how I didn't feel anything when I kissed you."

"Huh?"

"It didn't make me happy, or make my heart flutter in my chest, or anything like that." Which was all I needed to know. I got off my ass and stood up slowly. "You really are my little sister."

"Huh?"

Tsukihi stared at me suspiciously. She seemed to have no idea what I was talking about—the disturbance at our front door must have been completely wiped from her memory. I guess that made sense since her brain had been blast away, too—how convenient.

Better if she forgot.

Not just about the blond Lolita. The less she knew about those other two shady individuals, the better.

Or about who she really was.

A fake or real, she was still my little sister.

There was nothing—uncanny about it.

"Tsukihi, did I ever tell you there was a time when I wasn't your big brother?"

"…? What do you mean?"

"There was a time when I wasn't Karen's big brother, either. For the first three years after I was born, I was an only child, and for the next year after that, it was just me and Karen. I had to wait four years to become your big brother."

"Well—okay."

Tsukihi seemed confused.

It was only to be expected.

Even under the best of circumstances, this wasn't exactly the kind of conversation a person was used to waking up to—and after the wakeup Tsukihi had gotten, asking her to process everything I was saying was probably asking for the impossible.

I continued, regardless. I was only saying all of this because I wanted to get it off my chest.

"The thing, though, Tsukihi, is that Tsukihi Araragi was always my little sister, from the moment she was born. My little sister, and Karen's too. There hasn't been a single moment where that wasn't true."

"……"

"A kiss with me doesn't count. That's part of being brothers and sisters, all right? Just think of how many times I promised to marry you and Karen while we were still little kids."

That would have been polygamy, of course, I noted.

Tsukihi pouted, unhappy that I'd stirred up ancient history. "What does way back then have to do with anything? You think you can distract me so easily?" Averting her eyes, she muttered, "You're making me dagnabbit mad…"

If I recalled correctly—that meant she was only a bit mad.

Not that I cared.

"Hahaha," I laughed again, telling Tsukihi she should get a little more sleep—and exited my sisters' room.

She probably didn't even know why she was asleep so early in the evening. Perhaps compelled by my peremptory tone, she nodded with uncharacteristic docility.

Next I returned to the front door.

I guess Karen had changed her mind while I was upstairs, because she was no longer sitting in the doorway. Instead, she was standing at stiff attention like some mythical gatekeeper.

She could be very capricious.

From the front gate to the front door, the whole entrance to our house was in shambles. And now there was some crazy person standing watch. What was happening around here?

What was up with our family?

"Hey, Karen. I'm going to head out for a little while."

"Mrr! Brother or not, none shall pass!"

"You're turning into a weird character, you know…"

"If you want to defeat this, you're gonna have to pass through me first!"

"I can pass through you?"

What did that mean exactly? What would count as passing through her?

Looks like the words got switched around.

Besides, if I defeated the doorway, our house wouldn't be half-wrecked anymore, it could totally collapse.

"Ah, forgive me, forgive me. This is a great time to try out that new gag you taught me the other day," Karen said as if she'd just remembered something.

She used the stoop of our entryway to bend over into a fairly difficult-looking upside-down bridge position, supporting her weight on her neck.

"If you want to pass, you're gonna have to defeat me first!"

"Bwahahahaha!"

Uhm…sorry.

Something about that gag cracked me up every time.

"Uhn…"

I reached out and honked Karen's chest, which was emphasized by the bridge position.

Hey, stop touching your little sisters' breasts so much!

"Ghakk!"

To judge from her reaction, she'd suffered critical damage.

She went head over heel across the front hall like she'd been electrocuted. Tumbling full circle, she stood back up with a dauntless grin.

"Hmph. You have defeated me, well done! You have passed the first test!"

"This skit isn't over?"

"The second gatekeeper will not be so easy… Indeed! Prepare to be shocked, for he is our older brother!"

"I don't have an older brother." *Just two little sisters,* I said, shoving past Karen and slipping on my shoes.

"Boo! Come on, play along, Koyomi. You should have said, 'Th-That can't be! My brother died five years ago, protecting me!' I'm doing my part here looking after the entrance like you said, okay?"

"I don't recall asking you to monitor it like some character out of a boys' manga. Just watch for people going out and coming in."

"Out and in, huh? Hurrm. Out and in? Out and in, did you say? How can they go out before they've come in? If they don't come in first, they can't go out!"

"......"

She was getting on my nerves, but since I didn't have an answer to that, I just ignored her. If Hanekawa was here, I'm sure she would have had a good response.

"Well, I'm going out, so let me through."

"Heheh. I might let you, but when you return, are you sure you'll be able to get back in?"

"You better let me in."

Did she have a brain attached to her shoulders or was that just a watermelon?

"Hold on, though, going out where?" she asked me. "I thought you were supposed to be studying? You've got exams, young man!"

"Since when are you my boss? Anyway, umm…I have to go buy a study-aid."

"Huh. Well then, godspeed."

Karen had accepted one of my lies without the slightest suspicion again.

No wonder she got played by Kaiki… This went way beyond simply trusting her big brother.

Maybe I'd been wrong all along. Maybe Karen was even more loyal to me than Kanbaru was.

What a scary thought.

"Karen?"

"Yes?"

"We talked about this before, but what do you think justice is?"

"Being just. What else?"

"I see. Then what is the enemy of justice?"

"Hrm? Evil, naturally. Like that ominous dirtbag from the other day."

"Yes, you're right." She was right. Karen's straightforward answer elicited a nod from me. "But obvious villains like Kaiki are a minority. It's hard to be so confirmed in your evil. Most people couldn't be a scoundrel without some aesthetic or rationale. They end up establishing their own notions of what's just."

Deishu Kaiki was an exception among exceptions.

A fake among fakes.

While he did give voice to his views, he never once tried to assert their legitimacy. Indeed—he was anything but shy when it came to assuming the mantle of evil.

No matter what names Karen and Senjogahara called him, he never once tried to suggest that you had no one else to blame for being a sucker.

"So you see, broadly speaking—the enemy of justice is a different justice."

"……"

"War is an excellent example. The Fire Sisters' justice, too, is the enemy of justice from someone else's point of view—as long as we insist on our own justness, there's no telling when, or for what reason, we'll wind up becoming an enemy of justice."

The world wasn't built on such simple binary oppositions—it was more complicated. It was freakier than that.

During spring break, during Golden Week, I learned that until I was sick of it.

I was still learning. It was a lifelong lesson.

"Karen. It can be hard to know the right time to say 'cheating,' don't you agree? I know that you hate cheaters, and I don't intend to affirm cheating. But when you think about it, being strong is like 'cheating' for the weak, and being weak is like 'cheating' for the strong. Strength can equal weakness. And being just is like 'cheating' for the unjust and evil. In which case only evil—isn't cheating."

Strength can be a weapon. Weakness, too, can be a weapon.

As for being just—it was a lethal weapon.

Only evil, the supposed polar opposite of justice—bravely came to the fight empty-handed.

"Surefire methods are cowardly, like you said, because it's cheating. Whether it's rock-paper-scissors or whatever. Only evil, which is fated to lose, isn't cowardly."

If justice always prevails, then evil is always vanquished.

Evil never prospers. Which is precisely why—

"Sorry, Koyomi. I don't really get it," interrupted Karen.

I guess it was too much for her—maybe she was too young for this kind of talk.

But if she was going to pursue justice, this was a hurdle she was going to face at some point, and sooner rather than later.

I decided to put it in simpler terms—so she would understand.

"Just by living, everybody becomes somebody's enemy at some point. That's all I meant."

"If that's true…" My words seemed to have hit their mark this time—but Karen responded with a question of her own, a look of uncertainty on her face. "What do you do then?"

"Hm?"

"When you become the enemy of justice. When you've done nothing wrong, and think you're actually correct, but still wind up as the enemy of justice, what should you do?"

"If you can answer that question—you're a defender of justice."

I wouldn't know, though, I shrugged my shoulders.

Maybe that didn't cut it at all, after I'd put her on the spot. Maybe I was just taking things out on her with my line of questioning.

Hanekawa had actually told me as much once. It was during Golden Week.

—*Araragi… You might become a star, but you could never become a hero.*

It was harsh, but she was right.

What Hanekawa said—was always correct.

I was no defender of justice.

I wasn't on the humans' side, and I wasn't on the aberrations' side.

I was only on my sisters' side.

An ordinary, dime-a-dozen big brother.

"All right then, off I go. Guard this place. Don't let anyone in."

"Just leave it to me! I am Karen Araragi, my brother's orders are absolute!" Karen threw her head back and beat a fist against her chest. "For it is my brother who inspired the hatred of evil that burns in my heart, my brother who instilled in me the love of justice!"

"That's a nasty responsibility..." I didn't know how to respond other than to grimace and tell her no thanks.

She clearly wasn't influenced by me.

Neither she nor Tsukihi were.

"Ah... I almost forgot. If Tsukihi wakes up while I'm gone, don't let her out. She literally doesn't go out or come in. Knock her out with a sleeper hold if you have to."

"Aye, aye, sir!"

Why was she accepting my terrible order to choke out her sister? Karen wasn't about absolute obedience so much as the type to just go ahead and do things out of sheer momentum.

Scary, scary.

Casting one last sidelong glance at her, I toed up my bicycle's kickstand, straddled the seat, and began pedaling—I pointed the handles in the exact opposite direction of the bookstore, of course.

I was heading toward that ruined cram school building I knew so well—the name of which, as I had learned just today, was Eikow Cram School.

It was where Mèmè Oshino had once set up camp.

And now the onmyoji.

An expert on immortal aberrations —the aberration roller.

Yozuru Kagenui and Yotsugi Ononoki were based there.

"My lord, ye are going, then."

Now that I noticed—before I'd even noticed, Shinobu was riding in my bicycle's front basket in the reverse ET position.

While I was waiting for Karen to come home, the sun had set—in other words, the hour of aberrations was now upon us, when the moon shone bright and impudent in the sky.

It was Shinobu's hour.

When night fell, her eyes sprang open, alert regardless of whether she'd been awake or asleep during the day. It was a testament to the fact that she was a monster and not an organism—even with her schedule all mixed up, she wasn't about to sleep the night away.

Hence, her eyes—those golden irises of hers sparkled, more full of life than ever.

Not alive—but still full of life.

"Yes, I'm going."

"Where? To do what?"

"To them. To fight."

"For what?"

"For my sister."

"And what will this gain thee?"

"Nothing. I lose a bit of time, that's all."

That was just our usual silly banter—I don't care how many anime or live-action adaptations they were going to make, they'd never make a serious character out of me.

If a situation seemed dubious and inequitable—well, you just kept dividing by seven.

"I see." Shinobu gave a nod. She looked somehow satisfied. "If ye choose to fight, there is aught I can do—after all, should thou perish, I too must share in that fate. I have no choice, then. For my own safety, I must join thee in thy fight."

"You mean you're going to help me?"

"But let me be clear, I disdain doing so—I find this odious, but I have no choice. I care not what becomes of thy littler kinswoman. I am only helping thee out of self-interest, to protect myself."

"Your tsundere is so annoying," I said—with a chuckle. "Ha, I thought you wanted to die? Whatever happened to you being the suicidal vampire?"

"Hmph. That was my original characterization, I've moved past that now. Nor am I taciturn now as I was in the middle act. I am a regular donut-loving mascot now."

She didn't even sound self-deprecating. Sarcastic, flippant—but optimistic, if anything.

"'Twas Tsukihi, correct?"

"Huh?"

"Thy littler kinswoman's name."

"Ah… I can't believe you remembered it. You never remember human names."

"Well, after hearing it rehearsed so incessantly… Not that I can distinguish her from other humans as a result—hmph. And 'tis a fine name."

"A fine name? How so?"

"The *tsuki* means moon. This pleases me. The sun is my enemy— but the moon offers many boons. Mayhap this would be a good opportunity to return those favors."

That is my excuse, she said—leaning back officiously in the front basket.

We hit a bump just as she did so, nearly causing us to lose balance.

"I see. Thank you."

"Thanks are not necessary."

"In that case, let me buy you more donuts next time. I may not be able to get you one of each, but I can probably afford to get a tray's worth."

"That is unnecessary. I do this only for my own sake—ergo, I will not seek any recompense."

If 'tis a mere kindness, then I accept, Shinobu appended with a pushy, evil grin.

A ghastly smile.

She smiled like she might be an enemy of justice.

"Besides, I have my own grudge in this matter."

"Huh? A grudge?" I asked her.

"Aye. That whelp of a maiden called me, a legendary vampire, a geriatric—I wish to teach her who she is dealing with."

012

An ironblooded, hotblooded, yet coldblooded vampire, the king and slayer of aberrations, Shinobu had her existence robbed by me and her name bound by Mèmè Oshino, and lost nearly all of her combat skills—however, the truth was that it was incredibly easy for her to recover those powers.

She could do so at any time she chose. All she had to do was to drink my blood.

That would return her to her former vampiric glory—and liberate her from the girlish form she detested. She could reign once more as a mighty and invulnerable creature of the night.

It went without saying that the inevitable byproduct, a necessary side effect, of her doing so was that I'd become a vampire as well—as long as she did not suck me completely dry and leave me dead, that is.

On the other hand—and since she was now receiving energy directly from my shadow it needn't be too frequent—if I refused to provide Shinobu with any blood, she would die before long. So easily that you wouldn't know she'd once been immortal.

As the side effect of that, I would return to being completely human. No more after-effects, just a plain and simple human—it was a constant possibility, with which Shinobu tormented me relentlessly.

Shinobu becoming a vampire again.

Me becoming human again.

The two were depressingly equal.

But at the moment I wished for neither—neither the effect nor the side effect, neither the effect nor the counter-effect. I couldn't fathom Shinobu's heart, but for the moment at least, as far as I could tell, she was with me on this.

Therefore.

It was important—*here*—to limit the amount of blood Shinobu drew to a mere tasting, no more and no less.

Just like when we faced off against Kanbaru's monkey—or further back when we faced off against Hanekawa's cat.

Shinobu Oshino had to become a sort of monster.

Koyomi Araragi had to become a sort of monster.

It was just a matter of tuning up.

We weren't going to be negotiating this time or talking things out. Unless we were more diligent about preparing for a fight, we'd wind up rehashing the battle at our front door—the conclusion to which would be far too painful for any amount of hindsight.

For my own part, I didn't want to be folded up any more than I had to in one day—and it was unlikely Shinobu's bluff would work a second time. No, even the first time, the bluff only prevailed thanks to the sympathetic vote.

To make matters worse, our opponent was an onmyoji specializing in immortal aberrations. There was no such thing as being too prepared—you might even say that no amount of preparation was going to be enough.

Shinobu and I fastened our teeth into each other's neck, back and forth, draining our blood to and fro—until we got as close to the perfect balance as we were going to get.

And.

All prepared.

All ready.

All set—we arrived at the ruins of the former cram school to face off against Yozuru Kagenui and Yotsugi Ononoki.

"I see we have uninvited guests—Oshino would probably gab, 'You're late. I've been waiting for ages,' but I'm not nearly the body for folk like he is."

We were on the fourth floor of the building, in the classroom Oshino used most frequently as his den—out of the three on the fourth floor, it was the furthest one on the left from the stairwell.

The makeshift bed he'd constructed by joining together several desks with packing tape was still there, just as he'd left it.

It was also the classroom where I'd undergone my terrifying kidnapping ordeal the other day at the hands of Senjogahara before her subsequent rebirth.

Although Kagenui referred to us as uninvited guests, when I opened the classroom door, they were already staring in our direction as though they were expecting us.

Her rule that she couldn't step on the ground only seemed to apply outdoors and not to the floors of buildings—the bottom of Kagenui's shoes were in firm contact with the peeling, faded linoleum below.

Now that I saw her standing on two legs like normal—I began to understand a little what Karen had meant.

Something about the way she stood was unnatural.

It was even a little creepy.

The central axis of her body—was disturbingly straight.

There didn't seem to be any degree of bend.

The way she was standing, if a bicycle ran into her—the bicycle would go flying while Kagenui, I bet, would remain perfectly still.

It wasn't that she had good balance—she was completely affixed.

Her stance wasn't the only thing... Probably because I'd increased my level of vampirism and narrowed the gap between us, I was able to sense how strong she was.

Now that I did, I couldn't believe I hadn't noticed earlier.

Yozuru Kagenui, this seemingly sweet, friendly lady—bristled with danger.

Dramaturgy.

Episode.

Guillotine Cutter.

She emanated an incredibly salient bloodlust that rivaled that of the three vampire hunters—

"Oshino…" To avoid tipping off how nervous I felt—and to put up a bold front, I responded to Kagenui, "Oshino never gave off such a hostile vibe—not once."

"Hm? Kakak, I bet he didn't—not Oshino. But you know, fiendish young man—you're one to talk. The way you're angling for a fight now, what did you expect? To be welcomed with a banquet?"

Kagenui laughed in amusement.

From the looks of it, she was enjoying this chance to gossip about our mutual acquaintance.

"The vampire there, in particular—the erstwhile Heartunderblade, has certainly changed her feathers," Kagenui observed, pointing at Shinobu who stood next to me.

That was true. Having drunk nearly as much of my blood as was safe, Shinobu Oshino no longer looked like an eight-year-old girl, a blond Lolita.

Which isn't to say that she'd reverted to her fully adult version. That would have been going too far—she looked around my own age, about eighteen, if you asked me.

Despite not being able to tell humans apart even after remembering their names, it seemed that when Karen beat the crap out of me the other day, Shinobu had taken real notice (or real damage, since she suffered along with me from inside my shadow). Her hair was styled after the ponytail that Karen had sported until this morning.

She was also wearing a jersey of some sort.

Reflecting her aristocratic lineage, though, the needlessly gorgeous jersey somehow had a luxury, designer-brand feel.

The same went for the sneakers on her feet.

Shinobu Oshino's golden eyes were fastened on Kagenui and Ononoki.

It was a quiet stare.

"You look pure slick, Miss Heartunderblade—you could hold a candle to my younger self. But I doubt you have my britches. It looks like you put all your effort into just the outwith, like a lion's mane or a peacock's train—or a mantis' axe."

"The only mantis axe here is thy little maiden. I advise thee, onmyoji—ye'd be wise not to wag your tongue too bravely now. I've not regained so much of my skills and power since I dealt with that vile cat—I am in the crucible of alarm and hunger. There is no telling what might prick me to kill thee."

Shinobu sounded quite proud of herself. Her voice, too, was no longer the lisping one of a little girl—I was reminded, for the first time in a long while, just how meaningless outward form was to a vampire.

"I am not to kill thee—do not give me matter to do so. Do not give me motive—I have no mind to betray this one yet," she said, pointing her thumb at me.

At me—as the one she did not wish to betray.

"I entreat thee, give me no cause to show my true mettle, my true nature, my true fangs—forbear, as I request, and I will drain only as much of thy blood as metes a fitting punishment."

"You're not to kill?"

It was Ononoki who reacted—even more than I did, to Shinobu's words.

"Is that the resolve you came here with? You make me laugh. Isn't that right, sister? We're more than ready to kill—he said with a dashing look."

As usual, there was no such look on her face.

Her features were as still as a lake surface on a windless day.

But she did seem to mean it in regards to taking offense at Shinobu's speech.

"Now, now, Yotsugi, don't say that—these folk are just obtuse," interceded Kagenui, reinforcing the impression that her shikigami was indeed ruffled. "Right. You just don't know—how dire heartless we can be. You have no damned clue how ridiculously far we've strayed from the fair path."

"……"

I did have a clue.

I'd figured that much out for myself.

Kagenui and Ononoki—shot first and asked questions later, if at all. They'd attacked Tsukihi Araragi, along with the house in which she lived, without even a cursory interrogation.

I knew exactly what kind of humanity such people possessed.

What kind of aberrations they were.

They represented justice.

And nothing else.

"Well? What now?" Kagenui asked me—her tone was casual, as if we were about to get a deck of cards and play President like one big happy bunch, and she was just asking about the local rules. "We tend to welcome a showdown—I'm all for violence, I reckon it makes things simple. And just our luck, we've got a human and an aberration each—myself versus you, and the erstwhile Miss Heartunderblade versus Yotsugi. How does that match card strike you?"

"……"

"Hmm? You don't like it? I can square off with Heartunderblade and you with Yotsugi, if you prefer—she's the one who whupped your sister, after all. Well, fake sister."

"No…"

The first suggestion was fine, I said, nodding.

In fact, it was what I had been hoping for.

That matchup was the one point I was most concerned about. I just didn't know how to bring it up—it was almost as if she'd read my mind.

I guess she was feeling pretty confident.

Maybe she meant it as a handicap.

Either way, I could only accept—what other choice did I have?

"Good. Maidling, thou and I will fight downstairs," Shinobu, who knew these ruins like the back of her own hand, invited Ononoki. "There's a fitting room for our melee on the second floor—we should be able to fight to our hearts' content there. Allow me to show thee the wisdom of age."

She probably meant the classroom where I'd battled Kanbaru's monkey—it did seem well-suited to withstanding a clash between two aberrations.

"Fine, I'm good with that. Acting like you'd taken me hostage to make my sister back down was annoying me to no end. Don't fool yourself, even after powering up this far, you're still not at my level. Respect for the Aged Day is still a month away, but if you're going to rattle your old bones to try and show me the wisdom of age, then I see no harm in doing my civic duty today—he said with a dashing look."

In response to Ononoki, I heard what sounded like a vein popping from Shinobu's direction. I have to say, she had it coming once she brought up their age difference.

"Keh… That's rich coming from a minor goblin of the Far East with barely a tome or treatise about her," Shinobu retorted, her voice dripping with loathing. "When I'm through, ye'll never make another dashing look again."

Um, Ononoki only said that and never wore such an expression to begin with… But in any case, Shinobu headed for the door.

Now that she had my blood for a battery, she was no longer confined to my shadow—she still couldn't go very far, but the second and fourth floors of the same coordinates were well within bounds.

Think of it like the relationship between Mobile Battleship Nadesico and the Aestivalis.

"All right, sister, I'm going to go do some volunteer work taking care of the elderly—he said with a dashing look."

"I leave it in your hands," Kagenui replied to her shikigami.

"In my hands?" Ononoki tilted her head. "Please don't put so much trust in me—he said with a dashing look."

She turned toward me, suddenly, as if something had sparked her interest.

"Kind monster sir."

"Yeah?" I shot back.

"What do you think of the world?"

Without giving me time to answer, she told me her own opinion.

"I wouldn't mind if this world of fakes got destroyed, kind monster sir—he said with a dashing look."

Saying so with a not particularly dashing look.

Declaring so with rare conviction.

Ononoki finally followed in Shinobu's footsteps—and the two aberrations departed from the classroom.

"......"

The bloody combat that was about to unfold between those two likely exceeded the human imagination—having restored herself to such an extent, there was no doubting Shinobu's strength. Ononoki, meanwhile, was still an unknown factor.

At the very least, judging from how she'd pulverized our front door (and Tsukihi's torso)—she could more than hold her ground against any aberration I'd encountered so far.

In which case... Shi—

"Is this any time to be gawking?"

In the blink of an eye, as I was glancing toward the door that Ononoki had shut behind her—Kagenui took her opportunity to close the distance between us, drawing so close I could feel her breath on my nose.

"Wha..."

"Our battle has already started. It began the moment we came mewling into this world—"

I didn't even have the time to pull back my gaze.

The very next instance, Kagenui kicked my knee out—literally kicked it out.

No, excuse me.

"Kicked out" fell short.

You might think that she smashed my kneecap or broke my bones or something like that.

That would be misleading and a lie. Hypobole.

To be precise, what she did was to kick her heel straight at my knee—whereupon the force severed my leg from the knee down like a surgical scalpel, jeans and all.

Kind of like snapping a twig.

Or maybe—plucking the legs off an insect.

"Gha…kk!"

The surprise hit me more than the pain.

It was my astonishment that was the more blistering.

Letting her get so close was just incautious—I had to pay a price for getting distracted by things I had no business worrying about at the moment. I could hardly complain about taking a blow in exchange.

But did it have to be such a devastating blow?

How could one human kick another human's leg off—especially when my body was fortified to the limit as it was now?

My bones, my flesh…

Heck, even my skin was tough as if it were coated in thick rubber…

"Did you reckon I'd go after your weaknesses as a vampire? Target your airways, maybe? Your internal organs? Bring crosses and holy water? Did you reckon I'd whip out a Super Soaker?"

As she spoke, Kagenui swung her left fist—diagonally across from the leg she'd just kicked with—at a dizzying speed against my jaw.

Her punch could set off an airbag, according to Karen—however, that assessment needed to be modified somewhat.

She had been surprisingly conservative in her estimate.

Forget about airbags.

If it was a compact, Kagenui could probably total the whole car.

My whole lower jaw popped off like I'd gotten hit by a major league fastball at point-blank range—this wasn't early-stage stuff like getting a concussion because your brain shook in your skull from a punch to the chin.

My brain didn't so much as tremble when my lower mandible was removed with pinpoint accuracy.

"I hate to break this to you, but I'm Japan's first fighting onmyoji—I don't care about the Komai arts or onerous erudite secrets or any mince like that. Aberrations or whatever they are? I just get pumped up and smash them like so."

The next blow was a palm strike.

The palm of her right hand, which she'd been holding in reserve—came hurtling in on a straight line, at a debilitating, impossible angle, striking me on the right shoulder.

My right arm was jerked from my shoulder joint—leaving only the part from the neck of the humerus and up.

She hadn't grabbed or twisted my arm.

She plucked it free with just the pressure of her palm.

Not even the greatest *yokozuna* in sumo history were capable of such a feat.

It was sheer force—and its concentration.

Power and skill.

The result of which—was extreme destruction.

Yozuru Kagenui, the Destroyer.

Back in front of our house, when she'd folded me up like a piece of origami, I had wondered what kind of submission hold she could have used—if only I had known. She'd simply used her freakish strength to stuff me into that position, as if I'd been reluctant to perform calisthenics and she'd forced me to.

Mere monstrous strength.

And now, that mere, monstrous strength was being unleashed and wreaking havoc.

Could this really be the handiwork of a human, and not an aberration, in the face of an aberration—no, actually, forget all that cumbersome talk, she simply wasn't any sort of onmyoji!

Everything apart from her fighting skills had been subtracted from her as a person!

No wonder Shinobu had been so equivocal.

There was just no normal way—to describe such a person!

"Hur... Guh, uh, ahh!"

I could only pull away—I jumped backward as hard as I could on my remaining right leg to put some distance between us.

Kagenui made no move to follow me.

Not that she couldn't keep up, but she seemed to know better than to chase me too far. She was clearly a pro.

There was no need for a pro to get sloppy against an amateur.

Kagenui had no reason to make a valiant, sustained charge.

As unserious as she could seem, she preferred slow, steady progress.

"Huff... Huff, huff."

But I was lucky—the fact that Kagenui's destructive power was so awe-inspiring actually worked to my advantage.

It hurt so much that it didn't hurt at all.

This was so unrealistic that my brain couldn't accept it.

The damage so surpassed the limits of my sense of pain that my nervous system refused to process it—meanwhile, my body, possessed of vampiric immortality, began to automatically regenerate itself.

My severed leg.

My removed jaw.

My plucked-off right arm.

They all began to be restored to their original state—like a system reboot.

Obviously, the regeneration didn't happen in a heartbeat like when I was a full vampire. Nevertheless, everything was back in place sooner than you could say A-E-I-O-U.

Unlike Shinobu, my clothing wasn't included in the scope of my recovery (I didn't have the ability to create matter, my clothes were just normal clothes), so I was left looking a little bit punk.

But the damage to my psyche from my body getting so badly mistreated wasn't healing.

"Huff… Huff, haah…"

Calm down, stay cool—and heat up.

Even this unexpected development was within expectations.

It was nothing I couldn't endure.

This was a small price to pay for getting to grab my sisters' tits all the time and continuing do so.

Anyway.

Back to square one.

"Kakak. You…"

My opponent, Kagenui, seemed to be enjoying herself.

Despite the fact that we were in the middle of a fight, her jovial attitude had barely changed—or rather.

According to her, our fight started the moment we were born, so it was only natural that her attitude wouldn't change now.

She didn't stop at always being ready for combat.

When she asked me for directions standing atop that mailbox, she was already standing on her battlefield.

"Do you reckon you know why it is I specialize in immortal aberrations?" Kagenui opened her mouth wide and lewdly licked her lips. "It's because you can never go too far—"

"……nkk."

I thought I was back to square one, but with one sentence, she broke my morale.

What was up with this lady?

The world was a big place… I'd never dreamed that it contained so intense a human.

I'd come here intending to fight and all—but only pictured a contest of unique skills.

Not that I'd doubted Karen's guarantee that Kagenui was intense—but I thought once I was more than half vampire again, it would be a fair fight at the minimum.

And yet—what was this melee?

What was with the brute force?

This Kyotoite onmyoji was overwhelming an aberration—via sheer physical strength.

"Huff, huff, huff, huff…"

Regulating my breathing, throttling the thundering beating of my heart, I desperately tried to think.

No, don't think. Remember.

This—right…

The former inhabitant of this room, the slacker in the Hawaiian shirt—if Mèmè Oshino had wanted, he could probably have gone nuts in this way, too.

He just didn't.

He—no doubt could.

Even Shinobu at the height of her power had seen something in him. Whether it was the crab or the snail or the monkey or the snake, he probably could have dealt with them in a simpler way. The only aberration that had truly been too much for him to handle was probably Hanekawa's cat.

Oshino.

"Ms. Kagenui… How do you know—Oshino?"

I wasn't just trying to buy time.

Indeed, I was pretty sure that the only chance an amateur like me had against a pro like her was to try for a quick, decisive victory—but one way or another, this was something I needed to ask.

If I didn't ask her—I wouldn't be able to focus on the fight.

It would nag at me.

"You're acquainted with that dude in the Hawaiian shirt…Mèmè Oshino?"

"Huh?" Kagenui cocked her head at my abrupt question. "What, you mean he's still wearing those shirts? I thought that was just to flesh out his character, but I guess they really mean something to him if he's still keeping the faith."

"......"

"Well, nothing special—we're just old mucks. Me, Oshino, and Kaiki were in college together."

What?

Oshino was one thing—but Kaiki?

Kaiki?

Did she just say Kaiki?

"By Kaiki...do you mean Deishu Kaiki?"

"Sure, Kaiki. We were in the same department and the same club. There was one more of us above our year, and we used to play four-man shogi."

"Shogi..."

Come to think of it... Kaiki had gone on a little digression with me and Senjogahara on the topic of shogi. I remember thinking it seemed a little strange for him...

"Kaiki never tried to win. He always fixed for profit. They say it's bad luck, but he loved to get his pieces in a column."

"......"

Why did he have to be ominous in every way?

That was worse than a stalemate.

"Oshino loved solving shogi puzzles. He was mean and loved to torment us with two-king problems. It wasn't Microcosmos, but he did reckon up many a near-stalemate."

"I don't imagine that earned him a lot of friends..." So Oshino had been like that even way back in college. What an ass. "So the club you mentioned was a shogi club?"

"No, the occult research club. Though I reckon the only ones who took it seriously were Oshino and our sempai. We played so much shogi we forgot to recruit new members. Once we were finished, I'm pretty sure the club went under—I say finished, but Oshino and Kaiki both dropped out. The only one to actually graduate was me."

"O-Oh..."

Only the one who seemed least likely to had graduated.

But putting that aside—she knew not only Oshino, but Kaiki as well.

Naturally, that meant Oshino and Kaiki—knew each other as well.

It was unexpected, but it also made sense—there'd been something odd about the way Kaiki spoke of Kagenui and Ononoki.

So after bilking me, a high schooler, out of my money, Kaiki didn't even given me accurate information?

That is even less believable, he said… *As long as you're on the straight and narrow, you're even less likely to get involved with them than with me,* he said…

That son of a bitch.

If I'd known they were acquainted, I'd have asked more questions.

"Actually, it was Kaiki who kindly let us know that we had prey in your sister."

"Kaikiiiiiii!"

So this whole thing was another one of your scams?!

This was all your doing?!

That ominous sack of shit was such a hopeless scoundrel.

"Of course, he set us back something fierce as is his wont. I figured it was all a bucket of pish before I got here, but I guess even Kaiki tells the truth sometimes. Fancy me pink."

"First you take money from her, and then you take money from me? Business sure is booming, isn't it, Deishu Kaiki?! Maybe next time we should crack open some champagne!"

What was it he said? *"Coincidences" as they're generally understood are a tricky affair—and, by and large, a product of malice.*

A product of his own malice, clearly!

Playing dumb and spouting that line, when he knew damn well!

At this rate, Shinobu and I just happening to run into Kaiki at Mister Donut must have been intentional—malicious, even.

Kaiki was a conman, but he was also an expert. Maybe he knew just around when we would visit Mister Donut and was sitting there eating his muffins waiting for us, almost like Oshino—and come to think of it, the fact that he'd returned during *Obon* while Senjogahara was away also seemed a little too convenient.

"Dammit…I can't believe it. Seriously, bastard?"

It made sense now how Senjogahara had gotten tricked by him back in freshman year—let alone a pair like the Fire Sisters, Karen and Tsukihi.

He played us like a fiddle.

Even Kagenui and Ononoki were dancing on the palm of his hand—it was so grand it wasn't nasty anymore.

I should have never called him small-time.

Deishu Kaiki was biohazard level.

No wonder Senjogahara didn't want me to have anything to do with him—in fact, I had to hand it to her again for mustering the courage to face Kaiki a second time despite her unpleasant experience with him.

"In fact, Kaiki was the source behind Yotsugi's name—which I linked to his. The *ki* in Ononoki comes from Kaiki."

The character meant tree. "You mean—you bound her with that name?"

"Right. Unlike Oshino, I haven't the courage to bind an aberration using my own name."

Ononoki.

So it wasn't a mispronunciation of Araragi, after all.

What a yucky web—there was some twisted backstory and karma behind the battle going on beneath us now between Shinobu Oshino and Yotsugi Ononoki.

"Still—Karen and I met Kaiki, but I'm pretty sure Tsukihi, who's at the center of this, never came face to face with him…"

"Kaiki was always obnoxiously clever. He's in his element at seeing hidden angles—seeing two of three siblings was probably enough for him to sound out the third. Until today, I never reckoned there might be a connection between the vampire Oshino certified as harmless and Kaiki's *shide no tori*. Unlike me, Kaiki must have known she was your sister, eh?"

"Well—probably."

Right.

Unlike Kagenui, Kaiki didn't think Karen and I just happened to have the same name—he was perfectly aware that she was my sister.

I doubted he grasped definitively that there were actually three of us—but it wouldn't be so strange if he had.

"He's cunning as ever not to have told us, fiendish young man—in fact, instead of just keeping it a secret, I suppose he actively led me into believing that you two only happened to share a name. Intentionally planted noise in his information. He probably reckoned that way he'd gin some money out of us both."

I had to agree with her.

Araragi was an uncommon name, and it was pretty unnatural not to suspect blood ties—there had to be intent and malice at play.

It wasn't by chance.

"You probably know this by now, but Kaiki's specialty is fake aberrations... The *shide no tori* may fix under my specialty, but it fixes under his as well..."

Kakak, Kagenui laughed lightheartedly even though she'd been deceived by an old friend.

"The cleverest of us, though, was Oshino. Even though he was also the least serious, always messing with different girls, what a joker. No one ever saw him do any studying to save his life, but we all reckoned he was the biggest genius the club had ever seen. Even Kaiki kept his distance when it came to Oshino..."

"......"

That was amazing.

I had Oshino all wrong.

I could give two shits about him being clever or a genius or whatever, but if he could make Kaiki think twice, then the man had my undying respect.

But…messing around with different girls?

I found that unimaginable.

I didn't want to be too hard on him because he'd been young back then, but men should strive to be honest and faithful with girls, you know?

Shame on him, I say.

"Heh, I can get ahold of Kaiki every now and again, but I never seem to get together with Oshino these days. Part of the reason I came to this building first is, I missed my old muck."

"So when Kaiki was setting up shop in our town, he must have known Oshino was here…"

He just wanted to keep his distance.

But maybe I just didn't know, and there'd been some contact.

Maybe the two old friends had met up.

The Gaen family, Kanbaru's mother's side, had something to do with this whole field—Oshino had known about them, and as for Kaiki, it was in front of Kanbaru's house that we'd first met.

Plus, Oshino had mentioned some nonsense about having staved off a great yokai war during his stay—and it was right after he left that Sengoku got mixed up incidentally in Kaiki's machinations.

In which case…

Perhaps something had happened—between those two.

Of course, even if it had, there was no way for me to know—Oshino didn't tell me anything, nor did Kaiki.

It was less than half a day since our encounter at Mister Donut, but Deishu Kaiki must have left our town for real this time. After all, he'd already pulled off his revenge scam against me (actually, I doubt he was motivated at all by feelings of revenge, he just took what was there for the taking).

Geez.

We were all handing him our wallets.

"Well, this is a place of power—just the kind I can see Oshino fixing to make himself at home." Kagenui glanced behind her at the makeshift bed made of school desks. "And then—there's you. A sot who starts reminiscing in the middle of a battle seems like exactly the kind of body to be saved by Oshino."

"Saved…"

"But I suppose he would have said, 'I'm not saving you, you're gonna get saved on your own.' You know, fiendish young man…" Kagenui turned a sideways glance my way, as if changing gears. "I doubt even X-Ray Oshino realized your little sister is a fake—if he'd known, what do you reckon he might have said?"

"Oshino…"

For the three months he was in our town, he never once came into contact with the Fire Sisters. In fact, I wasn't sure I had ever mentioned them to him—I didn't think so.

Even someone as insightful as Oshino (I wonder if X-Ray Oshino had been his nickname in college) had no way of knowing something we had never even talked about.

Perhaps meeting me had something to do with Kaiki figuring out Tsukihi's true identity, but I imagined his meeting with Karen was the bigger factor—the Fire Sisters.

The Araragi sisters were a set.

Since Kaiki had been targeting middle school students with his scams, naturally he must have picked up some of the rumors about these "defenders of justice."

But, hypothetically speaking.

If Mèmè Oshino had known about Tsukihi Araragi while he lived here—if he'd noticed the existence of the Shidenotori, how would he have reacted?

What might he have said to me?

Mèmè Oshino's approach.

Mr. Hawaiian Shirt always remained neutral and strived only to balance things out even if it meant becoming a double agent—

"Who knows?"

Asked by Kagenui, and pondering the question myself—I squared off into a fighting stance.

The time for talking was done.

I had already asked what I wanted to know—and this was obviously no time for another comic-relief segment.

I was ready for the battle to get well and truly under way.

"It doesn't matter what Oshino would have said. If our opinions clashed, Oshino would have become my enemy. It's that simple."

I no longer claimed to be on the side of justice.

I was ready to be the enemy of justice or of whatever else.

In fact, ever since the last day of spring break—I was always my own enemy.

Not a day had gone past.

Not a single conversation.

During which I ever forgave myself!

"Ms. Kagenui. I am on my sister's side."

"Your sister is a fake."

And not your real sister, Kagenui underscored—spreading both her arms wide as though to provoke me, unfazed by the fact that I had assumed a fighting stance.

"Not just a fake but a *shide no tori,* of all things. An aberration, a bird of omen. *Hototogisu* versus *Araragi,* the poetry of it is a damn hoot—how many years has it been? You've been deceived all this time by a filthy shape-shifter."

"What does it matter to you?"

"It doesn't. Only, cheers to my bumbling—or rather, cheers to Kaiki keeping the relationship between you two, the fact that you're siblings, a secret, you've discovered the *shide no tori*'s true identity. I reckon that a huge mistake on my part, a grave error—but."

Kagenui adopted a mean, testing tone to lob the question.

"Knowing that the dear little sister you thought was real is a fake, can you still love her like you did before today?"

"I can. In fact, I'll love her even more," I answered without hesitation, like Karen might have.

264

I dropped my hips low for a moment—and then rocketed forward, flying towards Kagenui with my hands outstretched in raking claws, screaming at her as I went.

"Because if she's a step-sister—that's just so moé!"

Screaming, body and soul, screaming as long as my voice would hold, I charged Kagenui.

Then I tried to clamp my arms shut in a pincer, with all my might—this was no time to hold back.

Unbridled devastation.

I was returning devastation for devastation—forestalling devastation with devastation.

I was ready to sponsor devastation day and night—however.

"Fine, then…"

Neither parrying nor dodging my arms, but instead grabbing my wrists head-on, Kagenui neutralized my attack.

Catching me, arresting me, foiling me—through sheer force.

If anything, it felt like the excess momentum I had built up was going to pulverize my own elbows—you've got to be kidding me with this.

Offense was one thing—but why did her defense have to be so insane as well?

Who ever heard of a strong-arm defense?

Partial or not, I was wielding the physical strength of a vampire, the most powerful aberration out there—I had the strength of the aberration slayer's thrall.

How could she stop me with her two little arms?

And she was still joking around while she did it, not even gritting her teeth.

"I reckon your position—your feelings on the matter. For what it's worth, a defender of justice like myself must admire you for them."

Kagenui squeezed my wrists even tighter. Her grip strength was tremendous, and it was like being caught in a vice. My hands were being stretched apart like taffy.

"There is no reasoning with illogic—I'll not try to persuade you anymore. I'm not Oshino or Kaiki, after all—the only way I know to gab is with my fists."

"......nkk!"

"Still—I don't know, even if you're fine with it!"

Holding my wrists, Kagenui followed with an instant upward kick using the tip of her foot—I managed to sway backward, barely in time, but wound up getting a fair chunk of my face shaved off.

Thanks to my half-ass dodge, this time I felt real pain—but Kagenui's assault obviously didn't end there. Next, she brought the same leg back down in an axe kick.

Her strike traced the exact same arc as the one I had received from Karen the other day, but in terms of speed, force, even the way she reversed her upward and downward momentum, Kagenui's technique was a whole different can of worms than Karen's.

I wanted to bend my body backward even further to avoid it, but since she had a firm lock on both my arms, I couldn't even do that.

My shoulders were ripped loose from the force of the blow, along with my clavicles.

By this point some of the damage to my scraped face had healed—but Kagenui's next move was to punish that same face once more with a head-butt.

Quite a move.

Kagenui totally fought like a street brawler.

When it came to violence, slow and steady could go too far.

"Even if you're fine with the way things are, what about the rest of your folk?!"

Kagenui finally let go of my hands, my two wrists—only to unleash a flurry of attacks, like a dam gushing forth.

She used her feet to sweep me like a scythe, but no sooner was I flying through the air than she hit my torso with a succession of rapid blows, like a storm of fireworks being announced in the sky—now I knew what a drum feels like.

There were sparklers shooting from my eyes.

I was pretty sure I even saw sound effects in the air.

"You may be fine with it—but you've already got the *grounding* for it. You've been an aberration yourself before and that's coloring your views—you've been immortal before. That's why you can forgive your sister for being a fake, an aberration and an immortal—it's all peaches and sunshine for you, isn't it! But what about the rest of your folk—the ones for don't have bump to do with aberrations?!"

".......nkk!"

"For instance, what about your wee Karen?! Do you think she could pure say the same if she knew her own sister was an aberration?! What about your mother! Do you think she could say the same if she knew the baby for whom she'd suffered pangs of childbirth was a monster?! What about your father!"

She was like a bone-knife working through a conger fish.

I could feel my ribs, or rather my ribs along with the meat around them, being crushed into pulp. Or rather, she was a hand mixer whipping my whole insides up into a milkshake or a smoothie.

I was still suspended in mid-air as Kagenui continued with her combo.

If this was some fighting game, my health bar would probably be long gone—surely "YOU WIN" would be flashing on Kagenui's side of the screen by now.

"Most of all, what about the child, herself? If your fake sister knew that she was pure an aberration—would she honestly be able to live on?! Could she stay your sister like nothing had changed?!"

My sister.

Tsukihi Araragi.

Real—fake.

"It's fine now because she doesn't know—but what do you reckon it will do to her when she finds out?! There's no way an immortal monster can adapt to its environment—you should know that better than anyone else!"

"Ngkk!"

"Or when, inhuman as she is, she still clamors after being a defender of justice? What is it they reckon themselves, the Fire Sisters? Think how uppity, how cruel an immortal monster can be in the face of human folk—that, too, you should understand better than anyone else."

I did understand.

I knew—what Shinobu Oshino had been like before.

I knew the whole of her.

If an immortal aberration were to dedicate itself to justice, there was no telling just how obscene, how over-zealous that justice would be—

I knew that.

"It's our job to take care of these things before something like that happens! You can't quench a fire with oil. It must be stamped out quickly before it becomes a blaze—as Nobunaga Oda once said, if the cuckoo will not sing—it must be killed! You're alone in your stance, in your feelings on this matter! Don't fool yourself into believing that everyone is so open-minded! Whatever values, whatever sense of righteousness you hold, is your business—but don't shove your ideals down strangers' throats!"

I doubted Kagenui was really as angry as she sounded—I think she was just shouting to better punctuate her flurry of blows.

But.

It was clear that something in my words had set her off—had I said something wrong?

I could only imagine.

Since Kagenui was actually travelling with her own aberration and monster, Ononoki—there seemed to be some contradiction at play in her.

A familiar, a shikigami.

But also sisters—a two-man cell.

A step-sister.

"SHO—RYU—KEN!"

She just said *shoryuken.*

Almost like a finishing move for her combo, Kagenui released a flying uppercut, driving straight into my heart—naturally, since I didn't even have a foot on the ground, I was tossed up from the momentum, heart splattered to goo, and my whole body struck the ceiling.

So hard that my clear impression was made in the concrete.

I almost expected to crash through to the floor above.

"Ngh...ugh..."

Urrk.

I remained that way, pasted to the ceiling for a moment—before finally obeying the law of universal gravity and dropping to the floor.

Obviously, I was unable to make a graceful landing. This time, I landed face up in a hard back-flop.

Now I knew what an over-easy egg felt like.

I'd go great on a piece of toast.

"Don't relax yet—I'm not done!"

Relax? Who was relaxing? Kagenui didn't even give me enough time to worry before she straddled my supine body—in what was known as the mount position.

"I wonder how Yotsugi is doing—what do you say we go take a look at what she's up to?"

Take a look?

I wasn't sure what Kagenui meant by that, but I was soon to find out.

Through hands-on experience.

Tactile experience.

Before I could even intuit anything.

Her comment was just an opening salvo. She began pounding on me with her fists—devastating me to a pulp with her fists of devastation.

Along with the floor beneath me.

Her punches were passing through my body, or I should say my flesh and bones, like that was only normal, and hitting the floor—

until.

Kagenui's fists pulverized the floor beneath us—they were like heavy industrial machinery.

I hate to bring up anime at a time like this, but you know how in *Lupin III*, the character Goemon Ishikawa XIII is always using his Zantetsu blade to slice neat holes through the floor?

It was pretty much like that.

Only it wasn't neat or a circle—it was more of a ragged jigsaw-puzzle shape, as she sent chips of floor flying around crudely like a drill bit in every which direction.

Yozuru Kagenui punched straight through the floor of the abandoned building.

First the fourth floor, and then the third floor, in succession.

She was ruining our ruins.

Heck, I bet Kagenui could demolish this whole building with just her bare hands. We could turn it back into a vacant lot without even having to call in contractors.

She may have been human, but she'd long since surpassed human limitations.

This was combat art. It was like Karen's omnidirectional approach to karate, which gathered various techniques, but instead geared towards total destruction. You know that karate oath, "We come unarmed." Well boy, did Kagenui ever!

At this point, my body was acting like the dried towel laid across a stack of tiles in karate to soften the impact—I was acutely aware of all the bits of flooring getting mixed up in my flesh.

There was no time for me to heal.

If anything, it felt like before one round of damage could take shape, the next round was already starting—I bet I looked like a strawberry flavored McShake at this point.

Anyways.

After our preposterous elevator ride, Kagenui's fists finally ceased moving and she stepped away from my body, leaving me splattered on the floor—along the way, she had planted close to five hundred punches on me (since I didn't have anything else to do, I started counting halfway through to kill time).

We were on the second floor.

Ding! Second floor, arena—

"My lord and master, no wonder it felt like I was getting bobbed all over my upper body... Look at thee. Try not to hold me back so much. If it goes on for too long, it will get very irksome."

A vampire with golden eyes and hair.

Shinobu Oshino, I realized, was staring down at me with a look of utter contempt.

Judging from her words, Kagenui had aimed well—the classroom on the second floor that we'd fallen into was the very space where the two aberrations, Shinobu and Ononoki, were facing off.

The four of us were together again after a journey across the shortest conceivable distance.

Shinobu feeling what I was feeling even after being separated from my shadow proved that the loss of her vampirism was no trifling matter.

Oshino's approach was formidable, but it must have been very frustrating for her to have all these sensations thrust at her in the midst of a very serious battle segment.

However.

She wasn't the aberration slayer for nothing.

"Kakak," laughed Kagenui. "You were being such a loudmouth, but it looks like you took it fist and skull, Yotsugi..."

The scene was just as Kagenui teased.

In a corner of the dim classroom, opposite from where Shinobu and I were positioned, lay Ononoki. If not for the situation I was in, I doubt I could bear to witness her plight.

I didn't look human myself at this point, but clothes, hair, every bit of Ononoki was bloody and beaten.

You didn't have to look twice to see that, up until a moment ago, she had been on the receiving end of some very thorough abuse.

That is to say, Shinobu didn't have a single scratch on her.

Not so much as a strand of blond hair was out of place, and there wasn't a speck of dust on her jersey.

It wasn't a difference in healing abilities.

This came down to a difference in their fighting skills, plain and simple.

That said, as aberrations go, I doubted that Ononoki could be considered weak and helpless. Having experienced Kagenui's intensity firsthand, I could testify to that—there was no way any partner of hers could be a pushover.

Since I wasn't in the classroom with her, Shinobu wouldn't have been able to use her aberration-slayer blade… It made me realize afresh just how overwhelmingly monstrous Shinobu Oshino, the former vampire, was.

And just how utterly sadistic…

From the state of things, it looked like Shinobu had been toying with her… The stone-faced Ononoki's eyes were actually tearful.

Geez, if she could tell that I was getting put through the wringer, why not finish up quickly and come help me instead?

She was pissed off about being called a hag, but come on… If she was going to emulate Karen's style, she might try and be utterly masochistic as well.

Besides, this was a serious situation. It was no time for fun!

"I was just about to turn the fight around. I can handle myself, sister—he said with a dashing look," Ononoki insisted as Kagenui approached her.

Um, that wasn't what I called a dashing look.

That was a teary-eyed look.

"I see, I see. But how about you leave the climax to your big sister. Well, the erstwhile Heartunderblade, it seems the finals are between you and me."

Stepping in front of Ononoki as if to protect her, Kagenui laughed and patted her shikigami on the head before drawing herself up to face Shinobu.

"Come, Heartunderblade. We fight."

Kagenui showed no sign of being intimidated, at all.

No sign of wanting to flee even against a legendary vampire.

An expert on immortal aberrations.

Also known as the aberration roller—Yozuru Kagenui.

"Ha."

Shinobu laughed too, in response.

"Ha!"

And again—and again, like a howl.

"Ha"Haha"Hahaha"Hahahaha"Hahahahaha"Hahahahahaha" Hahahahahahaha"

Loud and long—laughing as only an aberration could.

Uproariously.

Savagely, wantonly, illicitly, belligerently, and baring her fangs, Shinobu laughed and laughed and laughed in response to the onmyoji Yozuru Kagenui's invitation until—

"No, I refuse."

She spoke those words and raised her arms like a champion.

Kagenui and Ononoki both did a double take at Shinobu's unexpected reaction. Ignoring their gazes, she helped me up—I had at least recovered enough to resemble a human being—and continued, "I fear my master is ill-pleased with me for bullying the maidling. I'd rather not purchase any more of his loathing. The finals, ye say? Do not be vain, human—my master has yet to be bested by thee. Is that not so, my lord?"

"Yup," I replied.

Meeting the demand Shinobu placed on me—the fire she lit beneath me, I borrowed her shoulder to help myself stand. Since the eighteen-year-old version of her was taller than I was, that shoulder was located pretty high up, but I did my best.

"I haven't lost yet—I'm not ready to submit. Neither your fists, nor your words, have done anything to persuade me."

"I already told you." Kagenui sounded fed up. She repeated, here on the second floor, the same thing she'd said to me on the fourth floor. "Whatever values, whatever sense of righteousness you hold, is your business—but don't shove your ideals down strangers' throats."

"They're not strangers."

I—

Although my outsides had knitted together, without holding onto Shinobu I doubt I could have managed to remain standing, my insides shredded to pieces like I'd swallowed a cyclone. Yet, even though I could barely move—I gathered every ounce of strength I had to rebut Kagenui.

The same thought had occurred to me earlier.

Strangers?

That, no.

I couldn't let that pass unchallenged.

"They're not strangers. They're family."

"……"

"And I do shove my ideals on my family."

Also…

I went on falteringly, hanging off of Shinobu like a wet sack. I was blatantly touching her breasts, but even such an act of God didn't concern me right now.

For instance, Hitagi Senjogahara. Accepting the calamity that befell her, she suffered bravely, keeping the truth of that matter a secret from her family.

No matter how much her father worried about her, she never thought of opening up to him—she decided that she was her own responsibility.

Even after being deceived by five frauds, her resolve remained unshaken.

For instance, Suruga Kanbaru. She still had an aberration residing in her left arm. It wasn't excessively harmful, but not exactly harmless, either—and yet her family knew nothing about it. If her sweet old grandmother, who was such a wonderful cook, knew, she'd definitely try to help, but Kanbaru refused to reveal the details—being thoughtful in her own way.

No doubt she wanted to reveal the truth and ask her grandma for advice—it had to be hard hiding such a secret from her family.

And yet.

Kanbaru was adamant about doing just that.

Not for her own sake, but for her family's.

The two of them, the Valhalla Duo.

I respected them from the bottom of my heart.

"Ms. Kagenui, what self-respecting brother would air his little sister's dirty laundry? I wouldn't tattle on her like that."

"......"

To say it like Mayoi Hachikuji.

The courage—to keep a secret.

"With your family, you lie. You deceive. You cause trouble. You inconvenience. Sometimes you incur debts and sometimes they can't be repaid. But I think that's fine."

That was fine.

Because that was what family meant.

"Ms. Kagenui—defender of justice."

I'd have loved to strike a pose and cut a cool figure as I spoke, but I still couldn't move—I had to lean on Shinobu instead as I croaked out my words.

"If being fake is evil, then I'll bear that burden. If faking is bad, I don't mind being a bad guy."

If my judgment was hypocritical.

If my resolve faked goodness.

If my feelings for Tsukihi Araragi were no more than that, then I would gladly be a hypocrite who wasn't even a scoundrel—

I wasn't Mèmè Oshino.

I wasn't Deishu Kaiki.

I wasn't Yozuru Kagenui.

I wasn't the Fire Sisters or the Valhalla Duo, either.

Koyomi Araragi—was Koyomi Araragi.

"Fuck favorability ratings. I'm fine being the worst."

He said—with a dashing look.

Big brother.

As long as Tsukihi continued to call me that.

It was all fine by me.

My healing was finally catching up with my damage—if I hadn't upped my immortality beforehand, Kagenui would have killed me close to a thousand times already.

It wasn't an exaggeration. It wasn't hyperbole.

Each and every strike was unmistakably lethal.

She hadn't used a single feint or setup or even a check—it was absolutely, one hundred percent, a striking style. Even her defense and submission moves were strikes, by the holy demon mother of Iriya.

Generally an opponent like that was the easiest type to face for a vampire—but she felt more like a natural enemy.

I moved away from Shinobu on shaking legs like a newborn deer—another five seconds and I would be all better.

But in those five seconds, how many times would I die again at Kagenui's hands?

Now that I was standing alone again, I expected her to launch round two at any minute with another wave of strikes—but she didn't.

"Man's evil nature, huh," she muttered instead, a sigh mingled with her words.

Her jovial attitude until just a moment ago seemed to have dissipated somewhat, which put me on guard.

Had I set her off again?

Man's evil nature?

Say what?

"Hm. You've never heard of it? I gabbed about it with Oshino and Kaiki often enough."

Kagenui gave her neck a few cracks, watching to see how I would react.

I read the movement more as a cool-down than a warm-up.

"As a high schooler, you must have heard tell of the doctrine that man's nature is good. That's what the Chinese philosopher Mencius believed. Folk are born with good inside. Benevolence is the heart of man, and righteousness the path of man—goodness is reckoned as the four beginnings, which are the feelings of commiseration, shame, respect, and conscience, and these can fix to grow into the four virtues of compassion, righteousness, propriety, and wisdom."

"Umm…"

Why was she force-feeding me the classics all of a sudden?

I may have been studying for college exams, but I hadn't chosen ethics as one of my subjects.

I did know Mencius, just his name—maybe from world history.

"So then…what's this about man's evil nature?" I asked.

"If the doctrine of innate good is an idealistic philosophy, then the doctrine of innate evil is a practical one. Our innate nature is greed, and greed governs human beings. That candid, faithless view was expounded by Xun Kuang—basically, folk are born with evil inside them."

"People are born—evil."

"Yes," nodded Kagenui. "So if people do good, it's not out of innate nature but rather deception—or so he proclaimed. Good is deception, fake—good is only done out of hypocrisy."

"Hypocrisy…"

Deception.

Deceit.

"Fake—in other words, man-made," Kagenui said.

The man-made, artificial.

Therein lay propriety—norms.

It was precisely man-made remedies that beckoned man to good, that led society in a better direction.

"Countering the prevailing notion of 'ruling by righteousness,' it equates to the principle of honor. All good is hypocrisy at its core, and precisely there—is an intention to be good."

Or so it goes, Kagenui wrapped up jokingly.

Then—

"Let me ask you something," she continued. "This is a thought game what Kaiki used to jaw about—fancy you have the real thing, and a fake that is so identical, in every way, that you can't distinguish it from the real thing. Which do you reckon has more value?"

A natural and an artificial diamond.

They were identical down to their atomic structure—but treated as distinct.

Indistinguishable, yet treated as distinct.

One was rejected—simply for being a fake.

Omitted.

"The real deal and—the fake."

"My reckoning on the matter was naturally that the real thing is more valuable. I think Oshino was of the opinion that they were of equal value. But according to the body what asked the question, we were both mistaken. According to Kaiki, the fake is far more valuable."

Kagenui went on without waiting for my reply.

"Because it wills to become the real thing, the fake is more real than the real deal—kakak! He may be an incorrigible scoundrel, but what he says can be glorious. Well, if I have to, I reckon that's the lesson I should take home from this. A lesson ten years in the making."

Laughing, Kagenui spun about and turned her back toward me.

Then she spoke to the bruised, battered, and half-dead Ononoki.

"Let's go. We've lost here."

Abruptly, unilaterally, without telling us, Kagenui had announced that our battle was over.

The bow was back in its bag and the sword was back in its sheath.
So then.

So then...

"Uh...umm. Ms. Kagenui?"

"I've lost interest. We're leaving. I would have loved to battle with the erstwhile Heartunderblade, but the peculiar way I'm feeling now, I don't reckon my heart would be in it."

Kagenui grabbed Ononoki by the hand and, dragging her, began plodding away—perhaps deciding that dragging was too hard, she switched to carrying Ononoki on her back before continuing once more toward the classroom door.

"W-Wait," I stopped her without thinking.

My body, of course, had regenerated during her lecture on Chinese philosophy (my clothes hadn't, so I was practically butt-naked), but it wasn't like I wanted to stop her and continue our battle.

But I stopped her without thinking.

"What? Did you have a parting gift for me?" asked Kagenui, turning around casually as if someone had called to her just as she was leaving some get-together—a friendly smile on her face, always ready for battle.

"N-No... It's just, where are you going?"

"To the next battlefield. There are plenty of immortal aberrations out there—they're immortal, after all. I reckon I can turn a blind eye to one. 'Rules consisting mostly of exceptions'—you bag the bird but you never bag the nest. Let's just say that your sister is an exception to our justice. You guide her, with your mentor's soul."

It does mean the money I paid to Kaiki was pure wasted, Kagenui regretted.

She sounded regretful but also amused.

"Besides, I reckon you were never quite serious about our battle in the first place..."

"Wha... N-Not serious?"

"It'd be an understatement if I said I sensed no bloodlust. I doubt you were slacking off—but it were hard to get in the spirit after that."

"If…"

In response, I began to say the first thing that came into my head. Until Kagenui mentioned it, I hadn't honestly been aware of this, except subconsciously. I'd been serious—I hadn't meant to be slacking off.

"If you didn't sense any bloodlust in me—that was probably because you treated me as a human being."

"Huh?"

"You said it yourself. We had one human and one aberration each—the only person who ever referred to me in *this state* as a human being was Oshino."

So…

Speaking of not getting into the spirit—I was the one to whom that applied.

The peculiar way I was feeling, I lost interest.

Yes, like the times when I'd dealt with ol' Hawaiian shirts himself— trying to get mad seemed a little silly.

"Hmph… So I accidentally took a page from Oshino's book— how embarrassing. What have I done? Now I'm depressed. In that case, why don't I end with something I reckon he would never say—"

There was a hint of nostalgia in her voice as she said it.

Just one word.

"Goodbye."

Yozuru Kagenui pronounced it in such a natural and fluent way that I realized—she might not be a genuine Kyotoite, after all.

013

The epilogue, or maybe, the punch line of this story.

Stuff that happened before I was roused from bed by my sisters as usual the next day.

Kagenui left the ruins with Ononoki on her back—obviously as soon as she set one foot outside, she could no longer touch the ground, so she walked away atop a series of walls, fences, guardrails, and such. Her sprightly movement and sense of balance remained impeccable even with Ononoki on her back. After sinking my teeth into Shinobu's neck and taking my blood back, returning her to little-girl form and getting me as close to human as possible, I got on my bike and rode home with her in the front basket.

By the way, Ononoki left with her clothes in tatters, but I wasn't nearly brave enough to pedal home butt-naked—needless to say, before returning Shinobu to little-girl form, I asked her to use her Create Matter skill to whip me up a set of clothes. She had good taste but could be unnecessarily upscale, so it took a fair amount of time for us to reach an agreement.

"I can't wear clothes this flamboyant! Can't you make something more normal?!"

"My pride does not permit me to create mere fast fashion! While

I am coordinating thy habiliments, ye shan't look slatternly!"

Remember, we were having this epic debate at night in an abandoned building, after the two-man cell had already left.

That was why it took us so long to get home.

Come to think of it, over that spring break when I went through hell, Tsukihi had texted a question to me: *Where was it that Mytyl and Tyltyl found the blue bird of happiness?*

Obviously I didn't reply, but even I knew the answer to that.

In their own home.

So my blue bird had been you two—the Fire Sisters.

When I arrived home (Shinobu had returned to my shadow by then) with that cool thought, Karen, still standing by the front hall, was arguing with her parents.

Her parents.

In other words, they were also my mother and father.

"You will not pass! The only one who is allowed to is my brother!"

……

This was all because of me.

My orders had been so narrow that Karen and my parents—nah, how the heck was it my fault?

Karen was the real thing, a real moron.

She was like a badly designed game script. I ended up wasting even more time then and there explaining to our parents why our front door had been destroyed.

Not that I had any real explanation to offer them.

I just made up some nonsense excuses as I'd done with Karen—obviously my parents didn't accept them as readily as she did, but being realists, they never dreamed the destruction might actually be the work of a shape-shifter (they seemed to suspect Karen was pranking them, as if something of this level could still be classified as such). In the end, though, I brought them around.

Indeed, my parents seemed to consider the fact that Karen had changed her hairstyle for the first time in ten years the more important matter—I was a little worried that she might pin the blame for that on me. However…

"Huh? What are you talking about? Wasn't it always like this?"

Karen, herself, sounded confused.

She'd already forgotten her ponytail era.

My sister really did worry me sometimes.

But—that was also the side of her that saved me at times.

In any case, once my parents began scolding Karen in earnest, I snuck away to the second floor.

To my other little sister, Tsukihi Araragi.

Tsukihi, for her part, was lying on the top bunk, still asleep like she'd been before I headed out, just like I told her.

Dressed in a yukata in place of pajamas.

With the left side over the right, my mistake intact.

Dammit, at least fix that.

Shidenotori.

Aberration, bird of omen, lesser cuckoo.

However much I tried to hide the truth, the time might come, perhaps through some accident where she suffered an injury serious enough to remove a piece of her body (indeed, much as I had suffered several times during my battle with Kagenui), when Tsukihi would discover what she was—but until that day came, just as I had told Kagenui, I would keep the truth about my little sister hidden safe in my heart.

If justice practiced by those who could not die was nothing but a fiasco, then likely Tsukihi, with an aberration from the sacred realm residing in her, had forfeited her claim to that principle. Even if she attempted to do justice, as with Shinobu and me, it would only be an obscene, purging justice.

It would be a heartless justice.

The human heart is not a vessel to fill with things but a fire to blaze and kindle—well said.

Brood parasitism.

Kagenui was probably right—maybe she did have justice on her side.

At the very least, not many people watching a TV segment on the rearing behavior of cuckoos would find it pleasant.

The inefficient breeding method known as brood parasitism would seem crafty and underhanded to most.

I'm pretty sure that would be my simple view of it, too.

Still, though.

Tsukihi wasn't like the cuckoo, little or otherwise.

To say the least—she'd never tried to push Karen or me out of the nest.

She'd always been our little sister.

From the moment she was born—always.

Real or fake, she was still just, and real or fake, she was our sister.

Even if she wasn't just, she was family.

The Fire Sisters.

My little sisters, my pride and joy.

So let me bother to answer now the question Ononoki asked me.

Even if it's full of fakes—I think it's a wonderful world.

Let that be my contrarian reply.

A la Deishu Kaiki.

"I was nervous you were going to kiss me again, but I guess not."

Tsukihi had suddenly spoken.

At some point her eyes had sprung open. She looked as sleepy as ever with her drooping eyes, but it wasn't because she'd just woken up. Apparently, she'd only been pretending to be asleep.

What a radical cue.

"If you did try to kiss me, I was going to ensnare you with my tongue," she revealed.

"That sounds like something some kind of monster would do."

"Morning. Welcome back. Where were you?"

"Ah. Actually, I was off fighting a monstrous human and a humanoid monster for your sake."

"Oh yeah? Good work. Don't overdo it, though."

"Let me. I do it out of love."

"I know, I know. Our big brother loves us so much."

"Don't put words in my mouth. I hate you both."

"Anyway, Koyomi, how long do I have to stay like this? You told me to sleep so I've been trying my hardest."

"You guys are way too faithful to directives coming from the likes of me. I really do worry about your futures," I grumbled, hopping off the ladder. "Sleep until tomorrow. And then tomorrow, come wake me up like you always do."

"Aye, aye, sir."

"When summer vacation is over, I'll introduce you to my girlfriend."

"Hm?" Tsukihi seized on my words and immediately raised her upper body. "What, you mean you have a girlfriend?"

"Yeah. Since around May, actually."

"That makes me dagnabbit mad."

My back turned to her frank comment and reproachful gaze, I warned, "Don't go tattling on me," and stepped out into the hallway. It wouldn't do to hang out in my sisters' room for too long, and it wasn't like me to linger. I'd go back to my room and change.

With everything that had been going on, it was getting pretty late—about time for a gracious monster to bow out.

Afterword

Obviously there are real and fake things in this world, but when you really think about it, the two concepts form a pair, and there can only be fakes because the real thing exists, and without the occasional fake making an appearance, I'm not sure you could call it the real deal. Just as how in superhero stories, an imposter always shows up eventually. The fake hero, as it were. But taking this a step further, it's important to note that even though fakes exist, it is not in fact necessary for the real thing to exist. If the real deal represents an ideal and fakes represent attempts to realize that ideal, then perhaps it is actually better if the real deal didn't exist. Well, maybe that's going too far, but if the real deal is an ideal, then we can also wonder if it is an illusion. Of course, what people idolize as the real thing must have begun as the pursuit of an ideal, which is to say that it wasn't the real thing from the outset. If we roughly define the real deal's value as the impact it has on people, however, perhaps it is the real deal, after all, that gives rise to real deals. Given the above, rather than say that the two concepts of real and fake form a pair, it may be more accurate to say that they are just two sides of the same coin.

As with the first part, I wrote this book two hundred percent as a hobby, but whether they form a pair or are two sides of the same coin, they've come out feeling fairly different. Fiction is a scary business. In fact, both of them having been written as epilogues to the main story, these novels were composed presupposing the existence of

BAKEMONOGATARI, and yet, as to whether they wouldn't stand up without having read *BAKEMONOGATARI* first, surprisingly enough that doesn't seem to be the case. Well, some people might claim that they don't stand up as novels at all. But the Araragi sisters were extremely fun characters to write about, and my proverbial pen flew across the page. As sheepish as I feel that so many people were willing to give me such leeway in pursuing a very personal hobby—including VOFAN, who provided such beautiful covers, and all of the readers—this successfully concludes the epilogue, with all the members of the Araragi harem doing fine despite ups and downs. And so that was "Final Chapter: Tsukihi Phoenix," *NISEMONOGATARI, Part 02*.

One more thing. For all of this book's insistence on it being the final chapter, I must confess that I've decided to write about two more episodes. I hope those of you who'd like to learn more about Mayoi Hachikuji and Tsubasa Hanekawa will keep me company. Now, how many of you might there be?

NISIOISIN

BAKEMONOGATARI
MONSTER TALE
NISIOISIN

PARTS 1 - 3 AVAILABLE NOW!

Story by **NISIOISIN**
Retold by **Mitsuru Hattori**

Imperfect Girl

Legendary novelist NISIOISIN partners up
with Mitsuru Hattori (*SANKAREA*) in this graphic
novel adaptation of one of NISIOISIN's mystery
novels.

An aspiring novelist witnesses a tragic death, but
that is only the beginning of what will become a
string of traumatic events involving a lonely
elementary school girl.

Coming This October!

ATTACK ON TITAN

ATTACK ON TITAN:
BEFORE THE FALL
The first of the franchise's light novels, this prequel of prequels details the origins of the devices that humanity developed to take on the mysterious Titans.

ATTACK ON TITAN:
KUKLO UNBOUND
Swallowed and regurgitated as an infant by a Titan, an orphan seeks to find and prove himself in this official prequel novel to the smash hit comics series.

ATTACK ON TITAN:
LOST GIRLS
LOST GIRLS tells of the times and spaces in between the plot points, through the eyes and ears of the saga's toughest—but more taciturn—heroines.

LEARN MORE AT

IN NOVEL FORM!

ATTACK ON TITAN: THE HARSH MISTRESS OF THE CITY Part 1

A stand-alone side story, *Harsh Mistress* tells of the increasingly harrowing travails of Rita Iglehaut, a Garrison soldier trapped outside the wall, and her well-to-do childhood friend Mathias Kramer.

ATTACK ON TITAN: THE HARSH MISTRESS OF THE CITY Part 2

In this concluding half, Rita Iglehaut struggles to turn her isolated hometown into something of a city of its own. Her draconian methods, however, shock the residents, not least Mathias Kramer, her childhood friend.

ATTACK ON TITAN: END OF THE WORLD

In this novelization of the theatrical adaptation, the series' familiar setting, plot, and themes are reconfigured into a compact whole that is fully accessible to the uninitiated and strangely clarifying for fans.

VERTICAL-INC.COM